THE HALLOWED ONES

LAURA BICKLE

*G*RAPHIA

Houghton Mifflin Harcourt
Boston   New York   2012

Graphia and the Graphia logo are trademarks of the Houghton Mifflin Harcourt Publishing Company.

www.hmhbooks.com

Text set in Bembo.

Library of Congress Cataloging-in-Publication Data
Bickle, Laura.
The hallowed ones / Laura Bickle.
p. cm.
Summary: Amish teen Katie smuggles a gravely injured young man, an outsider, into her family's barn despite the elders' ruling that no one can come in or out of the community while some mysterious and massive unrest is wreaking havoc in the "English" world.
ISBN 978-0-547-85926-2 (pbk.)
[1. Amish—Fiction. 2. Christian life—Fiction. 3. Coming of age—Fiction. 4. Bioterrorism—Fiction. 5. Terrorism—Fiction. 6. Communicable diseases—Fiction. 7. Family life—Fiction. 8. Horror stories.] I. Title.
PZ7.B4727Hal 2012
[Fic]—dc23
2012014800

Manufactured in the United States of America

DOC 10 9 8 7 6 5 4 3 2 1

4500377738

Acknowledgments

Thank you to my wonderful editor, Julie Tibbott, and fabulous agent, Becca Stumpf, for making this book happen. You've both been delightful to work with.

Much gratitude to my husband, Jason, for suffering through muse duty and my story angst.

Thank you to Marcella Burnard for the grounding and moral support.

And a special thanks to the book's fairy godmother, Jeffe Kennedy. This story is very lucky to have you to sprinkle fairy dust on it.

CHAPTER ONE

After the end of the Outside world, the Plain folk survived.

At the time, I didn't know that the end of Outside had happened. None of us really did. We knew that something was wrong, of course. That knowledge trickled in slowly, like a leak in a roof. The signs accumulated, and then there was no denying the dark stain spreading over the pale ceiling of our world.

My first inkling was on a day in late September under a cloudless blue sky. The ravens had begun picking at the corn that was drying in the fields, black specks in the gold. I leaned on the wooden fence post, watching the birds scratch and listening to them caw to one another in their inscrutable hoarse language. The wire fence was pierced here by a wooden gate, to move farm equipment and cattle. This was a remote part of our little settlement of Plain people, but it made a good place to get away from chores and parents.

Beside me, Elijah had picked up a rock to scare the birds away.

"Don't throw that," I said, automatically. "It's mean."

Elijah looked at the stone, shrugged, put it down. He was a

year older than me, but he would do anything I asked. Tall and lanky and sunburned from working outdoors, he cut a handsome figure: dark hair and hazel eyes that crinkled when he smiled. I wasn't sure what I thought about that yet. We had grown up together. But things were changing. We both could feel it.

He leaned against the fence beside me, staring out at the field. I knew what he was looking at, the same thing I was . . . at what lay beyond the field. At the black ribbon of road just beyond the corn that carried the English to and from their business Outside. They drove their shiny cars down the two-lane highway, intent on going home or to work or school. At this distance, we could barely make out the drivers. Sometimes men or women drove boxy sedans in pressed suits and blouses. Often they would be couples with children strapped into harnesses in the back seat. Other times the drivers would be people around our age, talking on their phones or chatting with friends in the passenger seat. We were too far away to see their expressions. But during the summer, with the windows down, we could sometimes hear snippets of their laughter.

Since the time we were children, Elijah and I had made up stories about the people in the cars. We imagined that they were driving to the movies or going to parties. Once, we spied a sleek black limousine and fancied that it contained men in tuxedos and women in evening dresses. Maybe a group going to prom. It was as far away from our everyday world as we could envision.

"Someday that's going to be us out there," Elijah said, gesturing with his chin toward the road.

"Soon. Three more weeks." I'd been daydreaming about

Outside for so long. And it was almost time for *Rumspringa*. Literally, it meant "running around." It was the time for young Amish men and women to go beyond the gate and taste the Outside world. After years of begging and pleading, my parents had finally relented and let me go Outside this year, on two conditions: that I wait until the harvest was completed, and that Elijah go with me. We wouldn't be formally living together, of course. I intended to room with one of the girls I'd grown up with, Hannah Bachman. And one of Elijah's friends, Sam Vergler, would go too. Sam and Hannah had been courting since Hannah had turned sixteen. We'd have a girls' apartment and a boys' apartment. Proper. But for all practical intents, Elijah and I would be going on *Rumspringa* together.

Though he could have gone sooner Elijah had declared that he wouldn't participate in *Rumspringa* without me. He'd been saving money, apprenticing to a master carpenter and helping out with his father's farm. He seemed content, though, with his day-to-day life, content with the waiting. And I knew that my parents hoped that Elijah and I would someday be married. Indeed, I couldn't picture myself being married to anyone else . . . though I admitted that it would be strange to see him with a beard like the ones worn by all married Amish men, rather than his handsome, clean-shaven face. It was the destiny I'd accepted. I was Amish. I didn't dislike my life and accepted the inevitabilities cheerfully. Still, I wanted the experience of Outside. To know that I'd made the right choice. To be absolutely certain.

There was a difference, I had decided, between knowing and believing. And I wanted both.

"What's the first thing we're going to do Outside, Katie?" Elijah asked, grinning. "Eat sushi?"

"Ugh. No." I wrinkled my nose. This was a game we played often: *When we are Outside . . .* "I am going to buy a pair of britches. Jeans."

He stood back and looked at me, considering. "You? In britches?"

"*Ja,*" I said, lifting my chin defiantly. "And I want to go to the movies."

"The movies?" he echoed. He was still fixated on the jeans; I could tell by how he stared at my rump. "What kind of movie do you want to see?"

"I'm not sure." I smiled slyly. I'd found a newspaper while Outside with my father earlier that day. He occasionally delivered fresh produce to a convenience store that catered to English tourists. If I picked the produce, I could keep the money. I kept mine squirreled away in a wooden box that Elijah had made for me, with the word RUMSPRINGA carved on the top. After we delivered the produce, I found the page of movies in a trash can outside of the store and had tucked it away in my apron pocket. I pulled it out now and smoothed it over the top beam of the fence. "See. There's a lot to choose from."

Elijah leaned over my shoulder, and I could feel his breath disturbing the tie on my bonnet. "Wow." His finger traced over the listings. There was one that showed an explosion and soldiers in uniform. Another depicted a cartoon dragon with wings wrapped around a castle. I was partial to that one. It seemed magical, dangerous, and compelling. Though he was only printed in black-and-white, I imagined that the dragon was blue—blue as the sky at dusk.

"How about this?" Elijah pointed to an advertisement for a film that showed a female spy in a leather suit. Her breasts strained to be released from the zipper that contained them, and she held a gun longer than her impressive legs.

I peered at the woman in leather. "If you want. As long as I can see the dragon film."

Elijah laughed. "I would think you'd object to that. But she *is* wearing britches."

I shrugged. The woman seemed very unreal, as two-dimensional as the paper she appeared on. I wasn't threatened by fantasy. "No. I'd be eager to see if she really looks like that in the film, though."

"So am I." He lifted his eyebrows. I swatted him playfully.

Our gazes gradually settled back to the horizon, at the black ribbon of road. The whine of an engine echoed in the distance, like a mosquito.

"Ooh, a speeder," Elijah said. He stepped up on the lowest rail of the fence for a better look. Sometimes the speeders were followed by policemen with lights blazing and siren howling—a special thrill.

I shaded my eyes with my hand and peered at the faraway road. To my surprise, it was not a sports car that zinged along. This was a square sport-utility vehicle, piled high with luggage and boxes lashed to the roof. The driver, a man, was yelling. His wife was turned around in the passenger's seat, and I could not see her face. Nor could I see the expressions of the children. But I could hear high-pitched crying.

"They must be in a hurry to go camping," Elijah murmured.

"I'm glad I'm not going on that vacation," I said.

The vehicle sped out of sight, and no police car followed it.

I frowned, feeling sorry for the family. That sense of unease was foreign to me. My parents had always given my younger sister and me a happy home. I had never been afraid of my father, nor could I remember him ever having a cross word with my mother. Like Elijah and me, they had grown up together. That familiarity had not bred contempt, and they didn't concern themselves with what lay beyond the gate.

I did. And I wondered if Elijah and I would ever be like them.

"Katie."

I jumped, hearing my father's voice behind me. I whirled, stuffing the newspaper page into my apron pocket.

My father was crossing the meadow to the fence. Under his straw hat and above his gray beard, I could see the glimmer of a smile. Though his voice was stern, he wasn't angry with me. And I had never given him reason to be, never been disobedient . . . that he knew about. He didn't know about the time that I'd spent at the county library when I'd been ostensibly studying to be a teacher. He didn't know that I'd read about dinosaurs and planets and plenty of other things not accepted by the Amish. He may have suspected, but he didn't *know*. And he was a fair-enough man not to punish me just for the simple suspicion of wrongdoing.

"*Ja,* Father?"

He nodded at Elijah. He never chastised me for spending

time with Elijah. "Mrs. Parsall is here to see the puppies."

I smiled, though my stomach churned. "She's at the kennel?"

"*Ja*. She stopped by the house first, and I told her to go on to meet you there. She's wondering how many puppies to expect for her customers."

"I'll see to her now."

"Good girl."

I gave Elijah an apologetic smile and hurried across the sloping meadow to the weather-silvered barn in the distance.

My father had given me the responsibility of managing the family dogs three years ago. I'd been very proud to have the job—he even allowed me to set the prices and keep a portion of the money. He'd told me that it would help make a businesswoman of me. I'd made a profit every year, tucked it away in my *Rumspringa* box. Maybe it should have gone into the sparsely filled hope chest my mother had given me. But *Rumspringa* was the apple of my eye, my immediate future.

Running the kennel was often a challenge for me—letting go of what I loved. Though we'd always been kind to our dogs, we'd heard stories of others who weren't so humane. Those tales made me very, very sad. I loved the dogs dearly, and it was hard for me to give them up. Even to Mrs. Parsall, who promised that she found them loving homes and showed me photographs that people had sent her of the puppies as they grew up. She sometimes told me what their new names were, though they were still classified in my head under the nicknames I'd given each and every one.

Mrs. Parsall was waiting for me outside the dilapidated

barn, dressed in jeans and a floppy sun hat. She was a plump, middle-aged woman with blond hair and glasses that slid down her nose. I adored her. She extended her arms out for a hug, and her blue eyes crinkled. She often encouraged me to use her first name, Ginger, but that seemed too disrespectful.

"Katie, how are you, dear?"

I grinned against her shoulder. "Good, good. And you?"

Mrs. Parsall smiled. "Wonderful. And how is Sunny? Is she ready to have her babies?"

"Come see for yourself!" I pushed open the creaky sliding door and led her into the barn. "I expect she might go another week, maybe two. But she's huge."

Mrs. Parsall grinned. "That's great. I have a waitlist . . . The more, the merrier."

The barn was cool in shadow, and it took a moment for my eyesight to adjust from the brilliance of the day. It was an old gray barn, not for any good use for cows and horses anymore, and more than distant from my house. It sat a stone's throw from the foundations of a house that had once existed decades ago. I'd been told that the house had been struck by lightning. The neighbors who once lived there moved east, and their property had fallen into disrepair. But it was my own little kingdom.

The Hexenmeister had painted a hex sign over the barn door years ago, when I'd started breeding dogs. The symbol he'd picked included sheaves of wheat, for fertility. That part was for the dogs. He'd also worked in spokes of purple tulips, signifying faith and chastity. That part was for me. I'd smiled when I saw it, but it felt like the Hexenmeister was giving me a lecture every time I saw the contradictory images.

Sunlight streamed into the barn through chinks in the old slats, and I smelled sweet hay. Though I called this place a kennel and there were wire cages, I rarely used them. The golden retrievers I raised were a good bunch and had free run of the farm, except when birthing or when the puppies were very small. It wouldn't do to have one injured or have a bitch give birth in an unknown place.

But Sunny was here, waiting for me. She ran up to me, her bulging body wobbling as she came to greet us. She licked my hands and arms, made an effort to jump on my shoulders, but she was just too heavy with puppies for that kind of horseplay. Mrs. Parsall crouched down at Sunny's level, and the dog vigorously washed her face with her tongue.

Mrs. Parsall ran her hands over Sunny's sides. "Oh my. You look about ready to pop, old girl."

Sunny wagged her tail. This was her third litter. She was a good mama, attentive and loving to her pups.

"Who's the sire?" Mrs. Parsall asked.

"The papa is Copper. He's likely to be around somewhere, maybe chasing chickens."

"Ah. They'll have beautiful pups." She rubbed Sunny's glossy stomach. "Just beautiful."

"I think so," I said modestly. "Copper has the broad chest and that dark gold. I'm hoping that the pups will inherit their mother's desire to stay home, though."

Mrs. Parsall kissed Sunny behind the ear. "A little wanderlust never hurt anyone."

I laughed. "You've not seen Copper being chased by the rooster. He isn't fond of the dog harassing his hens."

Mrs. Parsall looked up at me through her bifocals. "This will be your last litter before you do the *Rumspringa* thing?"

I nodded. As eager as I was to experience Outside, a pain welled in my throat at the idea of leaving the dogs. "It will be. But I've been training my little sister about the dogs. She'll care for them in the meantime."

"How long will you be gone?"

I shrugged. "I'm not sure. I haven't really thought about how long." The group of us had talked about going north, to the nearest large city, to rent apartments and find some work. We could be gone a week or a year.

Or . . . a small voice in my head prodded. *Or you could be gone for always.*

But as much as I wanted to experience Outside, the Plain community was all I'd ever known, and I didn't know if I had the desire or the fortitude to leave it permanently.

I suppose that was what *Rumspringa* was for. To test limits and make decisions. Most of the young people in our community came back after only a few weekends Outside, spent at amusement parks or camping. Some made no formal display of leaving. They just wandered to the malls and cities during the day, wearing jeans and makeup and experimenting with cigarettes and fast food in a halfhearted way before being baptized into the Amish faith and giving up those things for good. Very few Amish "jumped the fence" and stayed Outside. But it still seemed possible. Vague, but possible.

Mrs. Parsall smiled. "You are always welcome at my house. You know that." Her home was empty now that her son and daughter had gone away to college across the country. Though she was very proud of them, I could tell that she was lonely. But contemplating *Rumspringa* at Mrs. Parsall's house seemed a bit like a sleepover at a favorite aunt's . . . not the full experience of Outside that I craved.

I gave her a spontaneous hug and a grin. "Thank you."

She patted my cheek. "You just have to be careful. There are a lot of dangers out there for a young woman."

"Don't you mean for a naive young woman?" I didn't bristle; my tone was teasing.

"For anyone." Mrs. Parsall's pretty moon face darkened. "It's not like it used to be."

"My parents went Outside for their *Rumspringa,*" I said. "They told me to be wary of the intentions of strange men. And smoking and drinking and staying out late." My parents had raised me to be a so-called nice girl; they wanted me to return as one.

"Not only that. Things have become more violent." She frowned. "There was a mass murder, not too far from here, last week. A whole family slaughtered in their sleep."

I shuddered, though the idea seemed unreal as the movie advertisements. "I will have Elijah."

"Just be very, very careful," the older woman said. "It's a dangerous world."

"You sound like my parents."

"All parents love their children. You should have heard the lecture I gave my kids before they left the house." She grinned. "Though they were well-armed with cell phones, checking accounts, laundry soap, and condoms, I still worried."

"Mrs. Parsall!" I could feel the blush spreading beneath my

pale cheeks. Though I had seen the dogs breed many times and knew perfectly well what caused children, I was still uncomfortable with the idea of myself having babies. Or experiencing sex, for that matter. And love . . . love was a mysterious thing. I saw a lot of couples marrying out of a sense of acceptance, of duty. That was a kind of love, but not the passionate love that I saw people emphasize Outside.

"These are the facts of life, m'dear." Mrs. Parsall chuckled. "Love and lust and laundry soap. Just ask Sunny."

Sunny grinned her inscrutable canine grin, her pink tongue protruding beyond her teeth. She was a dog and already more wise than I was about such things.

I walked Mrs. Parsall outside the barn, through the golden field back to my house. No one but she and I and the dogs ever came back here, and there was no path worn in the grass. The sun had lowered on the horizon, shining through the leaves of sugar maple trees just beginning to yellow with the coming of fall. I could still feel the warmth of the day through the dark brown cotton of my dress. If I didn't look up at the trees, I could almost convince myself that it was still summer. Almost.

But our community was bustling with the work of autumn and the activities of harvest: younger children gathered apples from a small orchard; men drove horses with carts containing bales of hay to barns; a group of women was busy gathering grapevines to make wreaths to sell in the English shops for Christmas.

We were a good-size settlement of Plain folk, about seventy families, spread over half a county. We had heard rumors of other Plain communities that were shrinking, owing to the youth and the spell of *Rumspringa*. And there were tales of other communities that grew so fast, there was no farmland for young families. But not ours. Ours had remained the same size and shape as far back as anyone could remember. There always seemed to be enough land for everyone to have at least forty acres to farm, if they wanted it.

And everyone seemed happy, unaffected by the schisms that seemed so common in other Amish settlements. The Bishop said that was because we stuck to the old ways. Everyone knew what was expected of us. There was no renegotiation of rules every time some new technology flew up a bonnet. The Ordnung was the Ordnung. Period. And we had been rewarded for following the Ordnung: there was always enough work and food and spouses and land for everyone. God provided for his people.

The pumpkin patch that my little sister tended was nearly as ripe as Sunny with distended gourds. There was one particularly large monster of a pumpkin that Sarah had a special fondness for. Twice daily she squatted beside it, whispering to it and petting it. Whatever she was doing seemed to be working—the pumpkin was easily over a hundred pounds, with another month to go before it would be severed from the vine.

Mrs. Parsall leaned against the bumper of her old blue station wagon. She pulled her keys from her pocket, gave me a one-armed hug. "You take care of yourself, kiddo."

I grinned against her shoulder. But something dark against the blue sky caught my attention. I squinted at it, first thinking it to be a bird. But it wasn't a bird at all.

I stepped back from Mrs. Parsall, pointing at the sky. "Look!"

A dark dot buzzed overhead, growing larger. It was a helicopter, flying so low that I could hear the *whump-whump-whump* of its blades. It was painted green with a white cross on the side, seeming to wobble in the blue.

Mrs. Parsall shaded her eyes with her hands, shouting to be heard above the roar. "It's Life Flight."

"It's a what?"

"It's a medical helicopter. From a hospital."

"It shouldn't be doing that, should it?"

"Hell, no. It—"

The helicopter veered right and left, as if it were a toy buffered by a nonexistent tornado. The breeze today was calm, stirred by the helicopter blades and the roar. I thought I saw people inside, fighting, their silhouettes stark through a flash of window, then lost in the sun. The helicopter made a shrieking sound, the *whump-whump-whump* plowing through the air as it bumped and bucked. It howled over us, so close that I could have reached out and touched it if I'd been standing on the roof of our house.

Mrs. Parsall grabbed me and flung me to the ground. I shoved my bonnet back from my brow in enough time to see the helicopter spiral out of control, spinning nose over tail into a field. It vanished above tall tassels of corn.

For a couple of heartbeats, I saw nothing, heard nothing.

Then I felt the impact through my hands and the front of my ribs, bit my tongue so hard I could taste blood. Black smoke rose over the horizon.

"Oh no," Mrs. Parsall gasped.

I scrambled to my feet, began to run. I heard Mrs. Parsall

behind me, the jingle of her purse strap. I dimly registered her voice shouting into her cell phone. I ran toward the fire, across the grass. I swung myself up and over the barbed-wire fence, mindless of the scratching on my hands and in my skirt.

I plunged into the stalks of corn, taller than me, following the smell of smoke and the distant crackle of fire. I was conscious of the brittle yellow stalks tearing at me as I passed and realized that they were too flammable this far into the season. If the fire got loose in the corn, we'd have no way to stop it.

But my immediate concern was the people on the helicopter.

I ripped through the field and shoved aside blackened stalks of corn to view the site of the crash. The heat shimmered in the air, causing my eyes to tear up. I lifted my apron to cover my nose against the smell of oily smoke.

Fire seethed above me in a black and orange plume, curling around the husk of the dead helicopter. The bent and broken tail jutted out from the ground at an odd angle. The cockpit had broken open, flames streaming through the broken glass.

And I swore I saw something moving inside.

CHAPTER TWO

I squinted into the sizzle of the heat, sucking in my breath. A hand slapped against the cracked glass of the window, slithered out the broken edges. Something alive.

Instinctively, I stepped toward it. I clambered over a smoking piece of metal and climbed up on the bent nose of the helicopter. I cried out when I braced my hands against the metal—it was hot as an iron. Tears streaming down my face from the smoke and the fumes, I reached out to the bloody hand and clasped it in mine.

It ceased twitching and writhing at my touch, and for an instant all was still. I didn't feel the searing heat of the metal through my apron and dress. I even ceased to hear the crackle of fire. I only sought to give some bit of comfort to the person in the wreckage. For that moment, we connected. The hand felt still in mine, as if soothed by my presence. I could see that it was a man's burly hand. I saw a green sleeve of a jacket pulled past his wrist, slick polyester from a manufactured uniform. I thought that he must be the pilot. He gripped my hand tightly. I could feel the fear pulsing in his palm. I did not know what I intended to do, only that I could sense the desperation clasped in my fingers.

Suddenly, his arm jerked, and sound came rushing back to me. I heard him scream, and he clutched my hand tighter, so hard that I cried out. He pulled against me, and I felt myself sliding against the hot metal, into the wreckage.

But it wasn't the pilot pulling me. He was still screaming as he was dragged back into the wreckage . . . by something else. I peered into the smoke-encrusted glass and saw a pair of red eyes, glowing with reflected light like a cat's in the smoky darkness.

My heart lurched into my mouth. Whimpering, I struggled against the urge to extricate myself from the viselike grip—I wasn't sure if I was trying to pull him free, or *me* free of *him*. But his fingers spasmed around mine, and I was lifted off my precarious balancing point on the helicopter nose.

"No!" I cried, yanking back with all my might. I might be small, but I was strong from years of hard work. I braced my shoe against a crease in the metal . . .

. . . and a splash of blood struck me in the face like a slap.

I gasped. The blood and sweat in my palm slipped against the pilot's, and his hand slid free. His arm lashed back into the cockpit, like a fish on the end of a line, and I landed hard on my backside on the scorched ground.

My spine ached from the impact, and I stared up at the glass, dazed. I heard another short scream, then nothing. My fingers wound in the burnt grass, and my heart hammered. I knew, deep in the core of my being, that there was something terrible in there . . .

"Katie!" I felt arms around my waist, hauling me to my feet. I blinked stupidly at Elijah, who gaped open-mouthed at my face.

I looked down. My chest and apron were spattered with blood, as if I'd slaughtered a pig. My stunned gaze slid back to the wreckage. I could hear popping noises inside the metal shell, like popcorn in a kettle. "The pilot is in there," I whispered. "We have to help the pilot . . ."

"Get back!"

A familiar voice thundered over us. It was a voice from Sunday church service. The voice of the Bishop. He stood yards from us, holding a shovel, his salt-and-pepper beard damp with perspiration. Other Elders had materialized from the corn, sparks bright against their black clothes.

"Get back!" he shouted again, brandishing the shovel. "Get away from it!"

The others backed away, receding into the corn. Plain folk were supposed to be obedient; they did not question an order from the Bishop.

But I paused, as I always did. I never followed commands as a reflex. The Bishop had remarked on my lack of submission before, had said that was a failing in my character. I stared at the fire with my breath rattling in my throat, trying to understand why he would order us away when someone needed our help. God charged us to help those in need, and I had never seen anyone more in need of—

"Katie!" Elijah dragged me back into the tall stalks with the others. I struggled against him, transfixed by the fire and still hearing the echo of the pilot's scream in my head. I felt the shadow of the corn closing over me, my shoes scraping in the dirt . . .

And a *boom* thundered through the wreckage, shaking the leaves around us. I threw my hand over my eyes as I fell back against Elijah, tangled in his limbs and mine. He covered my head as bits of shrapnel rained down on the field. I heard him hiss and wince, slapping at an ember threatening to ignite his shirt.

On hands and knees, I crawled to the edge of the blackened corn, watched as an orange fireball raced to the sky, turned black, and dissipated.

I swallowed hard. The Bishop must have known that the helicopter would explode again. I should have listened to him.

But that was not my nature. I always questioned.

I stared helplessly at the wreckage. There was nothing left but a split-open, flattened bit of metal that burned, like a tin can in a campfire. I could see nothing in it. No glass, no pilot. No bodies.

Just a fire that burned black at the seams.

Our community fell upon the wreckage like ants.

We had to.

Above any other thing aside from God, Plain folk feared fire. We had no fire departments, no running water from bottomless city lines. We had no telephones to summon help from Outside. If a fire caught and fanned itself to life, it could devour a field, houses, barns. We were defenseless against it.

Except for the earth the Lord gave us. We had plenty of dirt, and we used it.

Unbidden, men and women streamed to the field with shovels. Someone handed me one, and I worked in silent fellowship beside them. We heard the sound of the flames crackling behind us, the slice and cut of the shovels in the skin of the earth, the hiss of dirt raining down upon sparks. When we ran out of shovels, women went into the corn and crushed down the smoldering stalks with their shoes, stamping out the leaves.

We worked the fire line for hours, interrupted only by the Bishop's orders to advance and retreat. A child brought me water, and that was the first time I paused to look back at the shell of the helicopter. It stunk of plastic and something like kerosene, but there was nothing in it anymore except for a fine gray ash that made me cough. The ash shimmered dreamily in the setting sun, like the haze of mosquitoes at a river at dusk. I smeared the foul-tasting ash across my face when I wiped my lips with the back of my hand.

And I realized that we were alone. There were no English among us. My brow creased at that. Surely they would have sent someone for their helicopter. Surely they would have responded to Mrs. Parsall's call by now?

"Enough," the Bishop called out. He leaned heavily on his shovel. Sweat stained the front of his shirt, dripped from his beard. "The fire is out."

I stretched, my back aching from the hard work. We gathered around the Bishop, smelling of dirt and sweat and that synthetic burning stink. This corner of the field was destroyed, but it seemed that most of the crop was salvageable.

"Let us pray."

I lowered my head, clasped my hands. Our voices murmured in the gloaming, merging into one, lifting beyond the stalks of corn into the darkening sky. This was the Lord's Prayer that the English knew, but it was our prayer for all purposes and all seasons, spoken in our own Deitsch tongue:

Unser Vadder im Himmel,
Dei Naame loss heilich sei,
Dei Reich loss komme.
Dei Wille loss gedu sei,
Uff die Erd wie im Himmel.
Unser deeglich Brot gebb uns heit,
Un vergebb unser Schulde,
Wie mir die vergewwe wu uns schuldich sinn.
Un fiehr uns net in die Versuchung,
Awwer hald uns vum Ewile.
Fer dei is es Reich, die Graft,
Un die Hallichkeit in Ewichkeit.
Amen.

As we finished, silence seemed to press down eerily upon our gathering. After the explosions, perhaps it was only my ears ringing. Or the soft shock of the death of the pilot.

I only knew that the weight of the sky had changed, that something was indelibly wrong. I could feel it on the walk back to my house. I couldn't articulate it, not even to Elijah, but I think that he felt it too. He walked beside me, head bowed, shovel slung over his shoulder. Our shadows stretched long in the sunset.

I opened my mouth to speak several times, but no sound came out. This was too far out of my everyday experience to understand, but I wanted to get home. Home to my parents and the familiar rhythm of what I knew. A lump rose in my throat. *My mother will know what to do,* I told myself as I approached the house.

She was waiting for us on the back step. Though in her forties, my mother could easily have passed for my grandmother: she had the same gray eyes and straight, light brown hair streaked with wiry strands of silver. Years of sun and laughter had freckled her face and etched a spider web of lines around her eyes and mouth. Looking at her was sometimes like looking into my own future.

When she saw us, my mother rose to her feet and ran toward me. She thrust the hair that had come loose from my bonnet off my face, eyes wide at the dried blood on my cheek and clothing. "Are you all right, *liewe?*"

Plain folk were discouraged from using terms of endearment on the grounds that they were superficial. But the rules were loosened for mothers communicating with their children. My mother often called Sarah and me *liewe*—"dear."

"*Ja,* Mother," I said.

Her gaze wasn't fixed on me, but on my stained apron.

"It isn't mine, Mother," I whispered.

She nodded, wiping some dampness that had fallen on my cheek with the heel of her palm. "Are there any survivors? Your father went to find Frau Gerlach—"

I shook my head, unable to speak. I noticed that there were no red ambulances or paramedics even here. Frau Gerlach was our midwife, and the closest thing we had to a doctor, but saving the pilot in the helicopter probably would have been beyond the scope of her skills.

Mrs. Parsall paced down the driveway, staring at her cell phone, stabbing at the buttons.

"Did you reach the fire department?" Elijah asked.

"I called them. Ten times." She sighed in frustration. "And the sheriff and the highway patrol."

"I don't understand," I said. "Why didn't . . . Why didn't they come? These are their people." My fingers curled into fists. How could the English leave their people here to die, how they could not come to help their own?

Mrs. Parsall frowned at the device. "I don't know. I got a dispatcher the first three times I called. They said that they would send someone. After that, I just got a busy signal. I've been waiting by the road to flag them down, but . . . nothing." Her shoulders slumped.

My mother reached out, patted my sleeve. "Katie, go wash up. Mrs. Parsall, it's almost time for *Nachtesse*. Will you stay for a meal?"

The Plain reaction to any crisis is always to feed everyone in sight. My mother was no exception. She knew what Mrs. Parsall's answer would be on an ordinary day. She had spent many an evening at our table in the last months.

I often felt a bit sorry for Mrs. Parsall, returning to an empty house with her children and her husband gone. He was in the military, stationed somewhere in Europe. The Amish didn't believe in military service, so the idea was utterly foreign to me. Though I wasn't sure I wanted my mother's life as an adult woman, I wasn't certain that I wanted Mrs. Parsall's, either.

Mrs. Parsall hesitated. "I——"

"Please stay," I said, reaching for her hand with my filthy one.

"*Ja,* Mrs. Parsall, you must stay," my mother decided. "We'll have a table full in minutes, as soon as everyone comes in from the field." She gestured with her chin to the corn beyond. Some figures were already beginning to disperse to their own homes, but she knew that she had a duty to feed anyone who stopped by.

"Okay. Thanks. But let me help you set the table."

My mother nodded in satisfaction, and the women disappeared into the house with the screen door swishing shut behind them. Elijah and I gathered around the backyard water pump. Elijah primed it, pushing against the squeaking lever until spring water rushed out into a bucket below.

I untied my bonnet and thrust my hands into the soft, summer-warm water. I splashed it up over my face, scrubbed my grimy hands and neck. I felt a sudden surge of nausea and braced my hands against my knees. I had never been squeamish about blood before, but the only blood I dealt with belonged to animals. I gripped the edge of the bucket with sweaty palms.

The pump stopped squeaking. "Katie? Are you all right?"

"*Ja.*" I nodded. "Just . . . more water, please."

Elijah resumed pumping, and I thrust my head under the flow of water. It felt warm against the back of my neck, sluicing through my hair and dribbling underneath the collar of my dress. I let it wash over me until the water ran clear beneath my chin into the overflowing bucket and my dress was all wet.

"Thank you," I said, breathlessly.

Elijah looked at me oddly. I was soaked, with my hair unbound. Plain girls did not make a display of themselves in front of men this way. A woman's hair was considered to be her glory, and it was vain to display it uncovered outside of her home. I watched his Adam's apple move up and down, and then he turned his back to me to wash himself.

I squeezed the water out of my hair, coiled it back. I pulled my apron off, shoved it in the rubbish heap. It was beyond the help of soap or bleach.

My mother had the laundry hung out to dry. I plucked a clean dress from the clothesline and headed inside to change. I knew that I would feel better now that I was clean, surrounded by the familiar scents and bustle of home.

The bottom floor of our house was a large room with a staircase in the middle. Our back door led directly into the kitchen area. Propane-powered appliances lined the wall: a refrigerator and stove, separated by counters and a sink, where my mother was chopping vegetables.

Mrs. Parsall set the long table in the center of the floor. She glanced up when I came in, her smile wan. My little sister trailed behind her, humming and folding the napkins, blissfully unaware of what had happened.

I would not be the one to tell her.

I headed up the stair, to the room I shared with Sarah. Our twin beds, swaddled in quilts, were set parallel to each other with a window between them. I changed quickly, hiding my dirty dress in the bottom of the laundry heap. I didn't want to see it, wanted to pretend that all was normal. I tied on a clean apron, stuffed my wet hair up loosely under a fresh bonnet. My hands shook as I tied the strings, and I stabbed myself more than once with the pins that closed my dress.

I took a deep breath before descending the stairs. I hoped that my mother wouldn't coddle me, that she'd give me a chore to do to keep my mind from the awful black stain in the corner of the cornfield.

Downstairs, the table was filling up. My father had returned to the house. He was speaking with the Bishop, Elijah, and Elijah's father in low tones. Our next-door neighbors, Elijah's family, often joined us for meals. His mother had died when we were children, and my mother had often filled that role for Elijah and his brothers, Joseph and Seth. Their father always saw to it that our kitchen was well supplied in exchange for feeding his children.

"What are we going to do?" I heard Elijah say.

The Bishop sighed, looked at all of us. His beard was damp from the outside spigot, but his clothes still smelled like ash. He lifted his voice, and it was clear that he meant for all of us to hear. "The English will come when they are ready. They will come with their policemen. They will no doubt want to see the field, investigate the crash. Ask what we saw. But that is their task."

He spread open his deeply lined hands. "We have done all that we can do. We shall simply . . . go on as we usually do. *Ja,* there is nothing to be done for it but pray and go on."

The men nodded, and the nods spread to my mother and even Sarah, who bobbed her head to watch her bonnet strings bounce. Mrs. Parsall looked down at her shoes and sighed. Maybe she wanted to talk about the tragedy, but rumination on such things was not our way. We Plain folk did not obsess over things beyond our own control. From the Bishop's perspective, we had done the work we needed to: We came to help; we stopped the fire. And it was done. We would surrender the rest to God's will.

But I still had something to say. I bit my lip. "Herr Bishop . . . I saw something inside the helicopter. I went to help the pilot, but . . ." My gaze slid to Sarah, and my mother immediately distracted her with an early piece of pie.

I squirmed as the Bishop watched me. My voice lowered to a squeak. "It looked as if . . . it seemed that he was attacked, dragged back into the wreckage by . . . another person. A strange-looking person." I struggled to articulate what I saw, even now doubting those red eyes burning in my memory. The Bishop was a good man, but his authority made me nervous. I knew he noticed that I was often the last one to follow his orders. I always did follow them—but I needed to think on them first. This was not a trait that was encouraged, and it bothered my parents.

The Bishop patted my arm. "It's all right, Katie. When the police come, you can tell them what you saw. But you're safe now. There's nothing left."

I swallowed and nodded slowly.

"There is nothing to be done for this," he repeated. "It is

done. And we go on, as we always have. It is a tragedy, but it does not have anything to do with us."

An awkward silence stretched, and I could feel the weight of the Bishop's pale stare on me.

My mother, more noisily than necessary, brought a bowl of mashed potatoes to the table. "Herr Miller has brought us more potatoes."

"Thank you, Herr Miller," I said politely. We were up to our eyeballs in potatoes, and Mother was getting creative with them, turning them into potato salad, mashing them, and shredding them into hash browns. I glanced sidelong at the bushel of potatoes that had materialized by the door.

"You're welcome, Katie." Herr Miller perched in a chair beside my father. He was a tall, thin man with a beard white as a chicken's breast. Somewhat sad, I suppose on account of his wife. I remember that his beard had gone white shortly after his wife died. He seemed much older than my father, but they were the same age.

When all the food had been served, we automatically looked to the foot of the table, at the Bishop. I lowered my gaze to my folded hands in my lap as we recited the Lord's Prayer. Mrs. Parsall didn't try; she didn't know Deitsch. But I imagined her following along in English. We always spoke in English around Outsiders, to be polite, but we lapsed into Deitsch when we prayed. That old habit seemed soothing now. I let myself fall into the familiar rhythm of the words. The Bishop's "Amen" and the sudden silence after caught me a bit by surprise.

But my father filled in that empty space with a veneer of normalcy. "How are the boys?" he asked Herr Miller, passing the mashed potatoes.

"Good, *ja*. Good," Herr Miller replied. "Seth and Joseph are working now at the furniture store in town."

Mrs. Parsall nodded. "Ah. They are turning table legs?" She seemed to be game to play along in this forced routine. I noticed that her hand shook on the serving spoon.

"Joseph is going to be a master carpenter, like his uncle." Herr Miller nodded to himself. Joseph was two years older than Elijah and had been carving since he was old enough to pick up a knife. I still had a doll made with one of Joseph's carved heads. "Seth is learning. I suspect that he will be a farmer, like his papa, though."

Elijah shrugged. "Joseph always wanted to be a carpenter. When he's not otherwise busy chasing Ruth Hersberger."

My father's eyes crinkled. "Joseph has been chasing Ruth for years."

"I know." Herr Miller sighed. Ruth had just turned sixteen. She was gorgeous: blond curly hair, blue eyes, and a singing voice that could make angels weep. "Hopefully, he will marry her and be done with all the pining."

"Ruth is a nice girl," the Bishop said. "Good family. They would be a good match."

Herr Miller held his head in his hands, though I could see his smile behind his fingers at the Bishop's approval. "I only hope he is successful in his courting. If she chooses another young man . . . he'll hang around the house until he's an old man. Like me."

The Bishop's expression was enigmatic as he tucked into the gravy. "These things will sort out on their own." I wondered if he had already mentioned this to Ruth's family.

"You're not old. Yet." Elijah grinned at his father.

Herr Miller gave him a sour look. "Wait until you have children. You'll feel old immediately."

I glanced at the empty places that Joseph and Seth usually occupied. "Are the boys coming?"

Herr Miller squinted at the long sun's rays through the window. "They should be here by now, but I told your mother not to wait on them. They know what time *Nachtesse* is."

"There will be plenty of leftovers," my mother assured him.

And she was right. She had baked a chicken and cooked a roast, mashed potatoes with gravy, corn, noodles, and spiced apple pie for dessert. By the time we finished, the sun had sunk below the horizon and we had lit the oil lamps. The Bishop took his leave, admitting that he still had not finished his chores on account of the afternoon's excitement, and I walked Mrs. Parsall out to her car.

The sky was streaked with a slightly paler violet and pink in the west. The evening star had burned through the veil of color, and somewhere in the distant countryside, I heard dogs barking at a sliver of moon that tangled in the treetops. Lanterns were glowing warmly in the faraway windows of other houses in our settlement. The light was comforting. All looked to be well.

Mrs. Parsall slid behind the wheel of her station wagon and rolled down the window to release the heat that had accumulated during the day. It hit me in the face like a warm breath. She cranked the engine to life.

"I'll come by next week. If you need me, for Sunny or anything else . . ." Her gaze flickered to the dark field, the site of the crash hidden by the corn.

I nodded. "I'll send someone to the gas station to call you."

Mrs. Parsall rolled her eyes at the inefficiency of it all. Someone would have to go by buggy or horse into town and then return with a message. The Englisher who ran Schmidt's General Store and gas station kept a bulletin board of messages for Plain folk to gather and leave. Mrs. Parsall opened her mouth to speak, but then fell silent.

The radio had buzzed to life when she turned on the engine. Mrs. Parsall listened to what she called "classic rock-and-roll." I would sneak a listen every once in a while. Though I didn't make out all the lyrics all the time, I enjoyed the music. Once, Father had caught me humming "(I Can't Get No) Satisfaction" while milking the cows. He may not have known what the tune was, but he knew it was secular music, which was disapproved of by the Amish.

But the radio wasn't playing music today. It was just a voice, broken up by static:

" . . . curfew has been imposed. Local law enforcement officers have instructions to arrest anyone found out on the streets after sunset . . ."

I leaned on the car window, and Mrs. Parsall turned up the volume.

" . . . again, the sheriff's office and the highway patrol is requiring people to stay in their homes until . . ."

The station faded. Mrs. Parsall played with the dial, couldn't find the station again. Her brow knit above her glasses. "I wonder if there was another accident? Maybe that's why no one came for the helicopter."

"What kind of accident?"

"I don't know." She chewed her lip. "I hope that it's not terrorism."

I knew about terrorism, in the broadest terms. I remembered when Elijah came running up the dirt road to tell us about 9/11. I'd been milking cows with my father. Well, I'd been too small to milk, so I had just held the bucket while my father did it. Elijah breathlessly announced that planes had killed a bunch of people in New York City. It seemed very remote and far away. Though our lives went on as they always had, I noticed that the English were afraid. Very afraid. Somehow, though, I couldn't imagine anything like that happening here. Not to us. Our sect of Plain folk had not changed for hundreds of years. It would take more than a handful of men with hijacked planes to affect our way of life.

Back then my father had looked at Elijah and me and told us not to be afraid. That God would protect us, that nothing would change.

I believed him. He was my father. And he was right. He was always right.

I leaned into Mrs. Parsall's window, watching her face wrinkle in the unnatural green light of the car instruments. I felt some of that same fear emanating from her now.

"Stay here tonight with us," I pleaded. "You can sleep with Sarah and me."

Mrs. Parsall nodded. She slowly turned the key to silence the engine. "I'm sure that they'll straighten this out by morning. But . . ." She reached into her purse and dug out her cell phone. I walked back to the house to give her some privacy. I never really understood the attachment that some of the English had to their devices. But then again, everyone I needed to speak to was within walking distance. Maybe I would feel differently if they were far away.

"Can Mrs. Parsall stay tonight?" I asked my father.

"Of course. What's wrong?" he asked, reading my expression.

"On the radio . . . it says that there's a curfew. Police will arrest anyone on the roads. But they don't say why."

Herr Miller rose partly out of his chair. "Seth and Joseph are at the furniture store."

"I can call them, see if they're all right." Mrs. Parsall had come inside. Her nervous fingers knit in her pink purse strap.

"Did you speak with your family?" I asked her.

She nodded. "I couldn't get ahold of my husband. But I spoke with my son. He's at school, hasn't heard anything strange. He says he's at the library." She rolled her eyes in skepticism. "But he says the Internet is down. He couldn't find any information on what's going on." She blew out her breath. "So maybe it's minor."

"I'm sure that everything is fine," my father said.

Mrs. Parsall held out her cell phone to Herr Miller. "I don't know if this qualifies as an emergency, but . . . do you want to talk to whoever picks up at the furniture store?"

The restrictions on phone use by Amish were complicated. We weren't allowed to have phone lines in homes. But we could use the telephone for business purposes and to summon help in an emergency.

"I think . . . that I would," Herr Miller said. "But I don't know the telephone number."

"I do," Elijah announced. His father looked at him sharply. "Bishop's gone." Elijah shrugged.

"Elijah," Herr Miller said. "The Bishop may be gone. But God is everywhere."

Mrs. Parsall gave the phone to Elijah, and he punched in the number, then handed it to his father.

Herr Miller cradled the receiver to his ear. I could hear the phone ringing. It rang for what seemed like a long time before someone picked up.

"Hello? Joseph?" A grin of relief spread across Herr Miller's face. "Are you all right?" He nodded to himself. *"Ja, ja . . . ja.* Stay there . . . I will see you then. Goodbye."

He handed the phone back to Mrs. Parsall. "They are safe at the store. A deputy came by and told them about the curfew."

"A deputy?" Elijah echoed. "What did the deputy say?"

"He said that there had been rioting last night the next town over. Many people were hurt and taken to the hospital."

We all looked at Mrs. Parsall. She was our conduit to Outside.

"I don't know. I haven't had the television on." She spread her hands helplessly. "I wonder if that's what happened to the helicopter. Some unhappy rioter . . ."

"There's no use in speculating," Herr Miller said. "The boys are staying at the furniture store tonight. Better that they stay there than spend the night in English jail. The curfew will be lifted in the morning. They'll come home then, and we'll hear all about the excitement."

My father turned up the wick on the lamp. "Everything will be all right," he said.

And I believed him.

CHAPTER THREE

That night I lay in bed and stared out the window.

Night and I were old friends.

The soft darkness wrapped around me, and I heard the familiar sounds in the stillness: the creak of the house settling as the temperature cooled, my sister's breathing beside me, the crickets that had not yet succumbed to the frost. Night was a time for rest, for reflection. Sometimes it was the only time I truly had to myself. In fall and winter, the sun stayed hidden for longer and longer. Rather than burn the oil lamps out, we simply went to bed earlier. And that left time to think. Maybe too much time.

Tonight felt subtly different. It wasn't just being crowded together with Sarah in her bed. It wasn't just Mrs. Parsall snoring softly from my bed. Part of it was the shock from the afternoon wearing off.

I looked out the window, at the dark hills and the slightly lighter sky. The stars shone down as they always did. But I heard no engines of cars on the highway. And it seemed that there were fewer lights in the distance than there usually were.

I pulled the quilt up close to my neck and shuddered, re-membering what I had seen in the helicopter. I did not sleep at all, feeling those glowing red eyes burning into my mind. Even working a prayer on my lips did nothing to drive them from my thoughts.

I rose in the dim gray light before dawn, dressed, and pad-ded down to the kitchen. I needed to see for myself that there was nothing there, that my stressed imagination had conjured something from nothing.

I grabbed my shoes, arranged in a neat line beside my fam-ily's shoes near the back door. I slipped outside . . .

. . . and into the realm of the ravens.

They were everywhere: perched on our gutters, in the trees, walking along the ground, swarming in the sky. I heard them calling to one another in their raspy language, a sound that swelled the farther I walked from the house toward the field. They swirled like vultures over the corn, cawing. They swept through the sky in large black swaths.

I stared up at them. This was wrong. Ravens were not mi-gratory birds. They stayed throughout the winter. While they formed loose affiliations with others, they did not flock. Not like this. Not in the hundreds. Not in the thousands of black specks that I could see on the lightening horizon. As the light grew, so did the cacophony of their voices.

They were smart birds. I gathered this from years of watch-ing them. They remembered faces, and gave Elijah a wide berth because they knew he'd throw stones at them. They avoided Herr Miller's fields because he'd shot one of them, and one dead was all that it took to keep them away. When the bird had been shot, there was a terrible cawing the next dawn, as if they mourned. My father called them "gossip birds."

I never hated them, not the way Elijah and the farmers seemed to. To my way of thinking, they were God's creatures, same as cows and dogs. I never shooed them away from the grain. And they never avoided me the way they did Elijah.

But something had gotten them riled, some contagious thought that had them on the wing, sweeping south. I frowned as I entered the cornfield, pushing aside the stalks bent from yesterday's activity. What did the ravens know that I didn't?

One raven hopped on a bowing stalk before me. I looked up at him.

"What's wrong?"

He stared at me intently, then cawed three times. I honestly felt as if he were trying to tell me something. He flapped his wings and disappeared into the sky with his fellows, the stalk he'd perched on bobbing in the gloom.

I bit my lip and kept pressing forward. I smelled the location of the crash before I saw it, smelled that dew-damp artificial burn stink that clung close to the ground. I peered into the battered clearing, anticipating seeing only the scorch mark pressed into the earth.

But I was not alone.

Ravens hopped through the broken bits of debris, puffing up their wings. In the center of the flock stood a man dressed in black, the hems of his trousers stained gray by the ash. He was turned away from me, and I could tell that he had been here for some time: a white circle was circumscribed around the crash site in something that looked like whitewash paint.

My palms began to sweat. I rubbed them against my skirt.

The man muttered to himself, and it seemed that the ravens understood some of what he said. They cawed urgently when he paused to take a breath. He was bowed in prayer, and one bird lit on his shoulder.

I was torn between asking him what he was doing here and looking on in silence. I watched him for some moments, before the wind kicked up and the ash blew toward me. I pressed both hands over my nose and sneezed.

The man turned around. I recognized him as the bent old Hexenmeister. He looked at me with glazed, cataract-covered eyes. "Katie."

"Herr Stoltz," I said, my cheeks flaming red at having been caught out for spying. "I didn't mean—"

"Go home, Katie."

"Herr Stoltz, I—"

"Go home, Katie. And do not speak of this. There is nothing here. Not anymore."

That phrase sank deep into my bones, seemed to chase away a bit of the memory of yesterday. Dawn began to spill over the horizon, in brilliant gold, and the ravens took wing in a furious flutter of black, like rotten leaves stirred up in the bottom of a bucket.

I shuddered.

But I obeyed.

Seth and Joseph didn't return by midmorning.

And the English didn't come for their helicopter.

I said nothing about the Hexenmeister's visit to the field, heeding his order. I felt that I had intruded on something sacred, fearsome, and intimate. I was ashamed and curious, both at once. No one noticed that the ravens had all gone.

Herr Miller had come to our house to use Mrs. Parsall's phone. His hands were pale and fidgeted nervously. "They said that they'd be back this morning," he murmured. And he kept saying it, over and over.

Mrs. Parsall redialed the number to the furniture store, then shook her head. "No answer." Her brow was creased with worry. "Do you want to come with me in the car to go looking for them?"

"Has the curfew been lifted?" my father asked.

"I assume so," Mrs. Parsall said. "I turned on the car radio this morning. All it was playing was music." I'd sat with her in the passenger's seat, listening. Everything sounded normal.

"Maybe they're just being poky," my mother suggested. It was almost five miles to town. By buggy, that could take a bit over an hour. If the boys were on foot, it would take up to two hours.

I squinted at the window. It had been daylight for three hours. They should be here by now.

"I'd be grateful to go check on them," Herr Miller said. "Elijah's doing the morning chores."

"Maybe we'll find them walking by the side of the road," Mrs. Parsall said hopefully.

I followed them out to the car. Mrs. Parsall started the station wagon up, and the Rolling Stones' "(I Can't Get No) Satisfaction" was playing.

I bit my lip. I didn't believe in omens.

My father's hand clamped down on my shoulder as I moved to sidle into the back seat. He shook his head. "Not you, Katie. There are chores to be done."

I stepped back and stared after the station wagon as it bounced down the rutted drive to the road, the music sounding tinny in the distance.

I'd helped my father milk the cows and was feeding and watering the dogs by the time Elijah located me in the kennel.

"They didn't find Seth and Joseph." Elijah sat down heavily on an upturned bucket. His hands were slack in his lap, and his eyes were dark with worry.

"They checked the furniture store?" I patted Sunny's belly, full of babies and meat scraps. I'd snuck her some canned hamburger, and she was still licking the gravy from her chops. I thought that gravy was good for the pups, but no one else shared my philosophy.

"Ja. The door was open, but no one was inside." Elijah's mouth thinned. "Father won't say anything else. He came back white as a ghost, and he and Mrs. Parsall went straight to the Elders."

I frowned. "Mrs. Parsall went with him?" They must have seen something very strange for Herr Miller to take an Englisher to the Elders.

"Ja." Elijah blew out his breath. "Either my brothers are in trouble, or . . ."

" . . . or they're going to *get* in trouble with the Elders." A certain amount of drift was expected, even tolerated among young Plain folk. But not the kind of disobedience that caused parents to worry so much they needed to go to the Elders.

"They didn't check Schmidt's?" I asked. The boys liked to visit the general store whenever they could slip away. It was the same place we swapped messages on the bulletin board with the Outside world. Schmidt's had chewing gum, soda pop, cigarettes, beer, and, most enticingly for Joseph and Seth, comic books. The boys kept a secret stash in their shared bedroom.

Elijah shook his head. "No. I didn't know that my father and Mrs. Parsall had left."

And he would have been reluctant to tell his father the secret. I understood. Though we loved our parents, we often kept secrets from them. The older we got, it seemed like the secrets multiplied.

Elijah stood up, nearly knocking the bucket over and startling Sunny. "I'm going to go look for them."

"I'll go with you." My morning chores were finished.

"You just want to visit Schmidt's," he teased as I followed him out of the barn.

"Maybe." I shrugged. "I *would* like a Coca-Cola. And maybe a magazine."

"What kind of magazine?"

"Maybe *Cosmopolitan*." I said it only to shock him, to test boundaries.

Elijah raised a brow. He'd seen the scantily clad women on the glossy pages and the covers that announced new sex tips — probably incomprehensible to both of us — every month. I'd shown him one the other week. His mouth had fallen open. He dropped the magazine three times before getting it back on the rack. It was a scandalous thing, that magazine. The women in it seemed obsessed with expensive clothing and makeup and horoscopes and sex. There rarely seemed to be much mention of the other parts of a woman's life: of work, of families, of being part of a community.

I smiled innocently. "I would like to smell the perfume samples."

"Ah. Naturally."

We walked the mile to the Millers' barn, where Elijah readied his favorite horse, Star. She was a Haflinger female, all golden with white socks and a white star on her forehead. Star was too old to breed now, but she'd been around long enough to be unfazed by traffic. I rubbed the gray flecks on her nose and murmured at her while Elijah hitched her up to his buggy.

Elijah had his own buggy, which he'd saved for with his carpentry and produce money since he was twelve. It was an open buggy, glossy black, that seated two people. It was what many called a "courting buggy" — there was no privacy whatsoever, which ensured that its occupants behaved themselves. It was terrible in rain. Elijah bought it used, and the wheels needed to be reset at least three times. But he worked on it himself, kept it as clean as any young man on the Outside would with his own vehicle.

"What if we find them?" I asked, as Elijah offered me a hand up into the seat beside him. There was no room for the boys in this buggy. I thought for a moment about suggesting that we take Herr Miller's surrey buggy, which could seat up to five, but stopped myself. That would be too much like stealing.

"Then we'll make them walk and follow along behind them," Elijah said with a grin.

"What if they're hurt?"

His grin faded. "Then we are the ones who walk."

Star pulled the buggy out onto a rutted dirt lane, and Elijah shook the reins gently. The horse cantered out into the morning, the buggy bumping behind her for a good two miles until we got to the paved roads.

Paved roads were smoother on the metal wheels, but almost as noisy, as the buggy squeaked along the blacktop two-lane highway. Sometimes the English had issues with the horse droppings left behind as we traveled. There were always some who would honk their horns or try to spook the horses.

I remember when I was a little girl and one of the boys from school was driving a buggy down the road. He was twelve at the time. His horse was frightened by a swerving vehicle, and the boy was thrown into a ditch and killed. My mother used it as a cautionary tale, and I still had some fear of the road each time I set out upon it. Cars often whizzed past so quickly that they shook the buggy.

But there was no traffic today. A breeze moved briskly, stirring the yellowing tassels of grass by the side of the road. There was a lot to be said for traveling by buggy. One could miss so much when riding in a car—I knew from the few times I'd ridden with Mrs. Parsall. Cars went too fast, and the details blurred away. I watched for more ravens but saw none. Only a groundhog chewing gravel by the side of the road and a solitary heron fishing at the edge of a pond. My brow furrowed. The ravens sensed something that escaped the notice of the other animals.

My gaze fastened on something by the side of the road. A piece of red glass. My eyes followed over a rise in the road, seeing that a car had gone off into a ditch and struck a fence post.

Elijah slowed. "We should see if anyone needs help."

I hopped off the seat before Star had come to a complete halt. Elijah continued forward a few yards to find a level place to pull the buggy off the road and activate the flashers.

I stepped down the grassy slope into the ditch. The windshield of the car was broken, but the headlights still gleamed. The engine was silent. I leaned into the car, peered inside.

I saw no people. Just a woman's handbag and some children's toys in the back seat. I swallowed when I saw a rusty stain that looked like blood smeared on the back of a baby's car seat. The passenger's side door was open.

"Looks like they got out," Elijah said behind me. "Whoever they were."

I reached into the back seat and picked up a pink plush rabbit with red plastic eyes. I held it to my chest as I studied the car seat. One of the seat belts securing it had been torn. I pointed at it.

"Maybe . . . maybe the police came and cut them out," Elijah suggested.

My eyes fell on the handbag. Plain women carried what they needed in their aprons and dress pockets. But English women were inseparable from these bags, in which they seemed to keep everything from medicine to money to makeup.

The breeze plucked strands of my hair from my white prayer bonnet, and I picked the tendrils out of my mouth when I spoke. I voiced what we were both afraid of on the empty, eerie road. "There was mention of violence on the radio last night. Rioting."

Elijah's mouth flattened, and he looked at the northern horizon. "Seth and Joseph will be all right. They would not have gotten mixed up in that."

"I know." Seth and Joseph were pacifists, like the rest of the Plain folk. I knew that they wouldn't be caught up in perpetrating a random spree of violence.

But it didn't mean that they couldn't fall victim to one.

We climbed back into the buggy and drove into town without another word passing between us. When we reached a sign that reduced the speed limit from fifty-five miles per hour to thirty-five, I knew that we had arrived in Torch. I said a prayer under my breath that we would find Seth and Joseph in short order and return home before our parents even realized that we were gone.

But my heart dropped as the buggy jingled down the road.

Torch had never been a large town. It contained less than five hundred full-time residents. During the weekends, it often appeared that there were more, since Torch catered to the tourist trade in this rural part of the state. The Olde Deutsche

Restaurant served hearty Amish fare; as we passed, we noted that there were no cars in the parking lot, and the windows were dark.

We passed English houses, which seemed normal enough, with cars parked in the driveways. But more than one still had the porch lights shining in the day. And I noticed that the mailboxes perched by the side of the road were full of yesterday's mail.

Schmidt's General Store and gas station was positioned at a crossroads where the highway intersected the main street in Torch. Lights shone within, including a neon sign advertising beer. A car was parked in the fire lane in front, but there were none at the gas pumps.

We parked the buggy behind the store and hitched Star to a telephone pole that many Amish used for that purpose. The owner, Schmidt, sold anything his store carried to Amish youth with a wink and a nod. We often thought that he kept the alley behind the store clear specifically so that young men and women would have a place to smoke out of sight. I half expected to see Seth and Joseph loitering in the back, eating potato chips, but no one was there. Not even pigeons.

The back door to Schmidt's was always open. We stepped around the ashtray on the back stoop and into the bright light of the store.

Music played overhead, something wordless and inoffensive. The English called it "elevator music," but I was never quite certain where the term came from. I'd been on a handful of elevators, and none of them was ever musical.

The cases containing dairy products, pop, and beer were all lit and humming. Everything from the buzzing fluorescent lights to the drip of a toilet running in the bathroom seemed to intrude on my thoughts. The English probably considered noises like this to be part of the background, but I found them distracting. Mrs. Parsall even told me that she sometimes fell asleep to the flickering television, which I couldn't imagine.

We wandered down the aisles. I paused beside the racks of comic books. I'd read many of the Miller boys' comic books over the years. Joseph had a preference for *Superman*.

But I had a different favorite. I squatted down at the bottom of the rack, my fingers flipping through the curling pages. I plucked up an issue of *Wonder Woman*. The cover showed a magnificent woman with curly hair soaring through the sky, wearing only the skimpiest of clothes.

I had followed the Princess of Themyscira's adventures since I was a little girl. I was amazed at how she was unconscious of her near-nudity and beauty, fascinated that she was stronger than the men. I also felt some pang of kinship with her, knowing that she came from a society closed off from the rest of the world. Paradise Island was, in its own way, frozen centuries behind in time. And it was even more cut off from Man's World than we were.

But most of all, I was intrigued by the idea of her purity. Wonder Woman was certainly not Plain, and not even any stripe of Christian. She followed the ancient Greek gods, who occasionally appeared in the stories.

But she retained her virtue. To my knowledge, Diana remained virginally pure. Despite her seemingly overt sexuality, there was a certain innocence about her. Power and innocence. It flummoxed me.

I was also easily stymied by the threats she faced: crime, hatred, war. In my peaceful life, I had never known any of these things.

But comic books were considered children's things. Though Elijah shared in my teenage rebellions now, I wondered if he would feel the same way if I was married to him. Would he still turn a blind eye to me when I picked up a comic or paged uncomprehendingly through *Cosmopolitan*? Would he hold me to a different standard, once we were adults?

"Katie, *come on,*" Elijah called from the next aisle over.

"*Ja.* Coming." I tucked the comic under my arm and followed him.

He glanced back at me. "What?" he asked.

I shook my head. "Nothing." I was embarrassed to admit I was searching for comics when we should be looking for the boys.

"It's something," he said. "You only get that look in your eyes when you're thinking."

I blew out my breath. He knew me well. Better than I wanted to admit.

"I . . . wondered what would happen when we do as the Bible says. When we leave childish things behind." I looked down at the comic.

Elijah shrugged. "That's on the other side."

"The other side of what?"

"*Rumspringa.* I figured everything would sort itself out then."

I clutched *Wonder Woman* to my chest, refusing to give her

up. I paused before the case of pop, opened it, and reached in for a Coca-Cola. I had a weakness for Coca-Cola—the bite and the sweetness were unlike anything at home. Maybe *Rumspringa* would dim that desire out of me. But not yet.

I walked up to the cash register, reaching for money in my apron pocket.

But Mr. Schmidt wasn't there. I peered over the counter, festooned in ribbons of lottery tickets. The clerk's stool stood empty, and the cash register was closed. Fear prickled along the back of my neck.

Elijah's arm reached around me to ring the bell on the counter. "Maybe he's in the bathroom."

I gestured with my chin at the open lavatory door. "No."

"But his car's out there," Elijah insisted. It was as if he was refusing to believe what we saw.

"He's not here," I said. "And neither are Seth or Joseph."

Elijah rang the bell again, out of frustration, before he walked to the back exit of the store to fetch the buggy.

I looked down at the pop and comic book in my hands. For an instant, I considered walking out with them. The thought gave me a rush that crept up to my cheeks in a flush of power.

But I put my money down on the counter, calculating the exact sales tax in my head and counting out the change to the penny. I left it in a neat pile beside the cash register before I walked out.

I might have been rebellious. Maybe a bit sinful. Maybe a lot sinful.

But I wasn't a thief.

The furniture store was a two-story building built to resemble a barn, the front porch crowded with rocking chairs. Connected to the store was a sheet-metal warehouse where furniture was constructed and finished by Amish men. Elijah guided the buggy down the gravel drive and stopped to tie up Star on a hitching post beside the building.

We climbed two short steps to the porch and wove around the rocking chairs for sale. I paused before the front window. The store usually displayed hope chests, china cupboards, and bedsteads in the large window. These things were still here, but the glass was broken out. A few shards were on the porch, but it seemed as if most of the damage reached within the display window. Glass sparkled like ice on a bedstead with a red-and-white quilt spread on it.

"Stay with the buggy," Elijah whispered.

I shook my head and followed him across the porch. The floorboards creaked under our shoes as we reached the front door, which still had its Closed sign turned out. It dangled slightly askew. Above the door frame, a carved wooden placard bade visitors "Welcome."

Elijah grabbed the door handle and pulled. It opened, and the bell jangled.

"Seth? Joseph?" he called into the darkness.

Only the echo of the bell answered him.

My fingers gripped the sleeve of Elijah's shirt as we crossed the threshold. The air felt cooler inside, as if the shadow of the building still held some of the darkness of night that it was unwilling to release into the day. Elijah turned on the light switch beside the entrance.

The fluorescent overhead lights flickered to life, casting harsh blue light into the show room. If there were shadows in my imagination, they scuttled away under that blisteringly clear light.

"Joseph!" Elijah yelled.

I pursed my mouth. If Herr Miller and Mrs. Parsall hadn't found the boys, then they weren't here. But I understood Elijah's need to see what had driven them straight to the Elders.

Glass from the store window crunched underfoot as we wove our way through the displays that smelled like cedar and sawdust. I'd never seen the store empty before. There were usually at least a half-dozen English stroking the grain of the wood or filling out custom orders for kitchen cabinets. It was a lucrative business. But not today.

Today a chest of drawers was upturned on the floor, drawers spilled out. As a credit to the workmanship, none of the wood had split.

Elijah's face paled.

"They might not have been here when this happened," I said. "They may have been robbed, run away . . ."

"They were here." He walked to a pair of bedsteads pressed up against the wall. The Amish quilts spread over mattresses for decoration, to help shoppers envision the pieces in their homes, were rumpled. Rumpled as if someone had slept in them.

I swallowed, said nothing. What I'd said still held true. Maybe.

Elijah walked back through the store. I paused before the cash register. It was one of the old-fashioned ones that didn't run on electricity, so that Amish employees could use it. The drawer was still neatly tucked beneath it, undisturbed, so it seemed they hadn't been robbed.

Elijah reached behind the counter for the telephone. He punched "911" on the buttons and waited. After a few moments, he shook his head. "No answer. Just a recording."

"What does it say?"

He stood close beside me so that we could both listen to the receiver. A female voice said: *"County Sheriff's Office. Due to an emergency, all personnel are temporarily unavailable. For motorist assistance, call the State Highway Patrol at . . ."*

Elijah put the phone down. "An emergency," he repeated, shaking his head. His breath disturbed a tendril of hair that had escaped my bonnet.

The knowledge seemed to race through him. I watched as his jaw hardened. He turned around, headed for the back door.

"Where are you going?" I asked.

"To find out what happened to my brothers."

Elijah and I searched the back storeroom, stacked high with finished chairs and special orders with yellow tickets taped to them. We made our way through a maze of furniture to the workshop in the back. The door to the workshop was ajar and pushed open easily.

One could tell that Plain folk worked here. All the tools were hand tools, not powered by electricity. Hammers and saws were hung neatly on pegs, nails and screws captured tidily in Mason jars. Half-finished skeletons of furniture perched on tables, waiting for turned legs or handles. The sawdust made me stifle a sneeze.

"Elijah," I croaked. I pointed at the floor.

A narrow keyhole saw lay there. It wasn't quite as long as my forearm and covered in serrated teeth with a grip like a pistol. The fact that the saw was on the floor and not put away was remarkable in and of itself. But the blade was covered in stale red blood.

The blood spattered along the floor and terminated along a freshly sanded cabinet.

Elijah's callused hands knotted into fists. They didn't even unravel when I tried to slip my fingers between his.

CHAPTER FOUR

It was as if all the people had been mysteriously taken up in the sky.

We rode in silence through town, staring at the empty homes and businesses, until I spoke. I was always the first one to break our silences.

"Do you think that . . . I mean . . ." I fumbled to find the right words. "The English occasionally talk about that Rapture thing." Plain people were more concerned with our works on earth and tended to think that the afterlife sorted itself out.

Elijah looked sidelong at me. "No. Not possible," he said, flatly.

"Why not?"

"It's just not. We weren't taken."

I opened my mouth, closed it. "But if the Elders were wrong . . . what if we are wrong? About God? About everything?" I opened my hand and gestured to the countryside and the larger world beyond it.

"Not possible." He shook his head, vehemently. "Seth and

Joseph are gone too. If God favored the English, he wouldn't take all the English and just Seth and Joseph."

I considered it. He had a point. But I didn't remind him of the bloody saw on the warehouse floor.

Star's ears twitched at a distant wail.

"Sirens." Elijah pulled the buggy over to the side of the road as far as he could. "Not everyone was sucked up in your Rapture," he said pointedly.

I turned around behind us, where the sound of the sirens grew louder. I stood and lifted my arms to flag down the policemen. The breeze whipped my sleeves and skirts like pennants, and my heart lifted at the thought of finally getting some help for Seth and Joseph. Some answers.

I shouted as the patrol car came over the rise in the road, but my shout was obliterated by the blare of the siren. And it wasn't just one patrol car . . .

There was a caravan of them, roaring down the highway at breakneck speed. The first one rushed past us in a roiling howl of wind and sound. I counted four more before I realized that they weren't stopping.

The cacophony spooked Star. The buggy lurched beneath me, and I lost my footing, falling forward. The metal rail at the front of the buggy drove the wind from my chest. Star lunged ahead, and I saw Elijah struggling with the reins from the corner of my eye.

A wheel caught in the ditch and shrieked as the buggy pitched right. I clutched the rail as the buggy tipped and lurched. It landed on its right side in the ditch with a crash. I tasted dirt and blood and grass.

I'd been thrown. I could feel the impact in my ribs and spine. I pulled myself up on my palms in the grass, drew an aching breath to shout: "Elijah!"

With the buggy caught in the ditch, Star stopped dragging it, rearing with a scream of fear. I saw Elijah's white shirt behind a wheel, saw him stumble from the wreck, and breathed a sigh of relief.

I looked beyond him at the road. The caravan of police cars kept charging on as if the Devil himself were after them.

"Are you hurt?"

Elijah picked me off the ground. A cut glimmered red above his eye, and his hat was missing. I touched his brow, and he winced.

"Nothing broken," I said as my fingers felt my ribs under my dress. "You?"

"I'm all right." But I could see that he was putting no weight on his left foot. "I've got to get this shoe off before my foot swells into it, and it has to be cut off."

"Sit down," I ordered. Elijah obligingly sat on the grassy embankment over the ditch while I stripped off his shoe. He was right: his ankle was hot and swelling already under his sock. He flinched when I touched it.

"Do you think it's broken?" I asked.

"Not sure."

I attempted to feel his bones through the swelling. Though I couldn't feel anything jutting out, it didn't mean that there wasn't a fracture in there somewhere. I took off my apron, rolled it lengthwise to form a bandage, and wrapped it around the ankle to stabilize it.

Elijah groaned as he looked at the wrecked buggy. "So much for sneaking out."

I walked to Star, speaking quietly. She let me touch her nose and her head. I stroked her sides, ran my fingers over her withers and legs. I unhitched her from the buggy and led her up the slope to a fence that I could tie her to.

Nothing seemed to be broken on her either, but I could see that she'd thrown a shoe. She let me pull out a piece of nail that remained in her back hoof, and she calmed down enough to lip at some clover that sprouted around the fence post.

I walked down the embankment to where Elijah hobbled. He hopped on one foot and circled the buggy, bracing his hands on the frame as he examined it.

"Star's okay. But she needs a trip to the farrier. How's the buggy?"

Elijah grimaced. "It'll take more than a trip to the wheelwright to fix it. But it might be drivable."

"Let's get it righted and find out."

We scrabbled to get a grip on the side of the buggy that was aimed skyward. It was streaked in mud, and purchase was difficult. Finally, we succeeded in rocking the buggy right and left, creating enough momentum to allow it to fall back on its wheels with a clatter and a crash. We scrambled back to avoid being trapped beneath the undercarriage.

The buggy stood, bent and creaking. I could already see that the right wheel was badly warped. Elijah limped over to it and ran his fingers over the rim. He put his shoulder to it, trying to straighten it out.

The back was dented, and one light cracked out. I didn't

think that it mattered that the safety lights were out; no one was out here who would pay attention to them, anyway.

I found my comic book blown up against the fence, caked in dirt. But there was no sign of my bottle of Coca-Cola. I looked for it for a few moments but gave up and returned to the buggy.

"Is it drivable?" I asked.

"I think so."

Elijah brushed the worst of the dirt from the seat. It took several tries and many promises of oats to get Star to back into the harness. I insisted that Elijah sit before he made his foot worse. Reluctantly, he climbed aboard while I finished cooing to Star and fastening her into the harness. I climbed up into the buggy beside him, and he stared between the horse's ears morosely. He elevated his sore foot over the front rail.

"It's going to be a bumpy ride," he warned.

He was right. He started the horse out at a very slow walk. The bent wheel, on my side, wobbled along, knocking my teeth together. I felt bad for Elijah, his foot thumping along the front rail, with his broken buggy and thinking of his missing brothers.

I reached out and patted his sleeve, though it seemed an ineffectual gesture.

It was afternoon by the time we'd made our slow progress back home. I'd hoped that we'd be able to slip back into the barn unnoticed, that Elijah would be able to break the news to his father about the buggy slowly.

But dozens of Plain people had clustered around Elijah's

house. I swallowed as they turned to stare at the mangled buggy as it creaked along the dirt road.

"Elijah!" Herr Miller broke free of the group. "Where have you been?"

Elijah's jaw was set in a hard line. "Looking for Seth and Joseph."

Herr Miller blinked, running his hands over the buggy and taking in our battered appearances. "Are you all right? What happened?"

"We were run off the road by policemen. Six cars."

"Elijah's hurt," I interjected. "His ankle . . ."

Herr Miller and I shoveled Elijah out of the buggy. He leaned heavily on my shoulder.

"I'll take care of the buggy and Star," Herr Miller said. "Will you see to him, Katie?"

"Of course."

I supported Elijah as we limped through the throng of people. I spied my mother and father at the edges.

"Katie . . ." My mother tied my askew bonnet strings firmly under my chin. It was a gesture she'd repeated since I was a little girl, whenever I made her nervous. "Are you all right?"

"Just bumps and bruises." I looked over her shoulder at my father. His expression was a combination of worry and disapproval. That expression punished me more than any verbal reprimand.

"I must attend to Elijah," I whispered, feeling guilty.

"I will help you," my mother said.

"And I will help Herr Miller with the buggy," my father said.

My mother and I got Elijah up the steps of his house, through the living room, and upstairs to his bedroom. Elijah shared a large room with his two brothers, and it seemed very empty without them. Too quiet. The three beds were covered with quilts my mother had made. Elijah's was in the middle and received the most sunlight from the thick-paned window above it.

Elijah groaned as we set him upon the bed. My mother began unwrapping his foot.

"Bring me some water, Katie," she said. "And take a moment to clean yourself, too."

I nodded, then scurried away to the kitchen. I carried the washbasin out to the pump in the backyard.

I spied Mrs. Parsall, lurking awkwardly at the fringes of the crowd. I waved to her, and she made her way to me. She looked distressed.

"Where did you go?" she hissed.

"We went looking for Elijah's brothers."

She paused. "You went to the furniture store?"

"Yes." I looked away, trying not to remember the stained keyhole saw and the broken glass. "We tried to call the police but couldn't reach anyone."

Mrs. Parsall reached out and grasped me in a fierce hug. "It's going to be okay."

"Does anyone know what's happening?"

She shook her head against mine. "I don't know. I can't reach Dan or the kids. I think . . . it's something big. I don't know . . ."

I muffled a sob against her shoulder, and she stroked my

mussed hair under my bonnet. But I felt like I should be soothing her, with her husband and children unreachable. I hiccupped, then asked her, "Are all these people here . . . to form
a search party?"

I saw some of the Elders talking in a tight knot. They would
have a plan, surely.

"I think that they're waiting for the Bishop. To decide what
to do."

"That's best." I clasped Mrs. Parsall's hand. "Stay with us.
Until it's over."

She wiped her eyes beneath her glasses. "Your parents have
already insisted." She tried to smile, but it came off crooked.
"Your mother has offered me some of her clothes."

The corner of my mouth turned up to imagine her in our
style of clothes. "You'll be a lovely Plain woman."

"You'll have to teach me about the bonnet thing," she said
self-consciously, reaching up to smooth her hair. Hers would
be black, for a married woman, not a girl's white one.

"I will," I promised. I worked the pump until water rattled
forth into the washbasin. I quickly scrubbed my face, hands,
and arms in the frigid water, emptied the basin, and then re-
filled it with fresh water.

I carefully carried the basin back upstairs to Elijah's room
and set it down on the floor at the foot of the bed. My mother
was perched on Elijah's bedside like a sparrow, clucking over
his injuries.

"Is it broken?" I asked.

She shook her head. "Just sprained, I think." She dipped a
rag into the washbasin and cleaned his foot, to prepare it for

some of her homemade liniment. I took one of the other rags and began to scrub Elijah's face and hands.

He made faces under our ministrations. "Don't fuss over me." But I could tell that he secretly enjoyed being petted like a prize calf.

"Will he heal well?" I asked my mother.

She nodded, showing me the ankle as one of her teachable moments. She believed that a mother should know the basics of first aid. She had helped Frau Gerlach at the births of many babies, and she knew almost as much as the midwife did about the body. "He should. The skin isn't broken, so there is no place for infection to set in. If it was infected, we'd need to take him to see the doctor to get some antibiotics."

"How would I know it was infected?"

"If there was an open wound that failed to heal quickly. If there was pus, red runners streaking toward the heart. Fever. Ripe swelling, skin hot to the touch."

I nodded.

"In bad cases, delirium sets in. Never let it get that bad with one of your children, Katie, especially the small ones. Find a doctor before that happens and ask for the antibiotics."

"I can always find you," I said, smiling at her.

My mother laughed. "You can, but I will tell you when it's bad enough to go see the doctor."

Elijah swallowed, probably remembering his mother, who hadn't gotten to a doctor in time to be saved.

Plain people avoided going to English doctors wherever possible. We did what we could with simple medicines and the knowledge of our families and midwives. Illness was God's will.

Yet when an injury or illness presented itself in one of our loved ones that we could not cure with our own knowledge or tools, we often sought Outside help. Fortunately, this did not seem to be one of the times it was needed. Not that we could have found an English doctor to help us under the current conditions.

My mother admonished Elijah to stay off the foot for a few days, coated him in eucalyptus liniment, and bound his ankle up tightly. Elijah nodded solemnly, but I guessed that he wouldn't take her advice. The instant he was out of her sight, he'd be hopping and pacing the room.

I didn't blame him. I went to the open window and looked down at the throng of people. There was easily at least one person from each family in the community here, and more seemed to be trickling in. I spied the Bishop with his white beard and dark hat, approaching the whispering Elders. They looked like the ravens from this morning on the grass, black and just a bit ominous.

After conferring for several minutes, the Bishop stepped away from the Elders and raised his arm for silence. The chatter of the rest of the Plain folk shut off, just as if someone had turned a faucet. Black hats, straw hats, white bonnets, and black bonnets turned toward him.

When the Bishop spoke, his bass voice carried. I'd heard him speak many times on Sundays, knew that he could make it a gentle rumble. But not today.

"The Elders and I have gathered as much information as we can about the situation Outside," he boomed. The Bishop nodded to Mrs. Parsall. "We have learned that there is unrest Outside and have concluded that this unrest poses a danger to our community. It may be disease, terrorism, war . . . We simply don't know."

A worried gasp lifted in the throng.

"As a result, we are closing our gate. No one will be permitted in or out until the situation is resolved."

Herr Miller stepped forward, and I could see his hands trembling. "But my sons . . . my sons are out there."

The Bishop inclined his head. "And we will pray for them. Just as we will pray for the Yoder girls and Frau Fisher. They have not returned, either."

"But if it's not safe here . . ." someone began.

"There's no point in considering leaving. This is our land." The Bishop scanned the crowd. "We must do as we have always done. Keep faith. Trust in God. We will be safe."

His eyes were dark, and I thought that he looked up at me as he said, "And no one goes beyond the gate."

———————

"You should not have gone."

My father doubled my evening chores to keep me busy. He gave me mine as well as Elijah's. I would have offered to do them anyway, but my father wanted to make a point.

I glanced back at him from my milking stool to where he sat on his own. My father had taken on Seth's and Joseph's chores. I could never say that he'd ever punished me in a way that he was unwilling to undertake himself, and he was never cruel. I could not resent him as we sat milking the cows in the cool silence of the Millers' barn.

I averted my gaze from the wreck of the buggy. "I know that you worry."

"And I know that your heart was in the right place," he said. "Seth and Joseph are like brothers to you."

I nodded, casting my eyes down at the bucket. "I couldn't let Elijah go alone."

I heard the smile in my father's voice. "And your mother would not have let me go alone, either." I heard the smile fade. "But times are different now. You must be careful. You both could have been killed."

I understood his concern. But I couldn't convey to him that, no matter how sore my ribs were now, I somehow felt indestructible. Nearly immortal, though I would have never uttered that thought to any living person. It was blasphemous.

"You've had enough of the Outside world for now, I think."

I glanced sidelong at him. "*Ja*. The Bishop has closed the gate."

My father stood to gather his bucket and move to the next cow. "I think that this thing . . . whatever it is . . . shall be short-lived."

"I hope so." I bit my lip. I selfishly hoped that the English would hurry and straighten out their business so that their cares and tragedies would not interfere with my *Rumspringa*.

But my father knew my thoughts well. "Still. I think you will have to wait for *Rumspringa*."

"Wait until the crisis is over, of course . . ."

"No. I mean that you've not demonstrated the judgment that I hoped you would have. Perhaps in spring."

My breath caught in my throat. "But you and Mother went . . ."

"*Ja*. And those were different times. Safer times." My father carried his buckets to the mouth of the barn. "I do not have confidence that the world is safe enough for you to roam about in it."

I stared into the bucket. My hands slackened, and I blinked back tears. Selfish tears, I knew. There was much more at stake than my solitary future. Outside was facing violence and God knew what else. Seth and Joseph were missing, perhaps dead.

But all I could think of was the soft sound of snow creaking on the roof above my room this winter as a tear splashed into the milk bucket.

I finished my chores at twilight and trudged back from the Millers' barn to our house in the falling darkness. I looked up, watching the stars overhead. They were the same as they always were. Despite what my father said, I couldn't believe that the world had truly changed.

I took my time, smelling the dew condensing to earth and the sweet smell of drying grass. I almost didn't notice a thin figure walking through the field, his back stooped with age and from the load of the paint cans that he carried.

"Good evening, Herr Stoltz," I greeted the old Hexenmeister.

He seemed lost in his thoughts, as well. He paused and set down his paint cans. "Hello again, Katie."

"Are you painting?" I gestured at the cans with my chin. I said nothing to him about his work at the crash site this morning.

"*Ja.* There is much work to do." He smelled of turpentine,

and wet brushes were tied in a bundle over his shoulder. Flecks of red paint in his beard looked like blood in the dim light.

"I thought that you had painted all the hex signs this spring?" I asked. The Hexenmeister was responsible for painting the hex signs on the barns. I was accustomed to seeing him at the fringes of the community, muttering to himself, planting seeds in haphazard places. When I was a small child, he had scared me, but I had become used to thinking of him as a harmless old man, practicing his art.

Until this morning. And I began to take him more seriously.

The Hexenmeister had always seemed to be just beyond the edge of the Ordnung—a bit mystical and not living entirely within our strict rules. He would not have been allowed to work as he did in other Amish communities: with graven images, with vain and complicated art, with the calligraphy he used in letters he wrote directly to God. These were the practices of a small group of Pennsylvania Dutch, immigrants from the Old Country. Our ancestors had somehow been unable to extricate themselves from that particular Old World root, even as they renounced other sinful and worldly practices. The old man's father and his grandfathers before him had taken on the role of Hexenmeister. Some thought that this was an inherited insanity. But the Elders had always been quiet where he was concerned.

I wondered what they knew that I didn't.

I noticed that, unlike many of the Amish who sold their furniture, quilts, and crafts to the English, Herr Stoltz never sold any of his beautiful paintings. He made them for us, and us alone. Any of the hex signs sold in stores run by the English were reproductions, ordered from English painters who mimicked old designs. They had no real knowledge of the symbolism in them. To them, they were just pretty pictures. To the Hexenmeister, they were images designed to beckon good fortune, friendship, and fertility—and to ward off bad luck.

"There are more to do. Different signs." He rubbed his gnarled, stained hands like they ached.

"Would you like help carrying the cans?"

He shook his head. "No, Katie. It's late. You run along home to your family."

His eyes stared out unblinking into the night, and I stifled a shudder. It was as if he saw something in the darkness that I could not.

"Yes, Herr Stoltz. Have a good evening." I left him in the field, looking up at the stars.

He wasn't the only one out this evening. As I approached my house, I saw an unfamiliar figure pacing outside. As I neared, I realized that it was Mrs. Parsall, dressed in my mother's clothes, but minus the prayer bonnet and with the addition of her own sneakers. Mrs. Parsall was stouter than my mother, and the buttons strained against her belly. I smiled for a moment, seeing my friend cast into our world.

But when she turned, the expression on her face wiped away my amusement. She held her cell phone, and her lower lip quavered.

"Mrs. Parsall, what's wrong?" I reached out to rub her arm.

She blew out her breath. "I spoke with Dan."

I perked up. "Your husband is all right?"

"Yes. He's all right. But . . ." She shook her head, and I

could see her reaching out for words. "He says that something terrible has happened."

"Come sit." I guided her to sit down on the back step of the house. Her hands were shaking, and she took three tries to get the phone back in her apron pocket, failed. I took the phone out of her hand and noticed that the battery symbol was blinking on it.

"Please shut it off," she said. "The big button on the right."

I pushed it, and the phone display faded with a musical chirp that sounded like a pale imitation of birdsong. The insects seemed unaffected by what had spooked the ravens. We listened to the crickets for some time, watched the last of the summer fireflies rise to swim in the field, before she spoke again. Her voice was stronger.

"Dan says that they think there was a terrorist attack. A biological weapon."

"Here?" In our little corner of the world, that seemed improbable. "How?"

"They don't think it started here. They think it began in DC, that it's spreading west. A contagion."

"A contagion?" I echoed. My skin began to crawl.

"Something that causes violence, madness. They don't understand it yet; they're just gathering intelligence from afar." Her words ran over each other. "Dan says they've closed the borders to the United States."

"No one gets in or out. Like here." My head was swimming.

"Like here. In quarantine."

"What are they going to do about it?"

"No one knows. The military has no idea how the contagion is spread, how much of the rioting is panic, and how much is due to the contagion itself. In the end, it may not make much difference. The U.S. military is operating largely out of ships off the coasts, where they are intercepting radio and television transmissions." Her eyes lowered. "From what Dan says, it's complete havoc. Philadelphia and Boston fell. Fell like New Orleans after the hurricane."

"And your children?"

She hiccupped back a sob. "Most colleges are on lockdown, according to Dan. The National Guard is there. He's trying to find out."

I threw my arm around her. "They'll be all right."

"I hope so."

I wrinkled my brow, trying to understand. "How can a sickness cause evil?"

"There are a lot of theories that suggest that evil is a sickness. Every time some twisted SOB in the newspaper kills his girlfriend's children, there's always some psychiatrist who comes forward to say that the guy's mentally ill." Mrs. Parsall held her chin in her hands, elbows braced on her knees. "They say that there's no evil in the modern world anymore. That it's all just psychological dysfunction. Sociological inequities. Disease and social maladaptation."

I chewed my lip. "Plain folk are taught that evil is spiritual. The absence of God."

Mrs. Parsall bit back a sob. "Well, it seems as if God's left the building, and we're left to our own devices."

CHAPTER FIVE

We prayed that night, until the moon rose high in the sky.

With the information that Mrs. Parsall had provided about disease, I spent the evening under my mother's stern eye, washing vigorously under the cold water pump. Though Plain folk generally believed that illness was an expression of God's will, my mother would take no chances.

Once we had all been scrubbed beet red, my mother, father, Sarah, Mrs. Parsall, and I walked over to the Miller house with casseroles in hand.

And to pray.

Plain folk held regular prayer services every other Sunday in each other's homes. We prayed before every meal and when it was needed. Like now.

As we approached the lone light shining in the Miller house, walking in the darkness, I wanted to be comforted by that light. I wanted some reassurance of God's will. That it remained constant. That it remained good. That he was still listening to us, even if he ignored the Outside world.

We prayed silently before supper and after. Then Herr Miller got out his tattered *Ausbund* prayer book, and we prayed and sang in Deitsch. Mrs. Parsall sat silently in the corner, absorbing the words with glistening eyes and hands clasped in her lap. I drew her down on her knees beside us and felt her leaning hard against my shoulder. I know that she understood none of it, though she was praying in her own way.

The Amish were not permitted to be prideful in prayer, and we made up no prayers of our own. We used the Lord's Prayer most often and others from the prayer book. Many religions used prayer as means to impress, but we were forbidden to. We hoped that God heard us using the old words or our silence.

At one point Herr Miller broke down in tears. Elijah clasped his shoulder and wept quietly with him.

Herr Miller was facing every Amish parent's nightmare. Not just the potential loss of his children—he was facing the loss of their souls. Amish people were not baptized until they were in their late teens or early twenties, after *Rumspringa*. Our community wanted them to choose the Amish life of their own free will and understand the decisions they were making, as adults. There was no point to us in forcing a small child to be baptized. They could not give consent, nor could they fully understand the rules to which they committed.

If, Lord forbid, Seth and Joseph died before they were baptized, they would be lost. Caught out. They would not enter heaven. Herr Miller would never see his sons again, and I could not imagine the depths of that grief. He, at least, had the hope of seeing his wife again after death. But without all of his children . . .

The thought of evil still permeated me, ignited by my discussion with Mrs. Parsall and fanned by the Lord's Prayer.

Much of day-to-day Plain existence kept me well insulated from evil—and those sins that I usually resisted were the things that the English took for granted as neutral parts of everyday life: driving cars, electricity, the pride of fashion and vanity. I was so accustomed to debating the evils of those things in my head that it rarely occurred to me to contemplate violence or destruction.

I knew that I was weak, that I sometimes failed to submit to God's will. But I didn't feel truly sinister. I'd never had the urge to harm another living thing, to do such violence that was supposedly caused by some piece of germ warfare. Illness, like everything else, was considered *Gelassenheit*—God's will. Disease was invisible, and it was easily attributable to his divine plan.

But was the loss of Seth and Joseph truly his will? Had the Outside interfered with his divine will by creating an evil that was not spiritual? If it was a disease, would any amount of spiritual virtuousness deflect it? Or did God choose who would be affected?

My thoughts rushed and collided together, not able to be soothed by even the familiar rhythms of the Lord's Prayer. I felt the loss of the young men who had been like brothers to me in an ache behind my breastbone.

That night I lay awake in bed with Sarah sleeping beside me, staring at the dark ceiling. I didn't understand. Maybe I wasn't supposed to.

Instead of snoring, I heard soft sobbing from the bed beside me. Mrs. Parsall was trying to muffle her crying in the pillow. I could see her blond hair pressed up against it in the moonlight.

I kissed Sarah on the forehead and slipped out of my bed. I padded over to Mrs. Parsall's bed and climbed in beside her. I wrapped my arms around the older woman as she sobbed.

Like Herr Miller, she may have lost her children for all time.

And there was nothing I could say to soothe that hurt. All I could do was be a shoulder in the darkness.

———

Evil arrived on our doorstep the next day.

At the time, I didn't see it that way. But that was the way the Elders saw it.

I was doing my chores and Elijah's, feeding the cattle. Star dragged bales of hay on a sledge, and I stopped her in the middle of the field to put the hay in the iron bale holders beside the watering tubs. The bales were heavier than I was used to, about fifty pounds each, but I was determined not to complain. There were bigger concerns now than my own comfort. Though an air of crisis hung low like a cloud over our community, there were still mundane chores to be done. I was grateful for them, for the ache in my muscles that kept me tied to the present moment; the activity kept my mind off of useless ruminating about the future.

The cattle had seen me coming and were heading in, mooing and grumbling among themselves. Unlike the black and white dairy Holsteins in the barn, these were brown and white Herefords. Beef cattle. Most of them were bulls, and I gave them a wide berth. They were never aggressive. But at two thousand pounds, they could accidentally hurt a person as they made a beeline for the hay and grain.

I stretched, stepping back, as the bulls clustered around the feeder. My back popped in two satisfying places, and I looked up at the leadening sky. I wanted to get the hay bales out before it rained. It would be much worse slogging through a muddy field with soggy bales that weighed more than they ought to.

Suddenly, I heard a distant roar.

Four sleek triangular gray planes flew in "V" formation overhead, streaking across the thick sky from west to east. They reminded me of geese, the way they flew. I lifted my arms to wave and shout, wondering if they could see me. I supposed that perhaps they were checking the damage, to see who had survived.

The low roar rumbled over the field. Instead of white contrails, the tails of the planes were spewing something bluish. Not smoke. The planes continued along their way, heading east, streaking the sky with that mysterious blue, and receding beyond sight.

The breeze pushed the smell of the blue substance down through the field. I wrinkled my nose. It smelled metallic, like winter. I hoped that the military had found a cure for the contagion. Maybe they were dusting us, like crops, to get it dispersed.

Whatever the reason, the sight lifted my heart. It meant that there were still people out there in the Outside world. Alive.

I smiled up at the sky.

And it opened up and began to rain. The rain tasted cold and sharp, like metal.

I sighed and returned to my work, dragging the last heavy

bale from the sledge. The bulls had crowded me out of the feeder, so I chucked this one on the ground, and the smaller, less dominant ones headed for it. As I surveyed the cattle, I began to worry.

The big ones were due to be slaughtered this fall. The small ones would be kept over the winter, to be slaughtered in the spring. Some of the meat would be sold to the English. But if Outside remained off-limits, then there would be a lot of cattle to feed. And we didn't have enough room to keep all the meat. I doubted that we had enough food to sustain them through the whole winter. Things could get ugly very quickly, I decided, scanning the backs of the bulls.

I spied a dark shape along one of the fence posts in the distance. I frowned. The cattle shouldn't be lying down at mealtime. A downer cow was a sign of illness. We would have to act quickly to protect the rest of the herd. Growing up Plain, I understood that the individual was weak, but the power lay in the collective. The group must be preserved at all costs.

I walked briskly to the edge of the field. Maybe this sick one could be separated in enough time. As I got closer, I noticed that the dark shape wasn't on the inside of the barbed-wire and wood fence. It lay on the Outside, just inches beyond.

And it wasn't a bull. It was too small.

It was human.

I approached cautiously, trying to stay upwind of the body curled up around the fence post. One foot was tangled in barbed wire, as if the man had tried to get inside but failed. It was an Englisher. He wore sneakers, jeans, and a black jacket with a great deal of zippers and flap pockets. His face and blond hair were pressed into the mud, rain tapping on his face. His eyes were closed. The rain rinsed blood from a wound on the side of his head, near his temple. He looked like he'd been struck with something.

"Hello?" I rasped. I couldn't tell if he was alive or dead. I was afraid of both.

The pale form lay motionless in the mud. I crept closer, studying his shoulder. I saw that it rose and fell slightly with his breath, a breath that passed through his lips and disturbed the matted grass under his battered face.

He was alive. My heart caught in my throat.

I ran back to the horse to get help as fast as my feet would carry me in the sucking mud.

———

"We have to help him!"

I exploded into my house, soaking wet. My father was eating lunch in the kitchen and stared at me. He pushed away from the table, grasped my arms.

"Help who? Herr Miller? Elijah?"

I shook my head, struggling to catch my breath. "No. There's a man out at the south field. He's been hurt. He needs help."

"Where at the south field?"

"At the fence."

I knew that once I told my father, he would take care of it. An important part of the Amish belief system was helping those in need. And this man clearly needed us.

"Is he English?"

"Yes. I think so."

My father reached for his coat. "Show me."

I drove Star back to the field, where the man lay. He had not moved. My father approached slowly, crouched down at a distance.

"He's outside the fence," my father said. "We must ask the Elders for permission to bring him inside."

My brow furrowed. "But he's hurt."

"He may also be sick. We must ask the Elders."

My hands wound in my soggy apron. My father looked at me tenderly. "You have a compassionate heart, Katie. But we cannot violate the rules. We must ask them."

I nodded slowly, water dripping from my nose. Surely when the Elders saw him, they would bring him in, take care of him. I could not blame my father. He was a good man and was trying to follow the rules.

"I will go get them," he said.

"I will stay here and pray."

"Don't get too close," my father cautioned. "He may be contagious."

"I understand." But I didn't, really. The young man appeared to be hurt, not sick. The violence facing Outside had seemingly chased him down. I hoped that if Seth and Joseph found their way to an English house, that the Englishers would help the boys.

I watched as my father took Star and rode away, then turned back to look at the young man, the rain tapping on the ground and my prayer bonnet.

I knelt against the bottom rail of the fence, several yards upwind of him, and prayed silently with rain sliding down my knuckles. He did not move, did not seem to sense my presence there. But as I stole glances at him, I hoped that he could feel God with him, that he would know that rescue was close at hand. Just delayed by a bit of procedure.

Almost an hour later, I heard footsteps in the muck. I lifted my head to see my father, the Bishop, and two of the elder ministers walking across the field, rain streaming off their hats. My heart rose to see them, to know that they would end the young man's suffering.

I stood respectfully, backing away as the Elders circled around the young man. I clasped my cold hands behind my back.

They stared for a long time, in silence, before the Bishop shook his head.

The Elders made as if to retreat.

A rebellious squeak came to my lips, and my hand flew to my mouth. "You're—you're going to leave him?" I whispered.

The Bishop looked me in the eye, and his gaze was sharp as steel. "We cannot bring him inside. No one goes in or out. The rule stands."

"But he's just beyond—" I protested. "He's suffering!"

"And we cannot bring that suffering upon ourselves," my father said, clasping a warning hand upon my shoulder. I was not being obedient. I blinked up at him in amazement.

"We will not allow him to suffer." One of the Elders slipped a hunting rifle from his shoulder.

I stuffed my fist in my mouth to stifle a cry as my father steered me away from the scene. I looked back, wet bonnet strings stuck to my face, as the minister raised the rifle and took aim at the young man.

Rifles were used for hunting in our community, never used against people. Tears sprang to my eyes. The evil of Outside had surely reached in here, in the guise of fear and mercy.

I struggled to twist away. "But if it's God's will that he should die, should we not leave him?"

The black figures stared at me for speaking out of turn again.

"Father," I pleaded. "It's *Gelassenheit*. Let God decide."

My father turned back, exchanged a glance with the Elder who held the rifle. The weapon trembled from barrel to stock. It would be a hard thing to ask a man to kill another. Even in the name of mercy.

The Bishop's gaze flicked among us, then to heaven. He reached out and pushed the barrel of the gun down.

"Leave him. Let God decide if he should go quickly, or if he should suffer."

The men in black walked back across the field, back to their dry homes, like crows returning to the nest.

I trailed behind them, a confused and drenched brown sparrow behind the flock.

Chapter Six

I returned to the fence before dusk.

The rain had stopped, and the sun singed a low bank of clouds at the horizon. The long rays of the sun illuminated the sheen of moisture glistening on the fence posts and grass in an aura of gold and shoved my shadow behind me.

I clutched a jar full of cold water close to my chest. It sloshed with every step as I advanced upon the fence. When I stopped before the prone wet form beside the barbed wire, I swore that the hammering of my heart thundered through the water and caused it to splash to the rim. I imagined that this was the sound of the sea, though I'd never heard nor seen it.

The rain had soaked the young man through, his hair plastered to his sharp cheekbone. The blood had been rinsed from his face. He had not moved since this afternoon.

I feared that *Gelassenheit* had been fulfilled, that he was dead.

I crouched down beside him in the mud, wet grass tickling my knees. Tentatively, I reached through the barbed-wire fence to touch his chest. Swallowing hard, I placed my palm flat against the cold zipper and soggy leather of his jacket, where his heart lay. I was rewarded with feeling his chest swell against my hand.

I chewed my bottom lip. It would have been easier if he were dead, I knew. But *Gelassenheit* wasn't about what was easy.

I reached under the barbed wire with the jar, pressed it to the young man's lips. Awkwardly, I tried to turn his head toward the jar. Water dribbled over his lips, and my hand shook. I couldn't tell how much trickled down the back of his throat, and how much ran down the side of his cheek into the grass.

I sat back on my heels and set the jar down on the ground beside me. After wiping my hands on my apron, I clasped them to pray. The molten light from the vanishing sun warmed my face. I held on to that warmth until it drained away.

I stood as the first stars began to prickle through the canopy of blackness. I knew that it was wrong of me to ask for a sign from God, to ask for anything. But I wished, deep in the bottom of my heart, for some indication that he would not turn away from me for what I contemplated doing.

But there was no sign. No word from God except what the Elders had said.

And for a moment, I wondered if what Mrs. Parsall had supposed was true . . . Had he truly left us? Left all of us?

And if so, did it matter any longer what we did?

I waited until the moon crept beyond the tangle of trees, until my sister slept and I could hear Mrs. Parsall's soft, fitful snoring.

I slipped out of bed, dressed noiselessly in the dark. I remembered where each and every creaky floorboard lay in the house and sidestepped them in bare feet. I felt a pang of guilt in my chest as I passed the closed door of my parents' room and stepped down the stairs into the kitchen. I put my shoes on and let myself out the back door, a shuttered lantern in my sweating grip.

The crickets and bullfrogs sang sleepily, and the moon burned through the tatters of clouds overhead. The cool night air slid over my face as I made my way to the barn just at the edge of our yard. This was the barn that was frequented by our family, the cows, and the horses. It was in good repair and freshly painted red—not the gray, dilapidated realm that I haunted a mile away with the dogs. I slowly opened up the lantern and turned up the wick, feeling the heat of metal in my hands.

In the highly flammable setting of a barn, with the un-predictable hooves of animals, fire was an imminent threat. I placed the lantern down on the bare ground and watched it like it was a living thing with its own volition as I reached for the barn door. The hinges squeaked as I opened the door, then propped it open with a brick. I gathered the lantern in a two-fisted grip and walked into the darkness.

I whistled softly at Star. She blinked and nodded at me. We were keeping her here since we had taken over so many of the Millers' chores. I rubbed the white mark on her forehead and kissed her nose. She blew questioningly at me as I led her to the sledge and placed the heavy harness on her.

"I shall bring you extra oats," I promised, trying to buy her silence.

I turned the lantern down and shuttered it, and we left the barn. I glanced fearfully up at the windows of my house. No lights burned, and it was just chilly enough tonight that the windows were closed.

I was thankful that the moon was waxing, that it provided enough light to see by. It cast spiky shadows of grass and fence posts and the lacy shadows of trees on the ground. It illuminated the clouds above in gray light, all color drained from the sky.

I led Star to the Millers' south field. The horse's ears flattened, and I knew that she assumed that we'd be throwing more hay bales. I reached up to ruffle her ear. "I'll be quick."

She snorted back at me. The sledge bounced along the ruts in the field. I saw the steers lying down in the moonlight, shadows nodding. But that wasn't the shadow I sought . . .

There. I advanced upon the form curled up beside the fence. I knelt down beside the young man, touched his shoulder. It shivered.

"Can you hear me?" I asked. My voice sounded very loud in the quiet of night.

The man didn't speak, and his eyes were closed.

"I'm going to take you someplace warm."

I reached between the two strands of barbed wire and grasped his arm. With all my might, I pulled his soggy sleeve beneath the lowest strand of wire. I dragged him over a hump of lumpy grass and poison ivy, trying to extricate his dead weight from the wire. His jacket caught, and I was forced to pause and work it free. I hadn't brought gloves, and the barbs scraped my hands.

I succeeded in pulling him to my side of the fence. Grasping his heavy arms, I dragged him toward the sledge.

Star's eyes rolled, and she whinnied, shying away. In the field a steer ear twitched, and there was an answering moo.

"It's okay, girl," I said soothingly. Star was a good horse but unaccustomed to human cargo on the sledge. I left the young man in the muck, tied Star to the fence post, and then managed to drag him up on the sledge by his feet. He weighed considerably more than a bale of hay, even wet hay, and sweat prickled my brow under my bonnet.

"*Ja,* let's go," I said to Star. She allowed herself to be led from the fence, but I could tell that she was on edge. It was as if she sensed that I was breaking the rules and she was demonstrating her disapproval.

"I know," I told her, through gritted teeth.

She hauled the man to my distant, little gray kennel barn, away from our homestead and the prying eyes of others. Hearing the clatter of gear and the grate of the sledge, Sunny waddled to the door. She snuffled my hands and apron, searching for treats.

I kissed her head. "No treats tonight. But I brought you a roommate."

Copper was sniffing over the young man with the vigor of a hound dog. He whined at me, as if he'd caught some of the horse's trepidation.

"You must keep him a secret." I relit the lantern with matches from my pocket. The golden light illuminated the interior of the kennel as I contemplated where to house our guest. I considered hoisting him up to the hayloft but thought that would be impossible. I finally decided on a paddock at the far end of the barn. I hadn't put the dogs in it because the wall was caving in. Instead, I'd blocked it off with cages and used it for storage. I grabbed a pitchfork and put down a good layer of fresh straw.

"It's probably not what you're used to," I said, leaning on the pitchfork. "But it beats spending the night in a wet field."

I wrapped my arms beneath the Englisher's arms and dragged him awkwardly from the sledge to the back of the barn. I had to stop more than once to remove the straw that gathered behind his limp heels.

Once I got him arranged on the bed of straw, I did my best to get him out of his muddy jacket. It was like trying to undress a giant rag doll. The coat finally peeled off, and I landed on my butt in the straw.

I moved to hang the jacket up on a peg for horse dressage on the crumbling wall. It occurred to me to look for identification. Englishers always seemed to carry their lives with them. I reached into his pockets and found a few coins, a key ring, and a silver folding knife. Curious, I opened it. The blade was stained with blood. I shuddered and put it back. It reminded me of the saw on the floor of the furniture store.

I found a sopping wet wallet in one of the zippered pockets. Tentatively, I opened it. It was half-full of English money, a credit card, and a foil-wrapped package. I read the wrapper: *Latex condom with spermicidal lubricant for contraception and STD protection. To prevent pregnancy, HIV/AIDS, and other sexually transmitted infections* . . . Repulsed, I dropped it. I wrinkled my nose and searched for a driver's license. I found it tucked in between some bills. I squinted at the license in the dim light.

It said his name was Alexander Green, age twenty-four. He lived in Toronto.

I paused and stared down at him. He'd come a long way. Why? Had he been fleeing the disaster? Or just passing through and gotten caught up in the storm?

I put the wallet back in the pocket, then knelt beside him to get a better look at his injuries. Brushing his straw-colored hair aside, I could better see the wound in his temple. The rain had rinsed the blood away, and it seemed that it had clotted. I was reluctant to disturb it further. I pried his eyelids up to check to see if he had a concussion. My sister had gotten a concussion when she was five, tripping on the back step. My mother had showed me what to look for.

His eyes were a startling shade of pale, icy blue, the color of winter skies. As near as I could determine in the lamplight, his pupils were unevenly dilated. Not much, but enough that it made me diagnose him with a concussion.

I carried a bucket of water that had been drawn for the dogs back to the stall. Using a clean rag, I daubed at the mud around his face. He did not stir, remaining disconcertingly still. I brought him a clean dog blanket. Copper followed me back and stared at him, perhaps jealous that I was making such a fuss over a two-legged creature.

I don't know what I expected. I guess I thought that the stranger would regain consciousness once out of the elements. But he remained stubbornly closed. An enigma.

And I hoped that he did not regain consciousness while I was gone. I filled a dog dish with water and set it beside him. On a scrap of paper I'd used as a receipt for the sale of a puppy from Sunny's last litter, I scratched out a note for him, and anchored it under the dish:

> You are safe. But don't leave the barn until I come back for you. No one else knows that you are here.
> —Katie

I had no way of knowing if he'd ever read it. But I didn't want him wandering out in the day, where he'd be found by the Elders . . . the ones who'd shown him no quarter earlier.

I stood, gathered the lantern to my chest, and walked out of the barn.

"Watch over him," I told the dogs.

I glanced back at the barn as I drove Star out of sight. It was then that I noticed that the hex sign over the door had blistered and was peeling. Shards of paint had begun to litter the grass, like snow.

If I believed in omens, I might have taken that as a sign.

———

I began to doubt myself by the next morning.

I'd lain awake the rest of the night. My heart told me that I'd done well, but my mind chastised me for going against the Elders and my father. I'd never been that rebellious before. I'd read comic books and taken a sip of beer before deciding that it was irredeemably disgusting. I had even gotten myself a library card and had spent more than one afternoon reading pulp fiction in a secluded corner carrel. But those were the little rebellions expected of a teenager. Those things hurt no one. But this . . . this was beyond rebellion. This involved a victim. Whether the victim would be the young man in the barn or some harm befalling our community, I could not pretend that this was a minor crime. I had been buoyed by my outrage, by my sympathy yesterday. Perhaps I wasn't thinking clearly. Perhaps, as my father said, I allowed myself to be led too much by my heart.

But it was done.

And there was nothing left for me to do but to continue on that path, wherever it led.

I went out in the early morning, just after the sun rose. I told my parents I was going to look after the dogs. That much was true. I took my breakfast with me in a basket and some scraps for the dogs. There was much work to be done with the Miller boys missing and Elijah injured, and my parents did not question me about not eating at the table.

I walked across the long fields with a bucket of water and my basket. My spirits gradually began to lift as the sun rose. Everything always seemed worse in the silence of night. Here, in the sunshine of the day, I felt justified in my actions. I raised my chin and walked to the barn, stepping through the paint chips that were beginning to accumulate on the gravel and grass.

I pulled open the barn door with a creak.

"It's just me. Katie," I announced to the shadows.

Copper bounded up to meet me, sloshing water on my skirt. Sunny waddled behind him, tail wagging. Straw was stuck to her fur, and I set my burden down to brush it away.

"How is our guest?" I asked, warily.

Sunny gave me an inscrutable look and whimpered.

I followed Copper back to the broken stall. Sunlight had crept through the chinks in the barn siding in broad golden slats that illuminated dust motes stirred up by my shoes. I stood and stared at the young man. *Alex,* I reminded myself.

Since last night he'd turned over, and the note I'd left him had been moved. Whether he'd read it, or whether it had been disturbed in his sleep, I couldn't tell. A couple of broad dents in the hay lay at his feet. I assumed that those were the dogs' work. It was good that they weren't afraid of him.

And I shouldn't be either, I told myself.

I took a deep breath. "Good morning."

He didn't stir. I knelt down beside him on the straw and placed my hand on his arm. His eyes fluttered a bit, like he was caught in a dream.

"Alex?"

His eyes opened for a moment, unfocused liquid blue.

I tried to smile reassuringly.

His eyes seemed to slide past me, through me. A chill crept down my spine. I had not stopped to wonder, in my haste, if his head injury had damaged his brain. His gaze seemed vacant. It fixed on my white bonnet.

He licked his lips. "Where?"

His voice was so faint, I had to stoop close to hear it. It was as if it were all he could do to summon that one word.

"You're safe. In Amish country."

"Eh. Bonnet." He reached up for one of my bonnet strings that danced in his face. I flinched.

His eyes clouded, and his eyelids shuttered over his eyes. I shook his shoulder, but he did not regain consciousness.

I pressed my hand to his forehead. It was scalding hot. I brushed his hair away from the wound on his temple. It looked infected, telltale runners of red reaching across his hairline to begin creeping through the body.

I swallowed hard. It was just the wound, I told myself. No more serious contagion than that.

I backed out of the stall to the dogs' area. I kept their birthing equipment in an old metal locker. I retrieved a bottle of antiseptic and clean cotton and returned to the young man.

"This will sting," I warned him, though I doubted that he heard me as I pressed the cotton soaked in antiseptic solution against his head.

I could see the hydrogen peroxide sizzling on the wound, bubbling and hissing, but he didn't flinch. I frowned, angry at myself for not having done this the night before. I had assumed that the wound was not serious, that he'd simply been suffering from the concussive shock of a blow to the head. A concussion would subside on its own, but an infection . . .

Awkwardly, I wrapped his head in clean gauze. It was a struggle to position it in my lap to get the gauze around the back of his head. As I bandaged the wound, I felt something hard like bone move in his temple, and my stomach turned.

I gingerly laid his head back down on the straw. I arranged a metal container of water beside him and my breakfast: thick bread with butter, jam, and one of the first apples of the season. They looked like sad offerings to a strange god.

I wondered what would happen if he died; I wondered where I would bury him.

CHAPTER SEVEN

After a morning kept busy with chores, my mother sent me to take the Millers lunch. On the walk over, I noticed how tall the corn was getting. The stalks and leaves were golden, time for harvest. Without the boys, our neighbors would need to pitch in to clear the field. The ache in my chest twinged.

Winding my hands tightly in the basket handle, I tried not to think too much about food for the winter. Though we had more than enough to sustain ourselves, there was a delicate balance to be had in consumption and trade. We didn't have enough storage for all the grain we sold to the Outside. And not enough shelter to last the whole winter for the cattle that were usually slaughtered in November. That meat and grain was sold for resources we couldn't produce ourselves, like salt, glass canning jars, gelatin, and pectin for preserving. I told myself that the crisis would be resolved by winter, that there would be a solution for all of us.

Herr Miller was gone, probably out with my father. I left him his lunch in the kerosene-powered refrigerator and a note on the table. I idly wondered at the refrigerator. Many Plain folk did own appliances, such as stoves, irons, and refrigerators, that were powered by kerosene instead of electricity. Electrical lines were a forbidden connection with the Outside world. But we still brought the kerosene in from Outside. It occurred to me that this crisis was perhaps God's way of removing those small luxuries from us.

I arranged two sandwiches and applesauce on a plate and carried a glass of milk upstairs to Elijah's room.

He was sitting up in bed, between the two empty ones. Sunlight streamed in on the quilts, and I saw that he was reading the Bible. Gently, I set the plate down on his lap and handed him the glass of milk.

"How's the ankle?" I asked. It was propped up on a pillow.

"Getting better," he said, closing the Bible and reaching for the glass of milk. He downed it in three greedy slurps.

I sat beside him on the bed and picked up one of the sandwiches. "Are you bored?"

"Of course," he said, grimacing. Then he looked at the Bible lying between us, and his expression drained away.

I chewed slowly, waiting for him to continue.

"I've been doing some thinking," he began. Then he stopped, reached for the sandwich. His fingers gnawed at the crust.

"About what?" A trickle of cold dread had formed in my stomach, like ice water. The last time Elijah had been "doing some thinking," he'd ham-handedly brought up the idea of marriage. I'd turned it into a joke, and he went along with it. We both knew that it would eventually happen, but I wasn't ready for that. Not yet.

"I was thinking about the future," he said.

Oh no. I glanced away, hoping that he would sense my unease and just *stop.*

"Seth and Joseph are gone." He rubbed at one of his eyes with a hand covered with bread crumbs. My first impulse was to place my hand on his shoulder in sympathy, but I didn't want him to take it as encouragement. I continued to chew silently.

"And . . . I'm afraid of my father being alone. In heaven. I know that my mother is there, waiting for him. And that has to be some comfort." He tried to meet my eyes, and I looked away.

He took a deep breath. "So, I've decided to be baptized this fall."

The bread turned to glue in my mouth. "You *what?*"

"I've decided to join the Amish church."

My head spun. Baptisms took place in fall and spring, after *Rumspringa,* when young people had tasted the Outside world and willingly committed themselves to the church. Elijah had never been in a hurry to join up after I'd pushed aside the idea of marriage. One had to be baptized to be married, of course, but he didn't like the idea of me going on *Rumspringa* without him. The shock of his brothers being caught out must have pushed him beyond his ordinary limits.

"But what about *Rumspringa?*" I asked. My voice sounded tiny, almost petulant to my own ears.

He shook his head. "I can't leave my father alone. He's lost too much."

"What about you and me and going Outside and seeing movies and . . ." My voice faltered, and tears blurred my vision. "You promised."

He took one of my hands. "You can still do that, in spring, after all this is settled. I'll wait for you. I promise." He kissed my cheek. "Nothing will change."

Yes, it will, I wanted to say. *There will be no more dreaming aloud of cars and movies and comic books. No candy bars and Coca-Cola. No imagining what the ocean looks like, or what it would be like to go someplace exotic like New York. It's all gone. You'll be like my parents, and yours, never dreaming of anything other than what you can see . . .*

My throat closed, and I couldn't put a voice to those selfish thoughts. It felt like my world was growing smaller and smaller, closing in on me.

———

I returned to the dog kennel after supper, under the guise of checking on Sunny. Glancing at my basket, my mother commented on how I was intending to make the dogs fat. Guilt hammered in my chest as I smiled weakly. I hated lying to my parents, but it seemed as if it was becoming easier and easier.

Maybe this was what it meant to be growing up.

I trudged across the field, my heart heavy with my own sins and with the knowledge that Elijah would no longer be a part of my life and my transgressions. Not the way he had been before. Little sins were expected of young people and largely ignored. But once you joined the church, such dalliances were absolutely forbidden. Nothing from Outside that had not been approved. Elijah would belong entirely to God. And I would not want to tempt him from any of that—but I could feel the chasm already growing between us.

I choked back a sob. My heart ached. It ached for the adventures that Elijah and I had dreamed up for ourselves since we were children. They were all gone now, lost. I knew that he was making the right decision. I understood his reasons . . .

But some selfish part of myself wanted to be first in his heart. Before God.

And that scared me, because that impulse felt truly evil. Ashamed, I placed my hand over my heart and recited the Lord's Prayer. But I could still feel the hot evil of that seed there, taking root.

"It's me again. Katie," I said, as I hauled back the heavy barn door.

As before, the dogs greeted me. I fed them their scraps and headed back to the paddock.

There were signs that the young man had moved during the day. Straw had been disturbed, and the blanket was gathered tight around his ears. I knelt beside him and peeled back the blanket. It was stuck to his hot cheek with a sheen of sweat.

He blinked at me as I did so. His teeth were chattering, but his gaze was lucid. "Bonnet. You're Katie. From the note?"

"Yes." I situated the basket between us, feeling suddenly pinned under that icy gaze. "I brought you some supper."

"Thank you."

I reached toward him, and he flinched.

"I mean to check your wound." I showed him my empty hands, as if I were dealing with a wild animal.

He licked his lips and nodded. I gently unwrapped the bandage. He winced as the gauze stuck to the wound. I didn't like what I saw. The rim of the wound was yellowing, and a red runner crept across his cheek. His skin was scalding under my fingers. I bit my lip. This was beyond my power.

He must have seen that. "How bad is it?" he asked.

I didn't want to lie to him. "It's infected."

He stared up at the ceiling of the barn. "No antibiotics here?"

I shook my head. "No. I'll wash it out again with antiseptic, but . . ." I knotted my fingers in my lap. "I don't know what else to do."

"It doesn't really matter, anyway," he slurred.

He seemed to be fighting to maintain consciousness, and I wanted to keep him talking. I brought a cup of milk to his lips. He dribbled it down his cheek. He was too weak to hold his head up. I propped my hand behind his neck to help him swallow. I forced down a cup of milk and another of warm broth.

"What happened out there?" I asked. "What happened Outside?" I thought of the stained knife.

"My motorcycle wrecked . . . I was chased . . ."

His eyelids began to fall, and I wiped the broth from his chin. "Chased by whom?"

"They were fast, faster than me . . . like birds . . ." His eyes became more unfocused, and I wasn't sure he saw me anymore as his pupils dilated in remembered fear. " . . . soundless . . . they smelled like blood . . ."

His head lolled to the right, and he passed out.

I shook his shoulder but was unable to revive him. I dutifully cleaned and rebandaged his wound. I didn't think he would last much longer. He had that smell about him — that acrid smell of illness, sharper than sweat. I'd smelled it on sick cattle, on Frau Miller before she died.

Frau Miller had been pregnant, about to deliver. My mother and I had gone over to the Miller house to help, with kettles for boiling water and clean towels. The midwife, Frau Gerlach, greeted us at the door with worried eyes. Frau Gerlach never looked worried. She was always starched, prim, proper, and in control. That morning her sleeves were rolled up past her elbows, and deep circles ringed her eyes.

"She's been in labor all night," the midwife said. "All night with no progress."

My mother and I climbed the stairs to Frau Miller's bed. She was covered in a sheen of sweat that stuck her nightgown to her chest. Her long hair was strung out on the pillow behind her. She did not look like the glowing picture of motherhood that I expected. She looked pale, sick, exhausted.

"The baby's a breech," Frau Gerlach said. "I've tried to turn the baby as much as I can, but she needs to go to the hospital."

My mother knelt down beside the bed, took the other woman's hands in hers. "You must go to the hospital. You've tried, but you can't do this alone."

Frau Miller shook her head. Her expression was peaceful but pained. "The baby will come."

"You're too exhausted to push any longer." My mother wiped her face with a cool washcloth.

At the foot of the bed, I saw her leg twitch and Frau Miller's face cringe as a contraction overtook her. The midwife bustled me out of the way, but I saw a runnel of blood dripping down the edge of the bed.

"Oh no," the midwife said. "It's coming. Coming all wrong."

Frau Miller turned her face to the pillow and howled as the flow of blood thickened and tapped on the wooden floor. I backed away from the widening puddle. My mother and the midwife were up to their elbows in it, shouting instructions. I grasped Frau Miller's hand. Her nails chewed into my palms like talons, and I did the only thing I could: I recited the Lord's Prayer, over and over.

My mother finally fled to the door, her sleeves and front of her apron soaked in blood. She looked as if she'd been butchering. She shouted down the steps: "Someone get an ambulance! Now!"

But it was too late. I felt Frau Miller's hand loosening in mine, saw her blank stare. She didn't blink.

And there was no lusty cry of a baby. The midwife was unable to wrestle the baby free before it suffocated with the umbilical cord wrapped around its neck. I learned later that the child would have been another son. An unbaptized son who would never join his brothers or parents in heaven.

The birthing room held the same acrid smell of death about it that I smelled now in the barn. It had taken days to air the Millers' room out and scrubbing the floor with lemon juice to release it.

I sat back on my heels. Light had drained from the day, darkening the barn, and there was little else I could do for Alex here.

He needed medicine. He needed it or he was going to die. Of this much, I was certain.

I trudged back across the field, my gait and heart heavy. I had interfered in things I should not have. This was an ongoing struggle for me. For the others in our community, following the Ordnung was a reflex, like breathing. It was almost as if . . . they were moved by others. Others' interpretation of the Ordnung. Not self-controlled, not their own interpretation. I knew that, deep down, I was not like that. I had to mull things over. I followed what I understood. And for that, I was both grateful and afraid.

Something pale moved across the meadow, like a sheet blown by the wind. I squinted at it, shading my hand from the last of the sunset.

It was a horse, riderless, pale as moonlight. I could make out some tack and gear on it. It was not an animal I recognized.

I stuffed my fingers in my mouth and whistled. The shrill sound made my ears ache, but it caught the horse's attention. It slowed, allowed me to approach it within yards. I saw that his sides were heaving, that he was lathered from running, that the white of his eye showed when it rolled back to me.

"Shhh," I said. I approached him from the front, showing that I was no threat. "Where did you come from?" I whispered.

The horse blew and pawed, agitated. He finally allowed me to reach out and grasp his bridle, rub his nose. I said soothing nonsense words to him. A stab of fear ran through me . . . If this was an English horse, I could not keep him. The horse, unconscious of the rules, had violated the Bishop's order.

But I set that aside for now. I could do him the kindness of leading him to water and strip him of his gear, so that he could be free and not encumbered by saddle sores.

I murmured to him in low tones, and he allowed me to remove the bridle. I let it fall in the grass, hoping that it would not be discovered. I think that he understood that I was trying to help him.

Then he turned his side to me, to show me the saddle buckle.

And I gasped.

The saddle was stained with blood, a rusty blotch that spread over the horse's left side. In the foothold, a torn boot dangled.

I stood still, shaking. The horse glanced back at me with a pleading eye.

I sucked in my breath, timidly unbuckled the strap at his belly while trying to keep the boot from bumping my shoulder. I think that there was still something in it: flies swarmed around it, and I could see a bit of bone peeking out of the top of the boot.

I shoved the saddle away, to the ground.

The horse whinnied, shook himself. I saw that the saddle had left angry red marks along his belly, saw that he was relieved to be free of that horror.

"You have to leave from here," I said. "Go away."

The horse stared at me, unyielding. His tail switched.

I made shooing gestures with my hands.

"They will kill you if you stay," I pleaded.

He snorted and walked away slowly, toward a distant tree line where a creek flowed. My heart broke to watch him go.

But it ached even more for that boot left behind in the saddle.

CHAPTER EIGHT

The next morning I rode my bicycle down the dirt road to the gate that separated our community from Outside. It was an old green girl's bike with a white plastic basket with flowers on the front and on the banana seat. I'd purchased it from an English garage sale for ten dollars when I was twelve. It was on the edge of what was allowed by Ordnung—bicycles were permitted, and the rules on rubber tires had been relaxed when I was a child. The bike wobbled on the ruts made by the metal wheels of the buggies. Determinedly, I rode slowly to the wooden gate. The gate closed the road, connecting a wood and barbed-wire fence on either side that stretched as far as the eye could see.

A meandering cabbage butterfly drifted through it. The fence was a flimsy thing. An able-bodied person would easily be able to climb over it. It was symbolic, every bit as much an illusion of security as the Hexenmeister's carefully crafted hex signs. I didn't understand how remaining behind a couple of two-by-fours was meant to save us from the end of the world.

I pulled up short before the gate. It had been bolted with a simple iron lock that was probably older than my parents. My heart hammered in my throat as I contemplated breaking the Elders' edicts . . . again.

But I found that each rebellion was easier than the last. Perhaps this was what they meant about the road to hell.

I lifted my bike up and set it down on the other side of the fence. I clambered gracelessly over the wooden beams and dropped down beside it. Money from my *Rumspringa* box clinked in my apron pockets. Money that could hopefully buy some medicine for Alex.

And I prayed I could avoid whatever that bloody fate was that had befallen the horse's rider. But I could not, in good conscience, allow a man to die when I could do something about it. All I needed to do was get him in good enough shape to walk, to get him out of here. Like the horse.

Righting my bike, I pedaled off into the sunshine.

Some things about Outside seemed utterly normal. Canada geese flew overhead in their tight formations. A red-tailed hawk perched on a telephone wire, watching me as I rode along the empty pavement. Black-eyed Susans and orange tiger lilies grew in profusion at the side of the road. The sun was warm on my back, and a breeze tickled through the tassels of grass.

As before, there was no traffic. I rode without fear, the wind rustling through my skirts. I pedaled fast up hills and allowed myself the thrill of going downhill at hazardous speed. It was like flying. No one could see me, the flying Plain girl with the wind tearing at my bonnet strings.

But other things were not anywhere close to normal.

I saw a trailer that had burned down to its foundations, the sharp smell of the melted plastic siding still in the air. Closer to the village, a car accident made the road impassible. I had to walk my bike on the shoulder around the abandoned cars.

Sobered, I continued on toward town, where there was more evidence of fire. Burned-out cars had slid off the road into telephone poles. All the glass was broken out of the general store, glittering on the asphalt like ice. Smoke billowed out of the structure.

I swallowed and continued. I was afraid to be Outside alone, without Elijah. But, no matter what, I would have to get used to his absence. I would have to prove to him and to myself that I could.

I stopped at the furniture store and pulled my bike up on the porch. I called into the darkness of the structure for Seth and Joseph, but no one answered. I reached into my pocket for a pencil and snagged a scrap of paper that blew up against the building. I left the boys a note:

Seth, Joseph:
    I don't know if you'll get this note. But your father and Elijah are looking for you. All they want is for you to come home.
    —Katie

I wedged the note between the door and the door frame. If they came back here, if they saw it, they would know.

I continued on, pedaling down the side streets. I saw a police car overturned on its roof, burned to a crisp that blackened the pavement. A truck carrying pumpkins had jackknifed in the road, smashed gourds painting the street a lurid shade of orange. Flies had descended upon the mess, and I wrinkled my nose as I walked my bike around it.

I finally arrived at the drugstore, next door to a Laundro-mat and bar. I didn't really expect to find anyone there, since the streets had been empty.

The door at the front of the drugstore was locked, and the sign on the window said that it was closed. I shook the door handle, rattling the glass.

I stepped back and looked up. The lights were on inside, so I assumed that the structure still had electricity, that the power lines to this part of town were still intact. I was certain the drugstore kept surveillance cameras on the property to deter precisely the kind of thing I was planning on doing.

I cast about the parking lot, and my eye fell on a cigarette receptacle. It was heavy, but I managed to lift it and swing it clumsily.

The glass door shattered in a glittering hail. My blood pounded in my ears. I couldn't believe the destruction I'd caused—not even when the alarm went off.

The screech of the alarm caused me to jump back, and my first instinct was to flee, but I fought that down. If the alarm brought police, that was good. They could look for Seth and Joseph. They could get Alex to a hospital. At the very least, they could tell me what was happening.

My shoes crunched in the broken glass as I walked into the fluorescent glare of the store. I picked up a large backpack in the school supplies area and began to shop.

I bypassed the makeup and glossy magazines, the bubble

bath and the candy, veering toward the back of the store where the actual health items seemed to be hidden. Strange arrangement for a store that had a purpose to sell medicine.

I picked up rolls of gauze, sterile bandages, antibiotic cream, ibuprofen, and hydrogen peroxide, stuffing them quickly into the bag. As I worked my way farther back, I found myself staring at the closed window of the pharmacy counter.

Antibiotics would be there. I tried to lift the steel curtain covering the window, but to no avail.

I set my bag down and began to think. There must be something to pry it up. I grabbed a cane from a nearby display and succeeded in wedging it beneath the steel curtain, bending it back enough to just allow space for me to jump the counter and wriggle through.

I knocked over scads of plastic baskets and rattling pill bottles before I found the light switch behind the pharmacist's counter. I was surrounded by a bewildering array of shelves of bottles and boxes. I had no idea what purposes the vast majority of them were used for. I picked up bottles at random. I didn't understand the labels.

There had to be some kind of tool here for pharmacists to tell . . . I went to a desk in the back that held a large red book. I opened it. To my relief, it was an index of drugs. I searched for "antibiotics" and carefully wrote down the names of several on a nearby notepad. The terminology was largely unfamiliar to me, but I could read through the lists and copy the information.

Carefully scrutinizing the shelves, I was able to find most of them: a bottle of erythromycin, packets of something called

Zithromax (which sounded like a comic book superhero), and some similar odd packages called Bactrim. I crammed as many as I could into a plastic bag and squirmed out under the counter.

I paused to think, my mind and heart racing. I might not get another chance to be Outside again. What else did I need? I wandered down the battery aisle. Several chargers and batteries that worked for cell phones were arranged on a plastic display. I knew that Mrs. Parsall's cell battery had been getting low. I'd taken a good look at it last night before we went to bed, memorizing the model number printed on the back. I found two extra batteries and a car charger that were supposed to work for that model.

Last, I went down the dog food aisle. I scooped all the cans of dog food that would fit into the backpack. I hesitated, then went back for a second backpack and filled that with dry food. I knew as well as anyone else that when food went short, the animals would suffer most. Not if I could help it.

On the way out, I emptied my pockets of all the bills I had and placed them next to the cash register. I had no idea how much the medicines cost, but knew that it wouldn't anywhere near cover the damage I'd done to the store.

I glanced longingly back at the pharmacy counter and the pet food display, briefly thought of loading up with everything I could carry. But I knew, deep down, that I should not take more than I could pay for.

Still feeling guilty, I stepped through the shattered door to my bike. I nestled one backpack in the basket and slung the other on my back. I began to push away from the curb, when something caught my eye.

Something red and white and delicious.

The glow of a Coca-Cola machine beckoned behind the door of the Suds 'n' Duds, the bar and Laundromat next door. I'd always thought drinking and laundry were a strange combination, but I had noticed that many people Outside required constant stimulation. Odd.

I looked away from the Coke machine, my tongue sticking to the roof of my mouth.

But I couldn't help glancing back at the seductive glow. Like a moth to the flame, I drifted toward it. In the bottom of my pocket, I fingered some loose coins. They clanked together, slipping against my sweaty palms.

The doors opened at my touch, and I stepped inside. Unlike the drugstore, the Laundromat advertised that it was open twenty-four hours. The washing machines and dryers lining the walls and aisles had long since fallen silent, and the fluorescent lighting buzzed and flickered overhead. I had never used machines like that. We used simple tubs, washboards, and lye soap. I couldn't imagine not having anything to do while laundry did itself. The cracked tile on the floor looked grimy, and I smelled a combination of stale beer and perfumed laundry soap. I stepped around abandoned plastic baskets full of clothes on the floor to stand before the warm red glow of the Coke machine.

I fed the machine a dollar in quarters and nickels, then punched the glowing button to release the soda. The machine clunked inside, and I reached down to retrieve my treat from the receptacle.

But nothing came out.

Gritting my teeth, I reached up into the mouth of the machine, trying to feel if it had gotten stuck. My fingers wiggled in air and darkness.

I stood back and pressed the button again. Nothing happened. The machine had eaten my money.

I dug into my pocket. I only had two dimes left.

My hands balled into fists. This might be the last chance I ever got to taste a Coke. Whether it was because of what had happened Outside, or my parents' rescinding of *Rumspringa,* I wanted the syrupy taste of this small rebellion. And this stupid machine was denying that bit of freedom to me . . . just like everyone else.

I slammed my hand against the face of the machine. It was the first time I'd ever struck anything or anyone out of anger. The blow echoed against the plastic, startling me with the force of it traveling up my arm to my shoulder. But the machine was unmoved. It continued to hum as if nothing had happened, smugly digesting my change in the face of my pathetic assault.

Shoulders slumped in defeat, I turned to walk away. The drugstore had caved under the force of my criminal will, but the Coke machine was virtuous. Inviolate.

I paused, glancing over the rows of battered washing machines to the bar. It wasn't much, just a long counter with chipped, mirrored shelves of bottles behind it and wobbly stools before it. But it was apparently enough to keep the folks entertained while they were doing their laundry. A television perched above the bar was tuned to the soft snow of static. They must have served some food here too, since flies swarmed over a paper tray of french fries abandoned on the counter.

My eyes narrowed. There might be Coca-Cola there.

And, after all, I *had* paid for it.

I circled behind the bar, scanning the bottles and cans. The spirits were colorless, brown, amber, and red. I didn't know why one would drink something called "extra dry." Nor did I understand why someone would drink something violent, as suggested by the "brut" on the label. And "Irish Rose" sounded entirely unappetizing. Flowers, in my experience, tended to taste bitter. My gaze roved over cans stuffed into a small refrigerator under the bar. Just beer and wilted lemons.

I frowned. I'd tasted beer once before and hated it.

I really wanted a Coke. Just a Coke.

At the end of the mirror behind the bar stood a shiny steel metal door. I grasped the latch. It was cold—I expected that it was a refrigerator of some type. A walk-in cooler that might contain what I was looking for.

Cold air blew into my face as I opened it, and my breath made ghosts in the fog. Something inside smelled funny, but I chalked it up to rotting food. I reached inside for a light switch, and a weak fluorescent light flickered on overhead. It illuminated metal racks on wheels full of beer, a couple of kegs on the floor . . .

. . . and a familiar stack of red and white cans, tucked behind one of the movable racks. I grinned in triumph.

A spider web brushed across my face, and I rubbed it away.

I should have paid attention to that, to that sensation that made me shudder. I pawed at my face and took two quick steps inside, trying not to imagine the spider that had created the string now caught in my hair.

I reached for the cans of Coke, victorious adrenaline surging through me. But that adrenaline soured, curdled as I became aware of something sticky on the floor that was sucking at my shoes.

I stared down.

A brown stain spread across the concrete floor to a drain. At first I assumed that some of the cans had frozen, exploded. But as I pushed the rack aside, I saw that it had trickled from a body on the floor.

Not just a body. I had seen dead bodies before, at funerals. Those bodies were neatly dressed in their Plain clothes, pale and sunken, usually old. Since we didn't embalm our dead, we buried them quickly, with little ceremony. Plain dead were peaceful, solemn.

This was . . . not peaceful. A man in a T-shirt and jeans lay on the floor. His head had been torn off, missing. I saw only white vertebrae glistening in that mass of gore that had been his neck.

I jammed my fist in my mouth. I was too terrified to scream, too shocked to do anything but utter a squeak.

And then I heard the clang of the cooler door slam shut behind me.

I scuttled back, tripped on a bucket. I fell down, backwards, on the floor, in the stain. I scrambled to my feet, whimpering in terror. I shoved at the door, but it was locked.

I sobbed, slammed my fist against it. The sound echoed just

like my blow on the Coke machine and was just as ineffective. I tried to control my breathing. There had to be an emergency release, some way to get out . . . my shaking fingers worked around the seam of the door, feeling for a lever or a switch.

Something made a scraping sound above me.

Swallowing hard, I looked up.

Behind the fluorescent light, I could make out shadows. I shaded my eyes from the weak light with my hand. I was able to distinguish shapes — shapes of people. They were suspended upside down from the ceiling, curled up in balls or dangling with limbs dragging in spider webs of silk that drizzled down in the darkness, holding the forms there in an ethereal embrace.

My breath disturbed a string of silk that trailed from the shadowed ceiling. It moved as intangibly as smoke. I was reminded of when I was a young girl and had disturbed a nest of corn spiders in the barn. The creatures had crawled everywhere, in my hair, my bonnet, down the neck of my dress . . .

Something up there moved, shifted. And glowing red eyes stared at me.

I saw the figure scuttle across the ceiling in a spider-like fashion, but it was human . . .

"Oh God!" I swore, jerking on the handle to the door. I rattled it, working my hands around the door, trying to find an emergency release I knew *had* to be there.

The creature on the ceiling approached as silently as those barn spiders, reached toward me.

My shaking hands found a cracked plastic button to the right of the door. I pulled at it, turned it, whimpering, finally slapped it hard . . .

And the door sprang open. I lurched through the doorway, running behind the bar.

I knew that *thing* was behind me. I ran past the line of washing machines, turned back to see it pawing along the ceiling. I didn't watch where I was going, stumbled over a box of laundry soap. The powdered soap spewed all over the floor, and I slammed against the wall of dryers.

The glass door of one of the dryers sprang open from the impact, and I found myself face to face with the contents of the machine. At first, I assumed that they were merely clothes, but . . . that smell . . . it was the same as in the cooler.

I could see pale, broken limbs turned in on themselves, a claw of a hand tangled in a sleeve. It was a crumpled, stinking body.

I whirled, only to find the creature from the cooler walking down the wall of dryers, hands behind knees, then dropping upright, on his feet. He was pale and filthy, and he smelled like blood. But what was most unnatural was the way his eyes glowed, like a cat's in the darkness. Behind him, I could see other shapes gathering on the ceiling.

I didn't bother to ask him what he wanted. I knew.

He wanted to kill me. Like he and the others had killed the man in the cooler and the man in the washing machine. It didn't matter why. There was no reasoning. This was the visceral fear of prey in the face of the predator, bitter like bile in my throat. But I was determined to run.

CHAPTER NINE

I sprinted for the door, breath burning in my throat. I felt the creature snatch the tails of my apron, drag me back from the door. I shrieked and flailed, my feet skidding on the sticky floor.

I heard stitches pop and give way, the sash of my apron shredding in the predator's grip. I lunged for the door.

I heard a snarl behind me. I knew that I had no hope, that even if I reached to door, he had me. But I was determined to try, to reach that golden threshold of sunshine before I was mauled to death, before my head was torn from my shoulders like that poor man in the cooler or my broken body was stuffed in the dryer like canned meat.

I straight-armed through the door, landed on my elbows on the pavement as I felt a hand latch around my ankle. I tasted blood in my mouth where I'd bitten my lip, twisted and turned to stare my fate in the face.

And the creature hissed. Abruptly, he released my ankle, his hand smoking in the sunshine.

I scrambled to my feet and ran toward my bike. I could see the shadows seething in the Laundromat, the glowing eyes behind the dark glass, mirroring the light of the seductive Coke machine. Somehow, they were trapped, pinned there by the daylight, I realized.

I struggled onto my bike, pumping the pedals as hard as I could down the street into the shining afternoon.

I could not stop shaking on my ride home. I quaked so hard that it was difficult to keep the bike from trembling under the uneven weight of the dog food and supplies in my basket. I pedaled so hard that it felt like my lungs were going to burst, swerving on the dark ribbon of road away from even the shadows of trees. I was afraid of what may lay in that soft darkness.

I am being punished for my sins. That was my first thought. Clearly, the gates of hell had burst open. Those creatures in the Suds 'n' Duds were not human. They radiated evil — evil like I had never known or could even have imagined before. When there had been news of a contagion, I had doubted the reality of a medical evil. What I had seen was clearly not the work of medicine. This reeked of spiritual evil, something beyond what could be fathomed by any technology belonging to man.

I licked blood from my lower lip. I knew. I knew what had happened to Seth and Joseph. And the rider on the white horse. They had fallen prey to these monsters. Tears blurred my vision. I longed to tell Elijah, but I didn't know that I would ever be able to form the words. There would be no kind, gentle way of telling him that his brothers had been torn limb from limb.

I wrestled with whom to tell, what to say. Any tale I could tell began and ended with sins I'd committed and the discovery of the man in the barn. Given the ruthlessness with which the Elders had chosen to leave him Outside, I knew that telling would result in certain death for him.

And perhaps also for me. They might not kill me outright, but if the Elders still believed in a contagion, they would probably throw me outside the gate, to be fed to those monsters. I shuddered. My sense of self-preservation eclipsed my desire to protect my community. I would not sacrifice myself that way, I decided. It was not God's will that I died. He had allowed me to escape, despite my sins. He had a plan for me and would not allow me to die, I reasoned. Not yet.

I pedaled back to the road where the gate stood. It seemed such a flimsy barrier against those shadow creatures. I heaved my bike over it, mindful not to damage the precious contents of the basket.

I paused here, at the border of our world and Outside. I stared down at my dress, sticky with splotches of the dead man's blood. I knelt down to the ground, smeared some mud over the stains. I gathered some stalks of yellow mustard at the side of the road, tucked them over my basket to hide the contents and walked my bike home.

At the kennel, I was greeted by Copper and Sunny, who sniffed me vigorously. Copper flattened his ears and whined.

I reached down to rub him. "It's okay, boy. I'm okay. I'm okay." It seemed that the more I said it, the more it had to be true.

Sunny licked my filthy cheek, and I broke down. The bit of sympathy that the dogs showed me was enough to cause me to sit on the ground and sob. The terror and adrenaline drained out of me in my tears, shaking through me.

After I reached hiccupping, dry sobs, I scrubbed my sleeve across my face. I forced myself to stand and walk my bike into the barn.

The darkness made my skin crawl, but I reminded myself that I was safe here. I was no longer Outside. I unpacked the contents of the basket. The dogs investigated the bag of dog food, noses quivering. I lifted it and the cans up high on a rack, where they couldn't reach.

"That's for later," I told them.

I gathered the antibiotics and headed back to the last paddock.

The young man—Alex—lay sleeping peacefully on the straw. I tore open a carton of the antibiotics, read the instructions twice. I removed three pills from the package, added a couple of ibuprofen. I propped his head up on my knee and forced the pills into his mouth. He gurgled and sputtered when I poured water past his lips.

"Antibiotics," I said, curtly. "Take them."

He did as he was told, swallowing the pills. His glazed eyes followed me as I sat back against the wall of the barn, a shaft of sunshine warming my back.

"There are enough for you to take for the next three weeks. Don't lose any. There aren't any more."

"Thank you," he whispered. His eyelids began to drift shut.

"No." I shook him, hard. Anger burned brightly in my voice. I wanted answers. My Amish reticence faded in the darkness of what I'd seen, the urgency of needing to know: "Wake up. You need to tell me what happened Outside."

His eyes opened, and he took in my disheveled appearance. "You saw?"

"I saw. Now, tell me."

"At first, I didn't realize there was anything wrong. I don't think that anyone did."

I loosened my grip on the young man's collar. His head thudded back to the straw, and his gaze landed somewhere on the ceiling. He blinked hard, and I thought for a moment that he was going to try to lose consciousness again. My hand balled up. I wouldn't let him. I wouldn't let him slip away that easily, leaving me without answers.

But then I realized that he was blinking back tears.

"You're not from around here," I prompted, my voice softer.

"No. I'm from Canada." That explained the slight rounding of his vowels.

"Why are you here?"

"I was looking at graduate schools." His mouth twitched. "I wanted to get my PhD."

"To be a doctor?" Plain folk didn't go to college. Children were educated through the eighth grade, most often in one-room schoolhouses like the kind I had gone to. I remembered my mother telling stories of forced busing to public schools back in the seventies, but the Amish had eventually won a Supreme Court case that allowed them to educate their children as they saw fit in the name of religious freedom.

I wasn't sure how I felt about that. Before, I'd resented it, wanting more than my teacher, the fifteen-year-old sister of a friend, could give me. I had to sneak away to the library and pester the librarians to answer questions that she could not. But right about now, thinking about Mrs. Parsall's children, I didn't resent it so much.

"Not a medical doctor. Not any kind of useful doctor. My undergraduate degree is in anthropology." His gaze flicked to me. It seemed that he was weighing me, deciding how much I would understand about Outside. Trying to figure out how naive I really was.

"I know what anthropology is," I said quietly. "You study people. Other cultures."

"Yeah."

"I *have* a library card," I said. What I wanted to say was *I'm not an idiot.*

"I didn't mean to imply that you were . . . that you didn't understand." It came out a bit haughty. "Sorry."

I nodded and waited for him to continue.

Eventually, he licked his lips and went on: "I came to the U.S. a week ago. I told my family that I was looking at schools."

My sharp ears detected the slight change in his story. "Why were you here, really?"

A smile crossed his lips. "Well, that wasn't the only reason. There was a girl."

I didn't prod him. There wasn't a girl now.

The smile faded. "I visited two schools. The first one was just . . . *meh*. They'd offered me a partial scholarship, but their program wasn't very good. Snotty private school. Even with the scholarship, I'd be paying off the tuition until I was sixty. Not worth it for a professor's salary."

"You want to teach?"

"Yeah. Folklore." He gave a small shrug. "The second school was better. The head of the department had published a lot, was a nice guy. Public school, cheaper tuition."

"And . . . the girl?"

"Cassia." His eyes softened when he said her name, and his eyes crinkled. I had never seen Elijah's eyes do that when he said my name. "She was there. Studying biology."

"How did you know her, if you were in Canada?" I was suspicious, looking to pick apart the threads of his story.

"We met on the Internet, fragging enemy soldiers."

I looked at him blankly. He didn't look like a soldier to me.

"Playing video games," he amended.

It was unfathomable to me to *know* someone who lived hundreds of miles distant. "You met playing video games?"

"Yeah. My parents thought it was pretty outrageous too, but"—he gave another of his small shrugs—"two of my friends met their girlfriends on online dating sites. I figured that it was just as legitimate as that. We talked every day for about six months."

"And you . . . fell in love when you saw her?" I knew about the concept of online dating sites from my peeks at magazines, but I had never actually used the Internet, so it was hard to understand exactly how they worked.

"No. I fell in love way before that. Love without first sight." He gave a grim chuckle. "I killed three batteries on my cell phone talking with her in those months."

I couldn't wrap my mind around falling in love with someone from afar. I was accustomed to seeing Elijah every day, felt affection out of sheer force of familiarity, force of habit. For me, that was love. Tangible. Love was what was in front of me, not a distant fantasy.

He blinked and looked away. "Anyway, I got to campus the day that the news reports started to come in. The reporters said that something had happened in DC. Some kind of dirty bomb. A biological weapon had been detonated in a bus station, supposedly."

"*Supposedly?* They didn't know for sure?"

"It was certain that something blew up. There were photographs of the destruction. Half a city block cratered. But there were other reports, unofficial reports on the Internet, that something had happened at the CDC."

"CDC?"

"Centers for Disease Control. They study infectious diseases, in Atlanta. Just rumors . . . there were all kinds of rumors. Rumors that aliens had landed, rumors that something climbed out of the Sarcophagus at Chernobyl."

I hated to admit my ignorance, but I needed to know what was happening more than I needed to protect my pride. "What's Chernobyl? And why do they have a sarcophagus?"

He explained to me patiently, without condescension. I could see some of what might make him a good teacher. "Chernobyl was the site of a nuclear disaster in the Ukraine. Hundreds of thousands of people were evacuated and relocated, and thousands of deaths were attributed to the radiation, depending on who you talk to. The ground is still contaminated with radiation. They covered the reactor with a lead structure they nicknamed the Sarcophagus. It's been degrading for years."

I nodded. It sounded like the plot of one of the movies from the newspaper, but I accepted it. "Go on."

"There was even a story that some bored Satanists got drunk at a science fiction convention and managed to summon some supernatural evil that took over the whole convention center."

My frame of reference was already stretched to its limit. I had no idea where to begin with questions about that statement.

"Anyway," he continued, "I don't know what was actually true. What I do know is that the news started showing videos of rioting. And not just in DC—it cropped up everywhere. I guess I thought it was some reaction to the terrorism, but it defied all logic. It wasn't just a religious or political site that was burnt. It was schools, libraries. When I saw an Internet report of a tour bus of senior citizens turned over and . . . and eviscerated . . . I knew that it was much worse."

"How did . . . how did it spread?"

"Cassia thought it was a result of transportation—airplanes, cars. It had spread within hours. And the contagion seems to have an absurdly short incubation period . . . less than two days."

"Cassia sounds like a smart woman."

"Yeah." The corner of his mouth turned upward. "She's freaking brilliant. That's what I love about her. Biology fellow at the university. Gonna be a scientist."

"Hmm."

His gaze met mine. "What?"

"That's just . . . the first time I've heard a man say he loved a woman for her brilliance." I was used to hearing about men who loved women for their eyes, for their smiles, for their ability to work hard, for their gentleness and kindness. Not for their brilliance.

"Yeah, well. Women are different out there." He let out a snort of derisive laughter.

"I don't mean to sound insensitive about your dating life." I lifted my chin in defiance. "But I want to know more about 'out there.' Why, with all those brilliant people, is there no more 'out there'?"

He flinched. I felt a momentary sting of satisfaction at taking him down a peg. We Amish did not suffer pride well. Normally, I'd have accepted his condescension with a thin smile, but not today. Not after the world had ended. No one was observing the rules anymore.

"It's not as if we weren't working on it. I went with Cassia to the biology lab, slept in the hallway while all these people in their plastic suits stared into microscopes."

"You went to protect her?" That was a feeling I could understand. Though I knew very little about his world and the things he spoke of, I understood human emotion.

"Yeah. And I had nowhere else to go. The university went into quarantine. I wasn't sure if it was to keep the rioting out, or to keep us inside. They closed the iron gates, blocked off the roads. Campus police started shooting anyone who wanted in or out. Hell, I didn't even know those guys were armed." His voice was thin.

I sucked in my breath, thinking of Mrs. Parsall's children, at their own distant colleges. "Go on."

"I thought it beyond barbaric, until I saw a pack of rabid cheerleaders take out some cops in a patrol car. It was like they peeled open a sardine can, then dragged them out and chewed them up on the pavement." He shook his head. "I've never seen anything like it.

"The lab was barricaded while Cassia and the other graduate students tried to figure out what the hell they were. The National Guard came in. They were better shots than the campus P.D.

"Odd thing was, they only came out at night. During the day, the streets were empty, almost peaceful. Cassia said that photophobia — extreme sensitivity to light — was a symptom of rabies. That perhaps we were seeing a mutated, sped-up version of that."

His breath quivered when he blew it out. "I've seen rabies. This was . . . Jesus. This was something else. Something more atavistic in its power. Something . . . beyond science."

"Something evil," I whispered.

"I said they were vampires."

My heart froze. "Vampires?" I wanted to say, *They aren't real* — but the destruction of a world didn't seem real, either.

"Yeah. Cassia laughed at me. A plague of vampires? She said that it would be impossible for the human digestive system to adapt to survive on blood in the space of two days. Eventually, the Guard brought a corpse into the biology department for them to cut up. She said that it had a gullet full of blood. Cassia thought it was due to internal bleeding, that the key had to be some blood-borne infection. Maybe rabies with a bit of hematological fever mixed in. I didn't understand all of it."

"But you thought of vampires."

"I wasn't the only one. It seemed as good a way to describe them as any other. Like I said, the violence was only at night. People were walking around with garlic strung around their necks. Some of them even found refuge in the campus church. That worked well for a while . . . until someone set fire to it. I remember watching the fire from one of the windows in the biology building. It was about three in the morning . . . People came streaming out of the building, right into the arms of the vampires. They ripped them limb from limb." His eyes squeezed shut.

"It was nothing like you see in the movies, these creatures. There's no seduction. No passionate luring of the victim to a dark side of velvet. This is just the stinking, rotting underbelly of evil without its makeup. This is exactly what the Undead were in the old folk stories, the world around. Every culture has a vampire—a creature that drinks the blood of the living. And it's not a pretty process."

"There's nothing . . . nothing human remaining of them?" I struggled to articulate the question. "Is there anything intelligent there?"

"I think so. Cassia said they're capable of speech, of strategy. They figured out how to burn down the church. They would circle the biology building at night, like moths drawn to the flame, calling out for help. Once, one of the Guardsman went to help a woman who was being attacked in the street. Turned out it was a ruse—she was a vampire too. She shucked him out of his body armor like a squirrel with a nut. Maybe they would be less frantic if there was enough food to go around. But they're smart enough to find it.

"I suspect that the corpse that the Guard brought into the biology building was also a ruse, that it was something planned."

"How?"

"I think that they infected the body, left it for us. They knew that we were looking for answers. They couldn't get in. The biology building was built to contain all manner of nasty bugs in the event of a grad student dropping a petri dish full of Ebola. So . . . they sent something in. And that's what got us."

"The corpse became a vampire?"

"I told them that it would." His hands balled into fists in the straw, broke the hollow stalks. "I told them what our ancestors did . . . that they stuffed the mouth with garlic, cut off the head, cut out the heart and burned it . . ."

"They didn't do that."

"No. Their microscopes told them that the pathogen was dead. And they believed what their microscopes showed them."

"Cassia didn't believe you?" I couldn't understand believing a machine over a person.

"Not at first. I pleaded with her to let me sever its head. She wouldn't allow me to damage their evidence. She believed . . . she believed that they were close to an answer when that damn thing crawled out of the cooler and chewed the head off of her dissertation advisor. I think she believed me then."

He lapsed into an opaque silence.

I prodded him. "And then? How did you escape?"

"Not everyone did. The monster woke up just before dawn. I was able to get my bike out of the basement, tried to convince Cassia to leave. She wanted to stay, study that monster that was sucking her advisor dry in the next room."

I couldn't fathom it. That kind of loyalty to an idea. I had felt some loyalty to my community, but not enough that I would never leave it. I would leave it for anything as entertaining as *Rumspringa*. For a moment, I was ashamed.

"What did you do?" I asked, dreading the answer. Had he left her behind? I wasn't sure I wanted to know.

"She was wearing one of those plastic suits. She's small, so she swam in it. The sleeves were extra-long. Long enough that I could straitjacket her in it. She fought me, kicking and screaming, all the way down to the bike. I heard gunshots upstairs, breaking glass. I knew that we didn't have much time, that if we had any future, we could work on the forgiveness part." His mouth turned up darkly.

"The vamps are fast. But not as fast as a motorcycle. Not that they didn't try. We got past the stadium just as the sun rose."

I stared at him, hard. He was here now. Without his bike, and without the girl. "That wasn't the last time you saw them."

"No. I had thought to head north, back to Canada. There are enough unpopulated places there . . . I thought we could evade them until someone figured it out. Somewhere." He shook his head. "We avoided the cities, stuck to the rural roads, slept during the day.

"But I underestimated them. We were riding not too far from here, at night, when we were ambushed. At first, I thought that it was a herd of deer blocking the road. I slowed down. And that's when I saw . . . I saw that they were just corpses of deer, propped up on the road. I tried to weave around them, but I saw the figures of men around them, like ghosts.

"I went off the road, through a meadow. They followed. I hit a barbed-wire fence, wrecked the bike.

"Cassia was easy to see in the dark, wearing that white plastic suit. They attacked her like vultures. I had a knife, but . . . it wasn't enough." He swallowed hard, and his gaze glistened. When he spoke again, his voice was low. "I ran. I ran until I couldn't hear the screaming anymore."

The hair lifted on my arms. "They didn't follow you?"

"They tried. But I stumbled, inadvertently, into a place they couldn't catch me."

"Where?" My brows knit together.

"An old family burial plot. A farmer's cemetery. Not more than six or seven graves, no larger than a small room. It was marked off by unkempt grass, no fence . . . but they couldn't go in. I passed in and out of consciousness. They circled me all night, like wolves, until they slunk away before dawn."

I wasn't sure whether or not to believe him. "They left you alone?"

"It wasn't me. It was the cemetery. It was holy ground. Vampires aren't supposed to be able to cross into it. Someone must have still believed in it. I found the skeletons of wildflowers there . . . I imagined that there was maybe a child who still visited the place, left flowers on those Civil War–era stones."

"And you found your way here?"

"I don't remember much after that." He touched the wound on his temple.

He saw me looking at him with dubious, fearful eyes.

"I'm not infected," he insisted.

I backed away, allowed the sunshine that had warmed my back to strike him in the face. He squinted through it quizzically, unlike the creatures I'd seen at the Laundromat.

"I'm not," he said. I don't know if he was trying to convince me or convince himself. He reached into the light, let the dust motes and sunlight drift over his fingers.

"It doesn't matter, anyway," I said. "They're in town."

He looked at my disheveled appearance. "They found you."

"I escaped." I shook my head. "It won't be long before they find us."

"They probably already know. Like I said, they seem to be pretty intelligent."

"Then why haven't they eaten us alive?"

"If I had to guess . . . your community is holy ground. Like the cemetery."

"Holy ground?"

"Well, yeah." He stared up at the barn. "If I recall my comparative religions courses, you Amish are pretty strict about the sacredness of the everyday, right?"

"*Ja.* I guess so." I'd never heard it put like that.

"Prayer services rotate from house to house, not held in a central church?"

"Of course."

"Your land may be holy enough to keep them away. You may just have the last fortress against the Undead. Right here."

I sat back against the wall of the barn, hard. "We're safe?" For the first time since the attack in the Laundromat, I began to feel the warmth of certainty again. Much like having God's favor made tangible.

"Well . . . if I'm right. As long as you don't do anything stupid."

"Like going outside the gate," I whispered. The Elders had known, on some visceral level.

"And don't invite them in. They can't get in any other way."

CHAPTER TEN

I took my time returning to the house, absorbing everything I had seen and heard. I felt numb, unable to process all the information. My mother saw me crossing the backyard to the water pump, where I washed my hands until they were red and raw.

"Katie! What happened to you?" she cried at my filthy appearance.

"I . . . one of the bulls knocked me down. He didn't mean it. He just didn't see me." I bit my lip down on the lie.

She grabbed my shoulders. "Are you hurt?"

"No. Just a bit shook up." The smear of blood had dried brown, indistinguishable from mud.

She put her arm around me. "Come and wash up. You'll feel better when you're clean."

My mother sat me down at the kitchen table and gave me a glass of fresh milk while she carried wood to the basement to heat the water for a bath.

I stared into the milk for what seemed like a long time before lifting it to my lips. It tasted cold, rich, and pure. It grounded me, brought me back to myself.

My mother returned to take me to the spring room in

the basement beside the root cellar, leading me by one hand. The other held a small kerosene lamp. We had a spring on our property, which was a blessing, but no natural gas well. Many Plain folk were able to jerry-rig a system that provided hot water with a natural gas well, but we relied on a wood stove in the corner of the spring room to heat water for the scarred clawfooted bathtub in the center of the floor. I remembered bathing in it since I was a child, feeling the cold porcelain under my hands and chin.

My mother began to untie my bonnet, but my fingers wrapped around hers. "No. I'll do it."

She nodded and turned her back to give me privacy while she poured a kettle of hot water into the tub. The boiling water steamed as it hit the cooler spring water. My mother topped the bathtub off from the hand pump in the floor, dipped her fingers in to check the temperature, as if I were a little girl. She'd even laid out a clean dress for me on a table against the wall we used for folding laundry. The one she picked she knew was my favorite: dark blue like the sky after sunset.

A lump rose in my throat at her kindness. It was Saturday, and bath day, anyway, but she was still trying to care for me.

She patted and kissed my cheek. "I'll be up in the kitchen. Let me know if you need anything."

I swallowed. I needed a lot of things. I needed to tell her what I'd learned, what I'd heard and seen with my own eyes. I needed her reassurance that all was unfolding according to God's will, that we would be protected.

But all I could do was nod and look away.

My mother took that for modesty and left, closing the door

of the spring room behind her. She left the little lamp behind to cast its yellow glow on the earthen walls. Red embers emanated from the belly of the stove, crackling with the last of the wood my mother had burned for the water. The heat caused sweat to prickle from my skin, even though my flesh was still covered in goose bumps.

I ripped the bonnet off my head, cast it on the floor. I peeled out of my filthy dress and my underclothes, kicked my shoes into a dark corner of the room where I couldn't see them. A sob caught in my throat. I wadded up my clothes into a ball and walked to the stove. I tugged open the cast-iron door with a potholder and stuffed the bundle into it. The fire sparked and sputtered, as if trying to reject the awful, blood-spattered knowledge I shoved into its gullet. Finally, the dress caught and curled, burning brightly.

I shut the door on it, tears blurring my vision. I climbed into the bathtub, hissing as the hot water licked my skin.

I grabbed a washcloth and a bar of homemade lye soap and began to scrub, hard. I scrubbed until I was red and raw, as if I could scrape my own skin off and remove all the terrible things I'd learned today that had somehow become a part of me.

Eventually, I stopped, the water cloudy with the residue of soap. I stared up at the wooden floor joists of the ceiling in the dim, flickering light.

Was Alex right? Were we safe here, safe from those terrible creatures? I had a difficult time accepting that they were vampires, though my logic could find no other way out of the forest of the problem. Was God still watching over us? Had he chosen the Amish to be safe, here in our little community? For how long? How long until we ran out of kerosene and patience?

And what could I say . . . what should I say? I wanted to tell my parents what I'd seen, what Alex had told me. But I knew that, no matter how much they loved me, they would not defy the Elders on my behalf. No one in our community ever did, not even for their own children.

I remembered that two years ago one of my classmates had been baptized very young. He had been sixteen, insisted that he was ready, that he had tasted enough of Outside—but then he returned to the ways of *Rumspringa*. He moved outside our community within six months. He had come around for a while to visit his family, wearing his English clothes of jeans and T-shirts, driving his car, and talking about the job he'd found Outside in a factory. He'd also found drugs—meth. His parents kept trying to talk him into coming back, where there would be no temptation. He could go through withdrawal at home, ask the church for forgiveness, go back to where he'd started.

But the Elders said that his visits couldn't continue. They said that the only way to bring him back into the fold was to reject him. He could not have the best of both worlds. He had accepted the rules when he was baptized, and he should know better. They were confident that the disapproval of his family and community would cause him to come back, dry out, ask forgiveness and rejoin the church, and to live happily ever after. With us.

And so they shunned him. The *Bann und Meidung*. Under

the *Bann,* he was not permitted on our property. We were not allowed to speak to him, not even if we saw him Outside. We were to turn away from him, cast our eyes and voices away. We were to do nothing to help him. We were to release him to Outside like a wayward bird and let him find his way back.

It was heartbreaking for his family. I remember seeing him pounding on the door of his house, distraught, but no one would let him in. On the second floor, I could see his mother peering through the curtains, weeping. The only one who greeted him was the family dog.

He drove away and never came back. News came months later that he had died in a car accident. Alcohol was involved. His parents were not permitted to bury their son, and it was rumored that the government Outside had cremated his unclaimed remains. He'd turned against us, and his parents would never see him in heaven.

The Elders said that was God's will. *Gelassenheit.*

And the Elders now said that no one was permitted in or out of the gate. I had defied those edicts twice. I had brought an Outsider in, and I'd ventured Outside myself. I could tell them what I had learned . . . that Outside suffered from a plague of vampires. But could they do anything with that knowledge that they weren't already doing? They had placed our community in quarantine. That seemed to be working. According to Alex, it would continue to work unless someone invited evil in.

I squeezed my eyes shut. If I told the Elders, I did not know what would happen. I expected that they would throw Alex out to the monsters. For myself . . . I had never seen someone placed under the *Bann* until after they were baptized. But that didn't mean they wouldn't. If they could shun someone for accepting and then renouncing the Ordnung, for the crime of being an addict, they would not hesitate doing the same to me for bringing risk to the community.

And, given what I'd seen and heard today, the *Bann* would mean certain death.

I sank up to my chin in the now-tepid water. I had failed to follow the Elders' wisdom. Though they didn't have all the information, they had chosen the correct course of action through faith.

I had no choice. I didn't want to die. I didn't want Alex to die. I would have to keep silent.

But perhaps I could make amends to God, and he could forgive me. Perhaps he would not bring disaster to our doorstep.

I began to murmur the Lord's Prayer, my breath pushing small ripples across the water. Maybe he would still hear me.

——— ———

I walked over to Elijah's house that evening to bring him and his father some supper. I left as soon as the bread had cooled enough to handle and the Jell-O had set. The sun was still above the horizon. I wanted to be back well before nightfall, now that I knew what dwelt in it.

I knocked on the front door, and Herr Miller called for me to let myself in. I found him sitting at the kitchen table, reading his Bible. He looked very pale and thin as his eyes moved across the page.

"I've brought supper. And I'll pick up your laundry."

"Thank you, Katie," he murmured as I put a plate of bread, ham, and baked apples before him.

"I'll put the Jell-O in the refrigerator," I said. "It has spiced apples in it." There wouldn't be much more Jell-O, or any groceries from the Outside, in the future.

His gaze flickered at me as I prepared Elijah's plate. "Katie, you know that Elijah will be baptized tomorrow."

I paused in slicing the bread. "So soon?" I blurted.

"The church will be doing their fall baptisms tomorrow."

"I thought . . . I thought that wasn't for a few more weeks." The Amish baptized their young men and women in fall and spring, at large church services for that purpose. That then allowed those who were intent on starting families to prepare for weddings after harvest or before planting, when there was a lull in the daily activities. And there was always a course of study for many weeks before.

"The Elders moved it up. They said it was best, given the circumstances."

I could feel his gaze heavy on my back as I assembled the plate.

"I am happy for you both," I said. "You must be very proud."

"I am. But you should consider it, as well, Katie. I will talk to your parents about it. I think that they would be strongly in favor."

I bit my lip. I wanted to make amends with God, certainly. The end of the world had come, and it did make sense to get baptized. But my conscience was not clear enough for me to take baptism. I still had a young man in the barn. I couldn't be baptized now and abandon him the instant the water touched my forehead. For, once baptized, I could not continue to care for him in any good conscience . . . never mind the *Bann*.

I smeared a gentle smile on my face. With Elijah's plate in my hand, I kissed his father's balding forehead. I hope that he took that as a gesture of respect. He smiled and patted my sleeve.

I climbed the stairs to the boys' room. The door was ajar, and I pushed it open. Elijah was lying in his middle bed, reading his Bible. He smiled when he saw me.

"I brought you some supper," I said, closing the door behind me.

He put the Bible on the nightstand. "Thank you."

I sat on the edge of his bed. "How's your ankle?"

He wiggled the foot at the edge of the quilt. "It's getting better. I've been up and around on it a bit. I found someone to lend me some crutches for . . ." His eyes slid away from mine.

"For tomorrow," I finished.

He stared fixedly down at his plate. "I want you to be happy for me."

"I am. But . . . I also feel as if I'm losing my best friend." I rubbed my nose. It was as close to explaining how I really felt: that he would be closer to God than he would be to me. And that was a good thing. It just left me feeling . . . lonely. Bereft.

He reached out and took my hand. "Don't feel that way."

"How can I not?"

"There's nothing out there for us, anyway. The Outside world took Joseph and Seth. Caught them out." His eyes were dark. "I want no part of it."

I could understand his anger. "You aren't the only one who's lost family. Mrs. Parsall may have lost her children and husband."

"They aren't like us." Elijah shook his head. "They aren't going to heaven."

I pulled my hand away. "What's happened to you?"

His mouth was set in a grim line. "The Elders came by yesterday. What they said made sense."

"What did they say to you?" Dread curled in the pit of my stomach.

"They said that something terrible has happened Outside. That it's all gone. That there's no point in hoping for *Rumspringa*. We must devote ourselves to God and build on what we have here. God has blessed us. He's saved us. And we must show our devotion to him."

I couldn't argue with that unimpeachable logic. "I wish you well," I said softly.

"Come be baptized with me," he said, not unexpectedly.

"That's what your father said."

"He means well. So do I. If you were to be baptized tomorrow, then we could be married before first frost." Elijah's hand tightened on mine.

My breath stuck in my throat, and I tried to pull away. "Don't."

He held my hand fast. "Don't you want this? Don't you want to be married, have children, go to heaven?"

"Of course, but . . ." I grappled with my thoughts.

"Don't you want me?" There was a pang of hurt in his voice. "Don't you want me more than what's Outside?"

I placed my free hand on his cheek. "Of course I do. But this is all . . . it's all too fast."

I felt the tension in his jaw relax fractionally. "*Ja.* I understand."

Just days ago Elijah and I were looking at movie ads, planning where to go, and roaming Outside as if it was our birthright. Now the crisis had hardened him, caused him to withdraw into the safety of tradition. I couldn't blame him, but I would not be pushed.

He rested his forehead against mine. "I will wait for you."

I blinked back tears. "If you want to be married quickly, it may be best if you don't."

He frowned. "How could I imagine anyone else? I have waited years. I will wait a season or two more."

He kissed me. It was not our first kiss; Elijah and I had kissed many times on the way back from the Singings. Amish youth gathered on Sunday nights, ostensibly to sing, without adult supervision. There was always something heady and romantic about the darkness and the music. On a couple of occasions, we'd forgotten ourselves, exploring each other with our clumsy fingers. We were not strangers. Not lovers—I would not give myself to him on those occasions. But we knew each other well.

He kissed me more deeply. I would miss this, after his baptism. He would be unable to touch me again until we were married. It felt cruel, the pressure of his lips on mine, his hands wrapping around my waist and pulling me into his lap. One of his hands slid up to cup my breast, and I felt his arousal under my right hip.

"Elijah," I murmured against his lips. He took that for

ardor, plucked the pin from the top of my dress to peel back the fabric.

"*Elijah,*" I said again, more insistent.

His hand slid beneath the fabric to my breast.

"*Stop.*" I grabbed his hand and tried to push myself off his lap.

He hesitated for a moment, then released me. I scrambled off the bed, pulled the collar of my dress together, and jabbed the straight pin back into the fabric to close it.

When I looked back at him, there was hurt in his eyes. I'd rejected him, and it had wounded him dearly.

"I need . . . I need some time." I backed away, reaching for the doorknob.

"There's nothing for you Outside," he said softly as I slipped through the door.

Maybe not. Maybe my destiny was shrinking, becoming smaller and smaller to one inevitable path. I could feel it tight around my neck, tighter than my bonnet strings, strangling me.

Chapter Eleven

My head hurt, my heart ached, and I knew that there was no hope of sleep tonight. I kept picturing those monsters I'd seen today, free to roam in the darkness. I struggled with the concept that an idea like faith could create a strong-enough wall to keep them out. My own faith felt tenuous and weak . . . I couldn't imagine it being powerful enough to keep the vampires at bay.

But I did not think that baptism would strengthen it enough. I quailed against the idea in the deepest part of my chest. My parents had broached the subject after that evening's *Nachtesse,* stressing the same points made by Elijah and his father. I stared at the floor, mute. They could not force me. I could not swear obedience before God. It would be a false promise. I had that much integrity left.

Sarah snored beside me, closest to the wall. She slept the sleep of one who had no real concept of what happened beneath the surface. Today was the same for her as yesterday and the day before and the day before that. Her life hadn't really changed, except for having to share a bed with me. She'd seen no raven evacuation. No riderless white horses. No brutal application of the Ordnung.

Mrs. Parsall sat up against the headboard, staring into the dark. Her right hand was slack around her cell phone. She slept with it, even though the charge was dead. It was her last tie to her husband and children. I slid out of bed and reached beneath it for the bag from the drugstore. Wordlessly, I padded across the floor and put it in her lap.

She reached inside, the plastic crinkling. Her glass-blue eyes widened as she pulled out the batteries and charger.

"Where did you get these?" she rasped.

"You can't tell anyone."

Her hands grasped my elbows, and she drew me down to the bed. "Did you go Outside?" Her gaze was fever-bright.

I swallowed and nodded.

"What did you see?"

I remained mute.

She squeezed my arm. *"What did you see?"*

My lip trembled, but I couldn't shape my voice around horror that I'd witnessed.

"Were there people?" Her fingernails dug into my arms like claws. "Did you see people?"

I shook my head. "No. Not people. Monsters."

I could see the whites of Mrs. Parsall's eyes widening in the dark. "What do you mean, monsters?"

A tear trickled down my face. "Ravenous. Bloodthirsty. Inhuman."

Her hand flew to my cheek, smearing the tear. Her brow wrinkled, in shadow. "I don't understand."

"They are like . . . like vampires." I told her, haltingly, of the terror I'd seen at the Laundromat, keeping my voice to a whisper so Sarah wouldn't hear.

When I'd finished, Mrs. Parsall threw her arms around me in a hug while I sobbed into her shoulder. She stroked my hair and muttered soothingly. "It's okay. Shhh. You're okay."

Spent, I drew back and pressed the heels of my hands to my eyes, as if the pressure could drive away what I'd seen. "You can't tell them," I whispered fiercely. "If they knew, they'd shun me."

Mrs. Parsall brushed a soggy strand of hair off of my face. "I won't."

Her gaze crept to the phone batteries, and I saw the twitch in her fingers.

"Call your family," I said, hiccupping back tears.

Behind me, I heard Sarah stir and mutter: "Katie?"

I went to her bedside, pulled the blankets up to her chin. "It's okay. Go back to sleep."

Her sleepy eyes watched me, though, watched me until the weight of her lashes pulled her eyelids down.

I looked back to Mrs. Parsall, laid my finger on my lips.

She nodded, gathering up the phone and batteries, and tiptoed from the room.

I followed her, creeping past my parents' door, down the steps to the kitchen. All the lamps had been doused, and the only light in the room came from the moonlight streaming in and the pilot light in the stove. It was all cold, blue light, and I shivered in spite of the warmth.

Mrs. Parsall reached for the doorknob of the back door.

I grabbed the sleeve of her nightdress. "Don't," I whispered. "They love the dark."

Her mouth was set in a grim line. "I have to talk to my family."

I knew that there was no stopping her; I had just given her hope wrapped up in a plastic bag.

She pulled away from me, opened the door to the night, and slipped out the back step.

I paused on the threshold, listening. I heard the sounds of crickets chirping, bullfrogs in the pond. In the distance, I could make out the sketchy figures of deer in the fields. A larger, lighter shape grazed among them: a white horse. My heart fell when I saw him. The white horse wasn't leaving. He was still in danger. But at least he had the sense to graze at night, with the deer. Maybe he could evade discovery until this whole mess was over. I dared hope that much for him.

My gaze swept the darkness for threats. I spied a light burning in the window of the Miller house. Elijah's room. My chest tightened. I wondered if, behind that light, he was reading his Bible. Brooding. Maybe masturbating for the last time. It was hard to tell.

I turned away from the light. Reaching for the knife block on the kitchen counter, I pulled out my mother's serrated bread knife. I put my bare foot on the cold stone of the step, hissing at the chill, and followed Mrs. Parsall out to the yard. The dew of the grass was cold on my feet, dampening the edge of my nightgown. I found her, sitting on the bumper of her car, out of sight and earshot of the house. They wouldn't be able to hear our conversation.

Maybe not even hear us scream.

I sat beside her on the bumper, watching as she removed the old battery and fitted the new one in with shaking hands.

The phone lit up when she hit the power button.

"It has a signal," she said.

"Does that mean there's still someone at the cell phone company?" I asked.

She shook her head. "It just means that the satellites haven't fallen out of the sky." She punched numbers into the phone, and I could hear it ringing against her cheek.

I stared out at the horizon, my hand sweating on the wooden grip of the knife. I knew that those creatures of darkness were out there . . . but I hoped that God had mercy on Mrs. Parsall's husband and children, even if they were English. I hoped that he showed them even a fraction of the mercy he'd shown us.

The phone stopped ringing when Mrs. Parsall hit the disconnect button. She tried another number that rang forever into silence. She sat huddled on the bumper, curled over the phone.

I looked up at the stars. I knew that we were never to ask God for anything, but at this moment, I thought at him:

Please have mercy. Please save her family.

And the horse.

And the man in the barn.

And my family.

And take Seth and Joseph to Heaven . . .

I cut off my thoughts that tumbled over one another. It was a slippery slope. I was beginning to treat God as a vending machine.

"Dan?" Mrs. Parsall cried into the receiver, cupping her hands around it. My heart lifted to hear her sob: "Yes, yes, I'm okay. I'm with the Amish. What about the kids?"

I could hear a voice at the other end of the line, going on for several minutes. Mrs. Parsall pressed the heel of her hand to her forehead and sobbed. I put my arm around her, the arm without the knife.

"Can't they search?" Her voice lifted in pitch. "Can't they do anything?"

I held her shoulders tighter. The voice in the background buzzed against her ear.

"Okay." Her eyes were squeezed shut. "I love you."

The voice rumbled something more, then fell silent.

Mrs. Parsall turned the phone off. She cradled her head in her hands.

"Dan's all right?" I asked.

She nodded. "He's on a battleship off the coast of North Carolina."

I didn't ask about her children. I was afraid to.

"The kids . . ." Her voice broke, and she tried again. "He found Julia. She's okay, okay for the moment. She's at a kibbutz, of all places."

"What's a kibbutz?"

"It's a Jewish community, usually an agricultural thing. Her roommate grew up at one in California and took Julia back with her. Dan spoke with her this morning." Her voice low-ered to nearly a whisper. "He hasn't been able to find Tom."

I hugged her hard, kissed her cheek. "He will be all right."

Mrs. Parsall rubbed a string of snot and tears from her nose. "I don't know. Dan said that the contagion creates . . . mon-sters. Like what you saw."

"The military is working on it?"

"They are trying, with what they have left. There aren't many people remaining here." She covered her mouth with her hand, holding back fear and terror and sobs. "Dan says the military thinks that more than two-thirds of the world's popu-lation is gone. It spread on planes so fast that . . . and they're gone."

It was hard to comprehend, a number that large. "Gone?"

"There are some who've survived. Some fled to the sea, like our military. Vatican City is untouched, and what's left of the UN is using that as a base. There are pockets of people still holding out in kibbutzim and temples . . . even Stonehenge. The Japanese at Mount Fuji have set up a makeshift lab, are trying to find a solution. In New Orleans, people have taken over the Cities of the Dead, and he says people are living in the catacombs under Paris."

"I don't understand."

"We have someplace to retreat. There are nuns in Britain who are sheltering thousands in convents, monks in Thailand holding these monsters at bay with fire. Mosques still standing. Dan said that there's even a coven of witches in New Jersey who've raised an army of pagans based out of a temple to Bast in a strip mall."

My mind chased that idea. Mrs. Parsall's daughter was safe in a religious community . . . one that wasn't a Plain community. I thought back to what Alex had said, about religious barriers being the only ones against the vampires. But there had to be a line that such things could be of God. I refused to believe that everything of human imagining could be the correct interpretation of God's word. It was simply not possible.

We Amish were taught to be respectful of others. I didn't *not* believe that other Christians went to heaven, only that their way of life made it more difficult to get there.

"How can they be safe?" I struggled to understand. "How can . . . witches fight off the darkness?"

"These places are sacred. Sacred to someone."

I shook my head. "But they are not . . . not of God." It didn't ring true to me. Didn't feel true. "They will not stand." I had no doubt that Mrs. Parsall was reporting what was told to her. But I did not blindly accept what she said, just as I did not blindly accept the Ordnung.

I rubbed my temples, confused. "If this is a disease of science . . . I don't understand how something spiritual could stop it."

"I don't think that anyone does. Not yet."

The thought gave me hope. It gave me hope that we might be able to hold out, to fight back against the monsters.

"But I'm afraid of what they might do," Mrs. Parsall whispered.

"Of who? The New Jersey witches?"

She let out a laugh, though tears still streamed down her

face. "The military. If they can't stop this anyway else . . . they'll do what they have to do to keep the last third of the population safe."

My brow wrinkled. "What does that mean?"

Mrs. Parsall stared up at the sky. "Nukes. Missiles. Chemical weapons. Whatever they have left in sealed-off bunkers. They will sacrifice the few to save the many."

"What does that mean?"

She smiled darkly at me. "The United States and Russia have enough nuclear weapons to destroy the earth five times over. If they can't find a cure, they will decimate all the contaminated land to allow the human race to survive."

A shudder traced down my spine as I remembered the planes flying overhead days ago spreading that metallic-tasting dust. "But . . . they know that people on . . . on holy ground are safe! And will the nuclear weapons not poison those who remain?"

She sighed. "They will run their figures and calculate the acceptable losses. Like Spock said in *Star Trek:* 'The needs of the many outweigh the needs of the few.'"

I began to protest. Mrs. Parsall seemed to have as much faith in the military as my people had for the Ordnung. And that was just as dangerous. Moreover, I didn't know who Spock was, but he had no moral authority over—

Something rustled beside the car. My head snapped up, and my grip on the bread knife tightened and quaked like a car antenna in the wind.

I saw nothing but heard scratching near the left fender. The

hair stood up on my neck. The sound echoed in the undercarriage of the car.

Mrs. Parsall and I both scrambled back on the dew-slick
hood.

"Oh God," she cried.

The sound seethed and scraped below us. A whimper escaped my teeth. I knew with all my heart that the vampires had
found us. That we were finished.

I held the knife in front of me as the noise slithered under
the engine. Mrs. Parsall wound her fingers in the sleeve of my
nightdress, pushing me behind her with the protective instincts
of a mother. I resisted, squirming forward. We may be finished,
but I would not go without a fight.

A pale, writhing form crept out from beneath the car, and
I clapped my hand over my mouth to stifle a shriek.

It was just an opossum. A mother opossum with babies
clinging to her, their tails woozily moving like the tentacles of
some undersea beast.

She glanced back at us with a weary eye and shambled
away into the darkness.

I began to murmur the Lord's Prayer in thanks.

"Shit," Mrs. Parsall said.

Chapter Twelve

I did not speak to my family of what I'd learned last night from Mrs. Parsall.

Neither did she.

I carried my silence with me, that heavy curtain of secrets, throughout my minimal chores of the morning. Mrs. Parsall stayed behind when we went to church, and I was forced to carry that silence alone, as my fingers knitted in my apron while I sat on a wooden pew at the Miller house. My mother sat on my left, Sarah on my right. My father sat across the aisle with the men.

It was church Sunday. Plain folk did no more chores than absolutely necessary, beyond caring for their animals, and spent the day in prayer, fellowship, and sharing food. Church services were held on a rotating basis at each house in the community. A wagon would arrive early that morning or the night before with pews and tables, and the women would descend upon the house to begin cooking.

A heartbreakingly clear blue sky stretched overhead. The benches were arranged in the Millers' yard in rows, and I watched the people settle like birds onto telephone wires, men on one side, women on the other. Two rows ahead of me, I saw Hannah Bachman's dark hair tucked under her bonnet. She was smiling and looking at Sam Vergler across the aisle. He was blushing under his freckles. I exchanged glances with Elijah from across the yard, looked away. Hannah and Sam had not changed, but something had shifted between Elijah and me.

My gaze landed on Ruth Hersberger, the girl that Joseph had adored. She sat close to the front, holding her sisters' hands, rising to kiss Herr Miller's cheek. Her eyes were red and swollen. It seemed that she missed Joseph more than I had thought.

I looked away bitterly. Perhaps a girl like Ruth would be better for Elijah as he stepped into the void left by his brothers.

I sucked in my breath to stifle a sob, then spied the Hexenmeister ambling to the back bench. He seemed to have been busy; even his church suit was spattered with a bit of paint.

I looked forward to the Bishop as he began prayers.

My fingers flipped the pages of the *Ausbund,* and my voice lifted in song automatically with the others. But my heart beat like a bird against the cage of my ribs as I snuck glances to the front, to Elijah. He sat with his head bowed in prayer and his crutches leaning against his shoulder, never once glancing back at me.

As the women and children sang, the men left the pews to decide who would give the sermons. My voice sounded dead to my own ears, and I was relieved when the men returned and the Bishop walked before the congregation to give a sermon.

The topic of the day was *Gelassenheit.* I cast my eyes downward at my clasped hands in what I hoped passed for meditative focus.

The Bishop's voice rolled over us like thunder:

"The world Outside is full of doubt, of violence and turmoil. It is natural to experience fear. And the answer to fear is not questioning. The answer to fear is faith—faith in the will of God."

I could feel the weight of the Bishop's scrutiny on me. I whispered *"Amen,"* and felt his gaze move away.

"*Gelassenheit* is not something to be accepted when life moves smoothly. We need to recognize the will of God when times are troubled. As they are now.

"We have experienced a great deal of loss in our community recently. The loss of Rebecca and Ava Yoder, Mary Fisher, Seth and Joseph Miller . . ."

I squeezed my eyes shut. The Bishop was admitting that they were as good as dead. A hysterical sob was muffled. I looked up to see Ruth crying into her apron with her sisters' heads bent over her.

Sarah stared up at me with round eyes and whispered: "Are Seth and Joseph really gone?"

"I'm afraid so, Sarah."

"Are they in heaven with their mother?"

I swallowed hard. I looked at her innocent eyes, thought of how devastated she would be by the idea that the boys who had been with her all her life were lost. I also thought of all the places that Mrs. Parsall had said that God had saved: the Vatican, the mountain in Japan, even the pagan temple in New Jersey. I could not believe that God would be unkind enough to leave Seth and Joseph behind.

I leaned in to kiss Sarah's forehead. "Yes, *liewe*. They're with their mother. She's taking care of them now."

When I looked up, I found the Bishop staring hard at me. I was certain that he could not have heard our whispered conversation over Ruth's weeping. But he sensed my rebellion, even from across the yard. I lifted my chin defiantly. I would not tell a little girl that the young men who had been brothers to her were gone for eternity. There was enough time for her to find out on her own.

"But, even in the face of these losses, God has given us a gift," the Bishop continued. "He has given us a great reward for observing *Gelassenheit*. He has given us safety."

A low murmur rustled through the congregation like dry leaves.

"Yes, God has blessed us and has provided for us. The world Outside has been devastated."

The murmur crackled. There had been rumors, and all were aware of the Elders' edict that no one was to venture beyond the gate.

"But he has saved us, saved us to reward us for our obedience. And as long as we remain obedient, we shall be safe."

My fingers chewed the hem of my apron. I knew that this wasn't true. We were not his chosen people. We were safe, to be certain, but so were others. The image of the pagan army in New Jersey kept popping into my mind. I imagined that they were much like us, dressed in black, fighting against the monstrosities at their own Laundromat.

I was brought back to myself when the Bishop gave up the floor to the next sermon—a lay sermon from Herr Miller.

My heart ached for him. Herr Miller had never been a public speaker. He stood at the front, his hands clasped before him.

"I want to speak today of fellowship, of the warmth and gifts that Elijah and I have received from the congregation during this difficult time. Since we've lost . . ." His voice broke, and he tried again. "Since we've lost . . ." Again he faltered, and he covered his eyes with his hand. His beard trembled.

Elijah leaped up to embrace his father. His father broke down in his son's arms, and the congregation lowered their heads in tears and prayer.

The Bishop intervened. "We shall take a short respite before the communion service. The men and women who will be baptized today are asked to leave, to take consideration of their faith. Only those who will take baptism shall return."

Sarah leaned into my side, and my mother and I wrapped our arms around her. I could not imagine what it was like to be in Mrs. Parsall's shoes, with no family. I bit my lip and stared at the ground.

My mother prompted me to stand and go with the others: "Katie."

Sarah looked up at me. "Are you to be baptized today, Katie?"

I shook my head and hooked my hands in the bench beneath my knees, as if I could root myself here. "No."

I could see the fear and disappointment in my mother's eyes.

A shadow passed by. I looked up, saw Elijah. He was in the group of young men and women who were leaving. I saw Ruth stand up, hesitate, and then sit down again. Hannah and Sam walked past, smiling at each other. This was surely a prelude to marriage for them. My eyes locked on Elijah's. I silently challenged him to sit, and he challenged me to stand. I did not break that hold until he passed into the threshold of the house.

The Bishop directed us to sing from the *Ausbund*. I kept one eye on the door. Only those who decided to go through with baptism at this time would return to the service. There was no penalty for reconsidering, and I hoped fervently that Elijah would take this chance to slow down, to wait for spring. There were always one or two who decided to wait.

One young man came back to sit on the front benches, then another. Two girls came next, sisters holding hands. Then Sam and Hannah, walking together . . .

I counted as each of them passed, in spurts and lulls as we sang. No Elijah. All the young men and women filtered back into the congregation, but Elijah had not returned by the time our hymn ended.

I looked up to the sky, smiled in gratitude at God. We would have time.

A shadow passed over me. I squinted up to see Elijah limping down the long aisle on his crutches, and my face fell.

I felt numb as he went to join the other young men and women who were kneeling at the front. Numb as the Bishop reminded them that they were making a promise before God and the witnesses of the congregation.

I wanted to close my eyes, not to witness this. But I had no choice.

The Bishop asked them the first of four baptism questions: "Do you believe that Jesus Christ is the son of God?"

Elijah responded in the affirmative. I could see his lips moving but could not hear him.

"Do you accept Jesus Christ as your Lord and Savior who died on the cross for you?"

He responded with the others, in unison.

"Do you renounce the world Outside, the devil with all his insidious temptations, as well as your own flesh and blood to serve Jesus Christ, whether it costs you your life or your death?"

I saw his lips say: *Yes.*

"Do you promise to walk in Christ's word and be faithful to the Amish Church for the rest of your life, never to depart?"

Yes.

The prayer bonnets were removed from the girls, and the Deacon followed the Bishop with a bucket of water and a tin cup. The Deacon poured water into the Bishop's hands and the young men's and women's heads, three times each.

When they came to Elijah, I wanted to stand up, shout at him, but I remained rooted in place, my voice jammed in my throat.

Water splashed on him three times: "In the name of the Father, the Son, and the Holy Spirit, we extend to you the hand of fellowship."

The Bishop lifted the men and women to their feet, one by one. "Arise as a faithful member of the church."

Elijah's face was glowing like the sun overhead.

I felt something in my chest break.

I had witnessed Elijah's baptism. It was real now, real as the vampires I'd seen yesterday. I tried to smile and make benign chatter with the rest of the congregation after the service, but I wanted nothing more than to flee. Elijah was surrounded by well-wishers, and I managed to avoid him and any questions about my own baptism by busying myself in the kitchen. Once the last plate was served, I made to slip away from the throng.

But one person saw me as I walked around the corner of the house, toward the open field and a good cry. The old Hexenmeister called out: "Katie!"

I paused. I could pretend not to have heard. But duty made me turn around with an artificial smile on my face. I anticipated that he, like much of the rest of the congregation, would want to say how proud they were of Elijah and the other young men and women.

"Yes, Herr Stoltz?"

He walked up to me slowly, as if his arthritis was bothering him. Crumbs of cobbler from the afternoon meal clung in his beard, and I could see that one eye was watering. He reached into his jacket. "I have something for you."

My brows drew together in curiosity. "For me?"

He handed me an envelope. "For you."

I stared at it. It was made of heavy linen paper, sealed tightly with wax.

Without another word, Herr Stoltz hobbled off back to

the house, humming to himself and veering toward the dessert tables.

"Thank you!" I called after him.

He did not seem to hear me.

I had no idea what it could be. I began to walk across the blond grass fields toward home, digging my fingers into the top of the thick paper. I opened the envelope, pulled out a heavy sheet of the same lumpy handmade paper.

I stopped in my tracks as my eyes scanned the page.

"Oh," I whispered.

In carefully inked letters the color of gooseberries, the Hexenmeister had written in Hochdeutsch — High German. It wasn't the everyday Deitsch that we spoke to one other. This was the language of prayers, the voice to heaven:

> Keep thine own faith. Wear love around thee like a shield, and no harm shall come to thee, even when thou walk in the valley of darkness. God bless and protect thee, and keep the road before thee straight and open.
>
> In Jesus' name, Amen.

His handwriting was a bit shaky but was still the most beautiful I'd ever seen. I clutched the letter to my chest and blinked tears up at the sky.

I knew what this was. It was called a *Himmelsbrief.* When I was a child, I had heard the old legends about the peasant of Cologne. The story was about a poor, illiterate boy who had prayed to God for help. The sky opened up, and a letter fell into his hands. From that moment forward, he became blessed.

He was starving, and a woman fed him. A man rushed out of a shop in the marketplace and took him to be a jeweler's apprentice. He grew wealthy and successful, eventually learning to read. The text of the peasant boy's letter was different than mine, but the idea of the *Himmelsbrief* was the same: it was a blessing from God, and it was to be carried with one always.

Hexenmeisters had the ability to craft such letters, working their prayers into the words — much like the magic of the hex signs they created. I had never known anyone else who had possessed one, had never seen or touched one.

And the Hexenmeister had given one to me.

I stared back at the house. How much did he suspect about my disobedience? How much did he know, through his strange connection with God?

I carefully folded the letter back along its original creases and placed it in my apron pocket. Perhaps the old man, having heard of the devastation on the Outside, had begun making them for the community. Maybe it wasn't just me he'd singled out to receive one.

Maybe.

————

Since no one would miss me from the afternoon's socialization at the Miller house, I decided to check up on my patient in the kennel. I went to the house to gather some things to take with me. Mrs. Parsall, exhausted from last night, was snoring in my room. I smiled and prepared her a sandwich and fruit on a plate in the kitchen for when she awoke. I could understand her reluctance to attend our church services, but if she was to remain here for any length of time, I thought it might be good for her to get out a bit and mingle with the others, so they would not fear her or feel awkward around her. But not today.

Carrying my supplies in a wicker laundry basket, I walked through the back field to the old barn. Copper met me halfway; I could barely distinguish his coat from the golden grass. I noticed that there were white chicken feathers stuck to his tongue.

"I see that you've been busy." I gave him a disapproving look that was lost on him. There was no use in telling a dog not to chase chickens. It was simply in their nature. Not evil. It just was.

Copper wagged his tail and sniffed my laundry basket vigorously.

"Yes, there's food in there. In good time."

Copper fell into step beside me, his tail slapping at my skirt as we walked.

The dilapidated barn looked undisturbed, and I set my burden down to haul open the doors. The dogs had their own dog door cut into the side, covered with canvas flaps. Sunny squeezed herself through the door, panting from the effort.

"Hello, sweet girl." I put my arms around her, and she licked my face. It felt good to bask in the unconditional warm slobber of the dogs, who would love me no matter whether I was baptized or not.

I rose and carried the basket into the dimness of the barn.

"It's Katie," I announced.

A voice echoed from the shadows in the back stall. "I'm glad it's you."

I was heartened to hear that Alex was conscious. I could tell that he'd been moving around in the barn; the straw was disturbed and the waste bucket I'd discreetly left for him had been emptied. He was sitting up in his stall with his hands folded in his lap, watching me with his blue eyes.

"I brought food."

A corner of his mouth quirked up. "Well, I'm glad for that. And for someone to talk to. The dogs aren't good conversationalists."

I reached forward to examine the wound on his head. He winced when I touched it, but it seemed as if the redness was beginning to recede.

"Did you take your antibiotic this morning?"

"Yes. And a fistful of ibuprofen. And I used part of the hydrogen peroxide."

I wrinkled my nose. I could smell a bit of the peroxide on him, but I mostly smelled the sour odor of someone who hadn't bathed in a few days.

"I brought you some things," I said. "Including soap."

Alex sighed happily. "I would really love a bath, Bonnet."

I frowned at him calling me "Bonnet" but decided to let it slide. He didn't say it with sarcasm; it was said with the affection of a nickname. "There isn't a spring room in the barn," I said. "But there is a pump out back. I'll bring you a washbasin before I leave this afternoon."

I set about unpacking the contents of the laundry basket: sandwiches, apples, a thermos full of cider, a fresh block of soap, a battery-powered flashlight, a toothbrush, baking soda, and a straight razor.

Alex picked up the straight razor. "Ouch. I've only seen these in the movies."

"Don't cut yourself. There are no more antibiotics."

I also handed him a set of men's clothes. "These are for you. They will make you less obvious if you are seen."

He grimaced. "Yeah. I know that I reek." He took the bundle and shook out a shirt, britches, socks, undergarments, and Plain shoes.

"I hope that they will fit. The shoes may be a bit tight on you, but they'll do until I can find something better."

He held the shirt up to his chest and lifted a chiding eyebrow. "Where did the clothes come from? Your husband? Your brother?"

My mouth flattened, and I said quietly: "I'm doing laundry for a family that lost two young men to Outside. I expect that the dead are less likely to miss them."

"Oh." His hands lowered the shirt to his lap. "Sorry."

I shook my head, ashamed for taking out my bad temper on another. "I'm sorry. I'm just . . . I've had a bad morning."

His eyes widened. "You didn't go back to town, did you?"

"No. I went to church."

"Ah, well. That explains it," he blurted. "I mean . . . well . . . Two hours of sermons is enough to dim anyone's sparkle."

I frowned, changed the subject. "I have news from Outside."

He stopped chewing, dropping crumbs onto his stubble. "Yeah?"

"*Ja.* I took some cell phone batteries with me yesterday."

He smirked. "Took or stole?"

I was silent for a moment. "I left money. Do you want me

to tell you?" I wasn't sure if he wanted information or to sim-ply continue goading me.

"Yes. I want to know." He lifted his hands in surrender, but his eyes burned hungrily for the news. "Tell me."

"The Englishwoman staying with us has a husband in the military. She spoke to him. The . . . the contagion has spread."

"How far?"

"Far enough that he estimates that two-thirds of the people everywhere are just . . . gone."

Alex set down his sandwich.

I continued, the words falling over each other. "There are people who have survived . . . he said in places like Vatican City. Stonehenge. Religious sites." I shook my head. "I don't believe it. Not all of it, anyway."

He looked up. "I was right. They offer some protection against the vampires."

"God cannot be with everyone. Not everyone is right."

"Maybe, in your view. But it seems like whoever's left standing will demonstrate his approval the most." His mouth turned down. "Short of hiding in monasteries, are they any closer to finding a way to stop them?"

"It doesn't sound like it. They are working on it. But . . . Mrs. Parsall says that they may be forced to use nuclear weap-ons to stop the spread."

His jaw dropped. "They can't. They can't do that. If they nuke us back into the Stone Age, to nuclear winter, no one will survive."

I cocked my head. I knew that nuclear weapons were poi-son, but I hadn't heard that term. "Nuclear winter?"

Alex leaned his head back against the wall. "The nukes would devastate our climate, plunge us into a winter like no one's ever seen. The dust would blot out the sun. All of us would freeze or starve to death. Never mind the rest of the mammals on the planet."

"Would that be a worse way to go than the vampires?" I couldn't imagine a worse way than having my head torn off by the creature from the Laundromat.

His mouth opened, closed, like a fish's over a hook. "I don't know. They have to find another way."

"It is out of our hands," I said, turning my attention back to the basket. I handed him a clean blanket.

"Is that what they call *Gelassenheit,* Bonnet?"

My blood curdled in anger. "What do you know about it?" I forced myself to say blandly. To turn the other cheek.

"That your people tend to surrender yourselves to God's will. I always thought it was kind of passive, but . . ."

I turned to face him with eyes narrowed. As conflicted as I felt about my own religion, I would not brook sarcasm from an Outsider who knew nothing about it except what he'd read in college textbooks. Plain folk were charged with being mild-mannered, but something within me snapped: "Let me tell you about how *Gelassenheit* saved your life. When I found you on the other side of our fence, I was forbidden to take you in by the Elders. They said that no one goes in or out of the gate. I asked them — begged them to reconsider. A man stood over you with a rifle, was going to put you down like a dog."

My voice lifted, and I could see him shrinking back, the armor of cynicism falling from him. "I begged them to leave you there, that it was up to God whether you lived or died. And they took their gun and walked away. I violated their rules to bring you back here, because I thought that was the right thing to do. If they were to find out, you would be exiled. Thrown out of the gate and fed to the monsters."

I put my face very close to his, so close that my bonnet strings brushed his shoulder, and hissed: "Don't dare to tell me about *Gelassenheit*."

His gaze fell from my furious one. "Look, I'm sorry. I'm a jerk." When he glanced up, the expression in his ice-blue eyes had thawed a bit, seeming as hurt as it had when he'd talked about Cassia and the end of the world. He swallowed hard. "I owe you. Thank you. I mean it."

I gave him a curt nod, crawled away, back to the basket. My cheeks flamed, and I was ashamed of my outburst. "You're welcome."

The anger drained out of me as I dug in the basket. I set a jar of apple butter on the floor and a wrapped-up loaf of bread. Though I seemed to be doing well at pilfering and provisioning for Alex, I had no idea what to do with him next.

I cleared my throat, and my voice was more gentle. "I thought you would be bored, so I brought you some things to read."

I gave him copies of the Bible and the *Ausbund*. Chastened, he took the books gratefully. "Thank you."

"And I also brought you some less boring reading." Hesitantly, I handed him a stack of well-worn *Wonder Woman* comics. "Just don't spill anything on them."

A brilliant smile spread across his face. "Diana, princess of the Amazons! I love her." He began to page through them. "'Beautiful as Aphrodite, strong as Hercules, wise as Athena, and swift as Mercury . . .'"

I hesitated and returned the smile. Maybe we had just found a small patch of common ground.

Chapter Thirteen

I managed to avoid Elijah until the Singing.

By then, there was nowhere to hide.

Sunday evenings were when the young unmarried members of our community got together to socialize in a pre-approved fashion. After *Nachtesse,* we all walked to the one-room schoolhouse with our copies of the *Ausbund* tucked under our arms, giggling in the gloaming. The Singing took place without adult supervision. It was our chance to be free each week. There was always something magical about it: the music, the shy glances passed between boys and girls, holding hands in the darkness.

But it wasn't magical tonight. I told my mother that I didn't want to go and busied myself with washing dishes. She took the dishes from me and dried my hands with the dishtowel.

"Go. It will be good for you to get your mind off things."

"But, Mother . . ." I protested.

"It's Sunday. No chores." She lifted her finger and smiled. "Go."

I sighed, then trudged up to my room to stare sullenly at the dresses in the closet. Mrs. Parsall watched me from the bed, peering over her glasses. My mother was teaching her how to crochet, to keep her occupied. She was not doing a half-bad job on the afghan she'd started with marled ombre yarn. The rows were quite even, though she did count the stitches under her breath.

She laid down her hook when she saw me. "Are you going somewhere?"

"Yes. To the Singing." I rolled my eyes.

"Are you sure that you want to go out?" she asked neutrally. But I could see the anxiety in her eyes. She knew what lay in the darkness as much as I did.

I sighed and stared into the closet. "My mother insists."

"I would like to go to the Singing." Sarah peeped into the room and stuck her tongue out at me.

"You're too young," Mrs. Parsall and I said automatically, at the same time. That made us both laugh.

Sarah bounded in and wedged herself into my closet. She liked helping me get ready for the Singing, imagining what it would be like when a boy like Elijah would come to the house to walk with her into the night. When I was her age, I stood on the back step and watched the older boys and girls disappear too. It was hard to tell her not to envy that.

I pulled out a plain brown dress and began to take off my apron. I wasn't much in the mood for this and wanted to fade into the background.

"No! Wear this one." Sarah pulled my newest dress from the closet, a twilight-blue one that I'd made two months ago.

I made a face. "I'd rather wear the brown one."

"But the blue one is prettier."

"I don't feel pretty today." I unpinned my dress, careful to put the pins in a pin box with a magnet on my dresser.

"I don't know how you manage those pins," Mrs. Parsall said, plucking at her own uneven neckline.

Plain women didn't use complicated fasteners on our clothing, like zippers or buttons. I could see that Mrs. Parsall was still trying to get the hang of the pins. A loose one glinted at her collar, and I could see a scrape on her neck from where she'd stabbed herself.

I stepped out of my dress and reached for the brown. I turned my back to them, then slipped the *Himmelsbrief* into my pocket. I don't think they saw, as their attention was fixed on the closet.

"Wear the blue!" my sister insisted.

"Sarah, your sister is old enough to make her own decisions." Doubtless Mrs. Parsall was thinking the same thing I was: the blue would make me more of a target at night. The brown would blend right in. "But maybe she will let you braid her hair."

"I think that's a fine compromise," I said, fastening the brown dress shut.

Sarah grinned and drew me down onto the bed. She tugged off my cap and began loosening the pins that held it in place. I stared down at the floor, resigned, as my hair tumbled over my shoulders. It hung now almost to my waist. It wasn't thick and lustrous like some of the other girls, but fine and straight, easy to braid and pin up. Flyaways occasionally escaped, despite my best efforts, but it was easier to deal with than recalcitrant waves. My friend Hannah complained about hers requiring a headful of pins to look tidy. My hair, on the other hand, was like a good Plain girl: obedient.

Sarah brushed my hair, filling it with static. She hummed a hymn from the *Ausbund*, a song that we had sung that morning. I shut my eyes against it.

"Will Elijah be coming by to take you to the Singing?" Sarah asked, beginning the plaits tight against my scalp.

"I don't think so. He's had a very busy day," I said. "I doubt that he will come, now that he is baptized and a full-grown man."

Mrs. Parsall watched the twitch at the corner of my mouth. "He went through with it, then?"

"Yes." I was mercifully able to lower my head and blink back tears as the braid became long and Sarah needed more room to work.

"It will be all right," I heard her say. But it seemed strange to hear her soothing me, for something as silly and ephemeral as romance, in light of the losses she faced.

"I'm sure it will." I bit my lip as Sarah finished the plait, pinning it around the circumference of my head.

"There you are." Sarah sat back, glowing.

"You look beautiful," Mrs. Parsall said.

I reached up and touched the braid. The back was a little uneven, but it felt tight as a halo. I had no mirror to inspect myself. My father had one for shaving, but to use one to admire oneself was shamelessly prideful. Even without the mirror, I could tell that Sarah had done a very good job with her little hands.

"Thank you," I told my sister, twisting to kiss her cheek.

She smiled and bounced off the bed. "I'll wait up for you."

I winked at her. She always said that, but she always fell asleep. "I know you will."

Sarah padded out of the room in her bare feet to find my mother. Sunday nights were their special time together. Mother was teaching her how to set sleeves in a dress, and I was certain that the treadle sewing machine would be thumping along in moments.

I stared out at the sun, drawing low on the horizon, stretching the shadows of trees across the fields. "I suppose that I should go, while there's still light."

Mrs. Parsall crooked her finger. "Come here."

I came to sit beside her, next to the nest of yarn she was working with. Mrs. Parsall dragged her purse out from under the bed, and I thought she meant to use her cell phone again. Instead of the phone, she pulled out a compact with a hand mirror and a shiny tube of lipstick.

She turned the point of my chin toward her and dabbed at my face with the scented powder. I began to protest. "Mrs. Parsall . . ."

"Hush. I'm using a light hand. And I'm going to insist that you call me 'Ginger' from now on."

I was never comfortable calling an adult by her first name before all this had happened, but the old rules seemed to be slipping away. "Okay . . . Ginger."

The powder puff whisked across my face. "Stupid boy," she muttered as she worked. "He doesn't know his ass from a turnip."

I grinned in spite of myself.

Mrs. Parsall—*Ginger,* I reminded myself—opened the lipstick, screwed up a pale pink color. "Like this," she said, sticking her lips out in a pout. I mimicked her, and she swept the lipstick over my mouth.

"Close your eyes." I felt the touch of the lipstick on my eyelids and my cheeks, then Ginger's soft fingertips rubbing the pigment into my face.

"Stunning." She handed me the compact to inspect myself. I had never been called stunning before in my life.

As I gazed into the mirror, my lips parted in a small *O* of startlement. And it was not just because Plain people never complimented each other on appearance. I had not thought much of makeup before. Though Ginger told me that the women in magazines were covered in inches of the stuff, I honestly believed that they looked like that naturally. But she had worked magic, changed me from a bland Plain girl to . . . a pretty girl. The powder covered my freckles and the hint of sunburn, dimmed the shine of my oily skin. The soft pink was a sheer flush on my cheeks, contrasting with the gray of my eyes. And my mouth was all of a sudden dewy and luscious, as if I'd eaten fresh strawberries.

"Show Elijah *that,*" Ginger chortled. "You'll have him wrapped around your little finger."

She tucked the makeup into my pocket. I protested.

"It's yours," she said simply. "I have no need of it."

"Thank you," I said, almost afraid to touch my now-perfect face. I couldn't resist plucking the compact out of my pocket for another look. I felt powerful, in some strange fashion.

"Be careful," she said, severely.

I nodded. "I will."

Ginger went back to her crocheting as I put my bonnet on, mindful not to disturb the braid. As I grabbed my *Ausbund* and left, I heard her counting: ". . . seventeen, eighteen . . . oh, crap." She went back to the beginning to count the stitches in the row. "One, two, three . . ."

———

I stepped outside, feeling the warmth of the setting sun on my made-up face. The wind rustled through the grass as I walked down the dirt lane from our house to the field. I made sure to keep to the brightest areas, where the sun drove my shadow long behind me.

In the distance, I made out other dark spots on the horizon. A group of girls hung together like a gaggle of geese, with a handful of young men racing to catch up to them. A courting buggy bumped down a dirt road between the fields, carrying a couple to the white schoolhouse perched in the middle of a meadow. The site for the schoolhouse had been chosen because it was pretty much the geographic center of the community. No child had to walk or ride farther to the school than any other.

Young people were streaming into the building. I had gone to school there until I finished eighth grade, when education for Plain children stopped. The only requirements to be a teacher was that one be good with children and have completed the eighth grade herself. I had considered becoming a teacher, but I strongly suspected that the Elders deemed me too rebellious to teach children. I had asked on more than one occasion, and the answer was always that I should stay close to my parents and redouble my study of the *Ausbund*.

Inside the schoolhouse was a large room, big enough to accommodate all the students in the community. The teacher would give assignments to different grades and provide attention to each group in turns. For school, wooden desks would be assembled on the floor in neat rows, facing the blackboard.

But for the Singing, the desks were shoved to the back of the room and long wooden benches placed against the east and west walls in rows. The boys sat on one side of the classroom and the girls on the other, facing them. The room was already beginning to get crowded, as jockeying began for the front benches, where one could see and be seen the best by the opposite sex.

Ginger's makeup had an effect, I noticed. One boy tripped over a bench looking at me. I looked away and covered my smile with my hand.

I took a seat in the back of the girls' section next to Hannah's younger sister, Leah, halfheartedly placing my *Ausbund* on my lap. I smiled at Leah.

"You look really pretty," she said. "Are you doing something different with your hair?"

"Yes," I said. "Thank you."

I glanced at the sparkle on her earlobes. She was wearing earrings. They didn't look to be pierced, which would be a major rebellion. But this was the place for small ones, like the little rhinestone daisies that shivered when her head turned.

"I like your earrings," I told her.

Leah lifted her hand self-consciously to her ears and blushed. "Thanks." She returned my smile before flicking a flirtatious glance at a boy leaning on the wall near the window.

My gaze roved over the throng as they began to take their seats. I knew everyone here in some fashion or another. There was no thrill of meeting anyone new at the Singing, unless someone's distant relative had come to visit. The thrill, instead, was making eyes at your neighbor without adult supervision.

Hannah rushed inside in a flurry of skirts. Her face was flushed, and I saw that her hair had begun to creep free of its pins. She sat down beside me, her fingers pressed to the smile on her lips.

"I saw that you and Sam were baptized today . . ." I began.

"We're getting married," she blurted, grabbing my hands.

I was struck speechless. I knew that this would happen too, but not so soon. Plain engagements required no rings. Engagements were kept very private, until a month or two before the actual wedding, when they were announced to the larger community.

"Isn't it wonderful?" She glowed.

"I'm happy for you both," I said sincerely. I hugged her.

"You will be my attendant, *ja?*" she asked, eyes shining. Plain weddings usually had only one or two, dressed like the bride in a new blue or violet dress made for the occasion.

I could not say no. Hannah was my dear friend. "Of course."

I listened as she talked of being married before winter and building a house on her parent's property in spring, after the ground thawed. I nodded as she clutched my hands and chattered excitedly.

It felt as if she was living a life I was meant to live and had rejected. The world was moving on, without me.

My breath snagged in my throat when I saw a familiar lanky frame leaning on crutches. Elijah. His crutches thumped awkwardly on the scarred wooden floor. He wobbled a bit at the threshold.

Our eyes locked. He stared at me, startled, taking in my transformed appearance. I felt a sting of satisfaction at that. A grin spread across his face. I remembered that look. He seemed like the old Elijah then. Maybe things hadn't changed that much.

I made to rise to greet him.

But then I saw that he wasn't alone. Ruth was beside him, clucking over him and taking his crutches as he settled down on a bench in the first row.

Perhaps her solicitude was because she missed Joseph.

But if she missed Joseph as much as her tears had shown at church this morning, she had no business being at the Singing, a small voice in my head growled.

I sat back down, nodding stiffly at Elijah.

He nodded back, but his eyes didn't move from my face.

The rustle of paper sounded in the schoolhouse like the flapping of bird wings. The youths brought their prayer books to their laps and turned to the page that one of the girls was marking on the blackboard. I primly flipped to the correct page and began to sing when the others started.

We sang without any musical accompaniment, without harmonizing. Our music does not sound like Outside music. We're told that it has something of a singsong quality to Outside ears, that the Hochdeutsch is impossible to understand. But it is beautiful to experience. Everyone singing the same song at the same time — you can feel the vibration in your throat and in the air. It's like being part of something much larger, part of a perfectly tuned whole. The song buzzes through your lungs, through you and the person next to you. It is the closest I've ever felt to God speaking to me or moving within me.

I was facing west, with the sun in my eyes. As it sank lower and lower on the horizon, the light grew more orange and luminous. I could see Elijah, his shadow driven before him, deep in the glare. As the peacefulness of the music settled into me, I wanted to believe that there was still some hope for us.

Ruth sat two rows ahead of me, twirling a tendril of blond hair around her finger. As she sang, I saw her lift her eyes to Elijah.

Perhaps she was too accustomed to male attention.

Perhaps he was encouraging her.

Perhaps she saw in Elijah what she missed in Joseph.

Whatever the reason, I wanted to see no more of it.

I slammed my *Ausbund* shut. Hannah turned to me, alarmed. But before she could ask me what was wrong, I stood up and strode briskly down the aisle and out through the open door, into the waning orange light. I could barely breathe as I fled down the steps, like something was stuck in my throat. I couldn't tell what flavor it was; it tasted salty like tears, but it was sharp as broken glass.

"Katie!" a familiar voice called from the door.

I plunged into the tassels of golden grass as tall as my thigh, stirred by a wind that was picking up from the west.

"Katie, *wait*."

I stopped, half turned, clutching the *Ausbund* to my chest. My skirt flapped around me like a boneless garment on a clothesline, and my bonnet strings streamed before me. I watched Elijah try to stump down the steps with his crutches. Ruth was not with him. I rubbed my nose with the back of my hand as he approached.

"What is it you want from me?" he asked when he reached me. My shadow fell on him, and I could see bewilderment in his eyes.

"Apparently you're getting what you want from Ruth," I said icily.

That stung him more than any slap. He actually flinched, looked me full in the face. "You've made it very clear that you won't."

"I never said that."

"What do you want? You want me to get down on my knees and beg? I'll do that, if it meant you'd say yes to me." He loosened his grip on his crutches, moved to kneel on the grass.

I dropped my *Ausbund*, grabbed his shoulders to keep him from prostrating himself like that before me. "No . . . don't . . ."

"Then, what is it?" There was hope and resentment and hurt in his eyes. "I've always loved you. I know that you love me. I don't understand what else you need. What else are you looking for?"

"Time. Time is what I want."

"We don't *have* any more time!" He shouted at me over the wind that ripped through the grass, lashing against our legs with a sound like rain on a metal roof.

I cupped his face in my hands, kissed him as we'd kissed so many times before. I hoped to convince ourselves that I was still me, that he was still who he'd always been. But Elijah's lips were immobile under mine. I stepped back, seeing the smear of my lipstick on his mouth.

The light dimmed out of his eyes, like water draining from my hands. He touched my cheek with cold fingers.

"Makeup."

"What?" I said incredulously. Whatever spell Ginger had woven didn't seem to work on him.

"It's a sign of vanity." His voice was flat. "You should wash your face."

I turned and fled from him. I ran as hard as I could, my fists pumping the air, wanting that burn to drive out the wet knot of grief in my lungs. I knew that he wouldn't follow me. Even if he wasn't hobbled on crutches, he would not pursue me. Not this time.

I'd lost him. I'd lost him forever.

Elijah had been a constant in my life, like the North Star. I couldn't comprehend the sense of aloneness, that part of my sky gone dark. The world—not just the world Outside, but *my* world—was falling apart.

Chapter Fourteen

I ran until I couldn't run anymore, until my hands fell to my knees and I gasped for air. I had reached the shadow of the kennel barn. I'd automatically come here when I was younger and was upset by some petty conflict at school or when I fought with my sister. It was my sanctuary. But not anymore. I'd even given my sanctuary away to the Outsider. I truly had nothing left.

I wrenched open the barn door with a savage creak of metal on wood. I was angry, spoiling for a fight. I was ready to take it out on the only person nearby whom I could be terrible to with impunity. I did not announce myself to him, but the dogs knew my scent, came to me, licked my hands.

I listened to the structure creak and sigh as darkness fell and the wood cooled. The shade was cold on my damp face. There was no other sign of life, just me and the dogs.

Part of me, the selfish evil part of me that Elijah loathed, wished that the Outsider had died. I could dig a grave for him in a few hours, be done with my guilt. My sin of defying the Elders would be erased, as if nothing had ever happened.

I heard a rustle and assumed it was Alex stirring.

I squeezed my eyes shut and lowered my head. I concentrated all my power on steadying my voice. "Just me."

I did not go back to him immediately. I scrubbed my sleeve across my face, knelt beside Sunny to rub her sides. I could feel puppies moving within her. Any day now. Sniffling, I lit a lantern and hung it on a hook beside the door. I went to check their water. The levels were low, so I began to top them off with a bucket I kept in the barn. The dogs nosed past me and began to slurp, splashing water against my knee. I did what I knew how to do, tried to focus on work, hoping that would drive out the despondency and hurt and fear.

"Katie."

I glanced up, tears dripping down my nose.

Alex stood in the straw, watching me. I was startled to see him vertical, clean, and dressed like a Plain man, in dark britches, a white shirt that was a little short for his long arms, and suspenders. He was taller than I'd thought, though he stood with a slight slouch with his hands in his pockets. His face was clean-shaven, and his freshly washed hair was the color of straw. I did not know how long he'd stood there, watching me snivel.

I smeared the tears off my chin with my knuckles, turned back to fussing with the dog bowls. I didn't want the Englisher to see me cry.

"What's wrong?"

"Nothing." I clanged the food bowls together, filled them with scoops from an open dog food bag. "I'm fine."

"No. No, you're not."

I couldn't look at him. "I am fine." I began shaking out the dog blankets. They would be due for a washing soon . . .

He came up beside me and caught my elbow. "Hey. What happened?"

I bit my lip. I could feel the tears prickling hot behind my eyes, and I couldn't trust myself to speak again. My hands shook, and I let the blanket fall.

"Did somebody hurt you? Did the vampires——?"

His eyes were bright with such sympathy that I couldn't stand it. I shook my head, covered my face with my hands, and sobbed.

He put his arms around me while I cried against his chest. His shirt smelled like soap and sweet straw and dog. Familiar. He didn't say anything, just held me until my tears faded to hiccups. I grimaced when I saw that a smudge of pink makeup had smeared his white shirt.

His hands rested lightly on my shoulders. "What happened?"

I released a short, bitter bark of laughter. The end of the world had happened, and I was bawling over a boy. Maybe, but that boy had been a very large part of my very small world. "It wasn't vampires."

His brow creased. "What, then?"

I drew back, and his hands fell. "I don't think you'd understand."

He folded his empty arms across his chest. "Try me. I've got nothing but time."

I blew out my breath. "The man I . . ." I couldn't bring myself to say "love." "The man I'm expected to marry got baptized this morning."

"Okay." He looked at me blankly. "That's normal in your

culture, right? You come of age, and you get baptized in the church?"

"Well, yes."

"A lot of places don't do it that way, you know. They baptize babies."

"So I've heard. But here you have to choose to join the church of your own free will."

"And . . . he joined the church?"

"When you join the Amish church, you are required to follow their edicts. It is putting an end to *Rumspringa,* to all earthly desires." My vision blurred.

"It put an end to your relationship."

"*Ja.* At least, it must change form." I rubbed my eyes. "It's stupid, I know."

"What's stupid?"

"Being . . . being jealous of God."

He shook his head and laughed. "No, it's not stupid. Religion is a big deal for couples. You guys have to be on the same page."

I sighed. "We always . . . we always dreamed of *Rumspringa* together. Our parents dreamed of us married. Now *Rumspringa* is impossible. And . . ." My hands fell open and I took a quavering breath. "It seems he has found a more suitable girl. Ruth is . . ."

"A more suitable girl?" Alex laughed softly. "What does that mean? More pious, more obedient?"

I nodded, staring down at the floor. That was it, exactly.

"Look, I, uh . . . don't know the guy. But he sounds like a jackass."

My gaze flickered up, and I cracked a smile. No one had ever called Elijah anything like that. "He has his moments."

"I mean . . . c'mon. Is he that threatened by a woman who thinks for herself?"

I'd never been called a "woman." I expected to be a "woman" after *Rumspringa* and marriage. I still thought of myself as in that in-between liminal stage: too old to be a girl, but without the responsibilities of adulthood.

"If he's looking for a . . . a mouse, I'm sure that there are plenty of them about. But you're not a mouse. You're intelligent, brave as hell, and you're cute."

I blinked at him. "I'm not any of those things. I'm supposed to be obedient. Yielding."

Alex shrugged, as if it were a matter of objective fact. "Well, you are those things. I'm no expert in relationships, but . . ." A shadow flickered across his face, and I supposed that he was remembering Cassia. "As cheesy as it sounds, if it was meant to be, he'll come back."

I lifted an eyebrow. "You're invoking *Gelassenheit?*"

"Yeah, I guess I am." A lopsided smile crossed his face. It was then I noticed that it was speckled in tiny cuts: two on his jaw, one on his cheek.

"What happened to your face?" I asked.

His hand flitted to his chin, and his smile turned sheepish. "I, uh, kinda suck with that straight razor you gave me."

I smiled. "You'll learn."

He stuffed his hands in his pockets. "So . . . would you like some applesauce? I still have some left."

"*Ja.* I would like some applesauce."

I carefully took the lantern from its hook and followed Alex back to his nook in the barn. It looked as if he'd been restless there. His blanket was folded in a corner, food in another, comic books stacked in a third, and soap and clothes in the fourth. I felt a pang of sadness for him. These were the four corners of Alex's world. And *I* mourned for how small *mine* was becoming.

He sat down, unscrewed the cap on the jar of applesauce, and handed it to me with the spoon I'd left him.

"Thank you," I said. I dipped the spoon into the sauce and tasted the cinnamon apple mixture. It soothed me, stopped the hollow rumbling in my stomach. After a few bites, I handed it back to him. He tucked into the jar with the same spoon clinking against the glass.

He gestured to the stack of books. "Interesting reading material."

"Oh?"

"Yeah. I tried to read your *Ausbund,* but my German's really bad."

"You speak some of it?"

"I did take it in high school. Don't remember anything but bits and snatches. But I recognized the Lord's Prayer."

"Ja." I nodded. "That's the one I think we use most."

"Read Revelations in the Bible again. Depressing."

I put my back up against the wall, curled my arms around my knees. "Do you think that's what's happening? The Rapture?"

"If so, it would be a funny kind of Rapture, with all the holy folks kept on earth, don't you think?"

"I suppose. But it still feels like the end."

"Since neither one of us contemplates God having a per-
verse sense of humor like that, I'm gonna have to stick with
'don't know' as an answer. At least until the Four Horsemen
show up. Then I'll revise my opinion."

"Do you . . . do you believe in God?" I asked. Everyone I knew
did, even Outsiders like Ginger, but I couldn't tell if Alex did.

His eyes narrowed in thought. "I think I do, after a fashion.
I've just never had any personal experiences with a god. God
has never spoken to me like he apparently spoke to Joan of Arc.
I've never seen an angel or gotten a warm, fuzzy feeling in a
church."

"God has never spoken to me, either."

"No angels?"

"No."

"How about the fuzzy feeling in church?"

"Sometimes, when we're singing. It feels like there's some
kind of spirit there. It's hard to explain. You can feel it moving through you, buzzing around you. It's like . . . when the
locusts come up in summer, and you can feel the vibration in
the ground."

He seemed to chew on that for a while, handed the jar
back to me. "Most cultures do pick one or more deities, so the
prevalence of the idea suggests that it could be real."

"Hmm. It wouldn't be easy to follow the edicts of more
than one god. One is difficult enough." I couldn't believe I'd
said that aloud, but here, in the small circle of light in the falling darkness, I felt like I could be honest.

Alex plucked a comic book from the stack. "Wonder
Woman has a whole pantheon to please."

"Well, not *all* of them. Ares isn't usually too happy with her."

"Ares was like that. He was the god of war. That was his shtick. But Athena and Aphrodite and Hera have her back."

"It's all fiction anyway."

"Hera and Aphrodite were gods that people actually worshipped for centuries."

"I could never imagine that."

"Imagine having a pantheon of gods?"

"Well, that. That and being able to call upon a god and . . . and to have them help you." My voice sounded very small.

"Yep. A lot of older Western religions tend to buy into the idea that God is the clock-maker. He sets the clock of the world in motion and then steps away from it. He created the world and let it run."

I rested my chin on my hand, considering. "*Ja.* I think that's what we believe."

"A lot of old pagan religions and some of what I call the shake-your-pocketbook forms of Protestantism believe that God can be appeased or bribed to grant favors. There's a whole idea that God is really concerned with personal happiness and he'll make you happy and shower you with riches if you tithe enough."

"We don't take up collections, except on rare occasions. Baptisms, yes. Money goes to buy church benches and things like that. When there's a death or when someone's house burns down, yes. The money then goes to the family or for building materials."

"Yeah, but you Amish don't have a physical church with big television screens and sound systems and a pastor who feels that God wants him to have a Mercedes. You guys don't have to support all that."

"Hmm. I can't see how God would need money." Nor could I imagine what place a television would have in a church.

"Yeah. That's my issue with a lot of organized religions, anyway."

I lifted a dubious eyebrow to him. "But Ginger says that many different religions were saved."

He nodded. "Yeah. Sounds like it. But if the human race survives, I'd be tempted to see if there's any statistical analysis done on whether megachurches were safe from vampires. To see if God really is indiscriminate."

"Will you also include the pagan church in the strip mall?"

"Yep. I'd study that. See if yelling, 'Hera, help me!' actually worked against the vamps." He put his wrists together as if flashing magic bracelets against an assailant.

I smiled. "It worked for Wonder Woman."

"Yeah, well, Hera had a lot on her plate. I'm amazed that she had time to spend helping Diana out."

"Well, being queen of Mount Olympus must have had a good deal of responsibility."

"There's that, sure. But I think she was busiest keeping an eye on Zeus."

"Oh?" I'd never seen Zeus appear in the comic books.

Alex scraped the bottom of the empty applesauce jar to get the last of the cinnamon from the bottom. "Zeus was a ladies' man, always chasing women and siring illegitimate children. He'd even go so far as to take the form of a swan or bull to seduce women."

"Ew."

"Yeah. That's how he got Hera. He took the form of a wounded cuckoo, one of her favorite birds. She felt sorry for it, picked it up off the ground, and the next thing you know, Zeus is up her skirt and on her."

I wrapped my arms tighter around my knees. "Lovely."

Alex continued, "Zeus was never satisfied with having one woman. He was really the scariest serial rapist of the ancient world. He had dozens of children with other women: Hercules, Aphrodite, the three Fates, Apollo and his sister Artemis, Perseus, the three Graces, all nine Muses . . . he was a busy beaver."

I shuddered. Though the Amish had many children and did not use birth control, we didn't violate one another like that. It seemed the very definition of evil.

"Hera was understandably the jealous sort. She was the goddess of marriage and unable to keep her own marriage together. She heckled Hercules for years, starting with sending serpents to kill him in his crib. When Zeus loved Lamia, a queen of Libya, Hera murdered her children and turned her into a monster."

I squirmed. I was a bit uncomfortable hearing this, these tales of other gods. But I convinced myself that they were simply fiction. Like Wonder Woman. None of the Greek gods were swooping in to save the earth from vampire attacks. But the thrill of hearing this bit of blasphemy quickened my blood.

"My favorite myth about her, though, was the story of Io. Io was a priestess of Hera who'd caught Zeus's wandering eye. Io wanted nothing to do with him and rejected his advances.

Zeus then sent the oracles to pester Io's father, who eventually kicked her out of the house. Poor Io was walking through the fields alone when Zeus came upon her and tried to seduce her.

"Hera very nearly walked in on this. To avoid being caught, Zeus transformed Io into a very beautiful white cow.

"Hera, however, was familiar with Zeus's shape-changing tricks and demanded that Io be given to her as a gift. Zeus was stuck between a rock and a hard place; he handed the cow over to Hera.

"Hera, determined to keep Zeus and his would-be mistress separated, gave the cow to a giant named Argus the All-Seeing. Io was chained to a sacred olive tree at one of Hera's temples. Argus was a pretty good guard, since he had a hundred eyes and never closed all of them. He could sleep with a few of them open at any time."

"What happened to Io? I mean . . . I imagine that Zeus moved on to the next conquest." I rested my chin on my knee. No one had really told me stories since I was a child. I knew all the old biblical stories by heart. This was new. While reading was a common pastime among Plain folk, that interest rarely extended into fiction. The dogs ambled in and lay beside me. Perhaps they liked the rhythm of Alex's voice. I thought that he would make a good professor.

"Well, Zeus ordered the messenger god, Hermes, to kill Argus. Hermes showed up to the tree in the disguise of a shepherd. He managed to lull Argus to sleep by speaking magic incantations, then slugged him with a rock, killing him."

"And Io? Was she free?"

"Eh. She was free but stuck in the form of a cow. Hera

sent a gadfly to harass her for the remainder of her days and prevent her from resting. So, Io wandered until she came to the ends of the earth. For the ancient Greeks, that was pretty much as far as what's now Turkey. Zeus transformed her back into a woman when Hera wasn't looking. She conceived a daughter by Zeus's touch. Io gave birth in secret and hid her daughter with a nymph who raised her while Io continued to flee Hera's wrath.

"Io continued to run—ran as far as Egypt. Pimp-daddy Zeus came by and laid the golden touch on her again—*bam!*—and she's pregnant with child number two. She gave birth to her son, Epaphus, in the Nile. Hera found out about this one. She had the boy abducted. But Io persevered. She searched far and wide to find him in Syria.

"By this time, Io had had truly enough of the Greek gods. She returned to Egypt and swore them off, asking instead for the protection of the Egyptian goddess Isis."

"Isis was gentler than Hera, I'd guess."

"Yep. Isis was a mother and nature goddess. She was all about love and kindness. Isis took her in. Io became a priestess of Isis and married an Egyptian king. She never came back to Greece."

I sat in silence when Alex wrapped up his tale. I absorbed the whole of it, then blurted out: "That's terrible."

He smiled. "Those were the old gods for you, though. Wrathful. And this was how Hera treated one of her priestesses, one of her most fervent followers, who never wanted anything to do with Zeus. The part that amazes me is that it took Io so long to renounce them and switch to Team Isis. I guess you stick with what you know."

"*Ja,*" I said. "You do."

"Yeah. But the thing that I like about the story is that Io eventually gets her happy ending. I don't know of another myth in which one of Zeus's mortal women gets one. And she does it through sheer determination. Perseverance."

He lapsed into silence. I stared up at the flickering lantern. Darkness had fallen soft and thick around us. The Singing was over by now, and I would be expected home.

"I should be getting back." I stretched, stood, reached for the lantern. I felt bad taking his only good source of light. "My parents will be missing me."

"I can walk you back," he said.

I looked at the wound still angry on his temple. "I'm not sure that would be a good idea."

"I'll go with you part of the way." He reached for the flashlight in the pile of his meager possessions and put it in his pocket. His sleeve hiked up as he did so, and I saw a black mark on his forearm.

I reached for his wrist. "Are you hurt?"

He shook his head, smiled. "No." He rolled his sleeve up farther for me to see. "It's a tattoo. See?"

The black mark stretched across his forearm, up to his elbow. It looked like something architectural, a stepped tower. I squinted at it, holding my lantern high.

"What is it?"

"It is a moment of folly from spring break one year. You might consider it my own *Rumspringa.*" He rolled his eyes at his own foolishness. "It's called a Djed pillar. The backbone of the Egyptian god Osiris."

"So you do believe in a god." My skin crawled at the idea of someone worshipping those wrathful gods of fiction—for real. I dropped his wrist.

"Maybe abstractly," he admitted sheepishly, rubbing at the tattoo.

We walked toward the mouth of the barn. I doused the lantern as he pulled the door shut.

"Osiris is a good god? Like Isis?" I wanted to believe that there was some nugget of good in Alex.

"Actually, he's the husband of Isis. Unlike the tumult of Zeus's relationship with Hera, there was no infidelity or jealousy between them."

The sky was overcast, and I could smell rain coming. The night was soft and thick as lampblack, blanketing the field. I think that the crickets could sense the rain too; I couldn't hear them.

"That's something, at least," I said, walking beside him. Some beauty in the fiction.

"Well, they weren't without their challenges. Osiris was assassinated by his brother, Set. His body was torn into pieces and thrown into the Nile."

"Again, your myths are terrible."

I could see his teeth shining white in the darkness. "But this one has a happy ending too. Isis picked up the pieces of his body from the Nile and put him back together. Osiris was resurrected by his wife and became god of the dead and rebirth."

I shuddered. There was something sinister about the idea of a god of the dead. "And you were moved to put his symbol on your arm?"

He shrugged. "I was going through a tough time. My grandfather had died, and I didn't want to believe in the permanence of death."

I thought about that. It was, in its way, similar to how Elijah was coping with the disappearance of his brothers. Trying to fight against the permanence of death. But I didn't understand why Alex would choose something so . . . dark.

I pointed at a light in the distance. "That's my house."

He squinted at it. "Okay. I'll watch from here . . . at least, as far as I can. To see that you get there."

I smiled. "I don't think you'll be able to see much of me in the dark."

He pointed to my white prayer bonnet and apron. "I can see you for longer than you think."

This discussion seemed like a useless display of chivalry. If there were vampires in our midst, we'd be ripped to shreds. But it seemed like a bit of ordinariness that was sorely needed.

"Good night," I said to him.

"Good night, Bonnet."

I walked into the darkness. I felt the splash of a raindrop against the bridge of my nose. It woke me up from that dreamy world of myth and magic I'd let Alex lead me into. I shook my head. Blasphemous stories. *I should not have listened to them,* the voice of the obedient Good Girl in my head insisted.

But I was not sure that I wanted to listen to that voice right now. I wanted to crawl into bed and let today go. Release it. Pretend as if it didn't exist.

I scanned the fields as I walked. I did not see any other people coming back from the Singing; it was too dark to even see the cattle in the fields. All I could see were the shadows of trees and the lighter shadow of grass.

Something moved. I froze. I thought I saw a flash of something pale flitting at the edge of the tree and the field. It could have been an apron, a white shirt. It could have been the white horse. Or it could have been . . .

I sucked in my breath and ran.

I sprinted toward the light of my house, scrambled up the back steps. I paused with my hand on the doorknob, scanning the blackness behind me.

I saw nothing.

Maybe it was my imagination, the guilty force of too many dark stories in my mind.

I closed the door behind me, leaned against it, and prayed.

Funny how the Lord's Prayer was the first thing to come to mind when I was afraid, even in all my rebellion.

I was a hypocrite. When the roof came down, it was going to fall on me first.

Chapter Fifteen

By morning I had talked myself out of the flash of white I thought I'd glimpsed last night. I'd chalked it up to my overactive imagination, ignited by grief and fed by dark stories of old gods that no one except Alex believed in anymore.

I'd gone straight up to bed, pulling the braid out of my hair and the covers up to my chin. When I came down to breakfast, my mother spooned extra oatmeal into my bowl, as if she sensed my unease.

"Elijah came by looking for you last night," my mother said.

Across the table, Ginger nodded approvingly.

I hastily filled my mouth with oatmeal so I wouldn't have to talk. "Mmmph."

"Ruth Hersberger was with him," Sarah chirped, poking at the slices of apple on top of her oatmeal with her spoon.

The oatmeal scalded my tongue, and I took a swig from my glass of milk.

Ginger lifted her eyebrows. "Isn't that Joseph's girl?"

I swallowed, set my spoon down. "She was."

My mother and father traded looks down the length of the table.

"How did the Singing go last night?" my father asked.

I stirred my oatmeal and watched the steam rise from it, not meeting his eyes. I was about to be caught in a lie if I wasn't careful. I didn't know what Elijah had told them. I settled on a partial truth. "I left early. Went to go sit with the dogs."

"Elijah and the Hersberger girl said that they were concerned about you."

"Oh?" I gritted my teeth.

"They said that you seem very emotional lately. That perhaps you might benefit from more prayer and devotion to the Ordnung."

"It's the end of the world," Ginger blurted. "Isn't she entitled to feel a bit out of sorts?"

My father and mother both shot her startled glances.

"Well, maybe it would be good for her to find some comfort in the word of God," my mother began, her voice tense. Plain folk would try to be diplomatic, but they did not brook any interference in child rearing. I wondered if Elijah had told them about the makeup.

My hand tightened around the spoon, and I set it down. "May I please be excused to begin my chores?"

I felt the weight of my father's gaze heavy on me. "All right."

"Thank you." I grabbed my bowl and scurried away to the sink to rinse my dishes out. I could not bear their concern or conflict between Ginger and them. And I was furious at the idea of Elijah strutting up to my house with that fickle tart and

telling my parents what was good for me behind my back. I
clawed at the crust of oatmeal on the inside of the bowl as if it
were Ruth Hersberger's face.

I snatched up my shoes beside the door and fled into the
backyard without looking back.

I was in no mood to deal with people. I hastily fed Star,
put together her gear, and harnessed her to the sledge. I loaded
two bales of hay, working quickly in case my parents decided
to come after me to have a heart-to-heart talk. I grimaced as
I lugged the heavy bales into the back of the wagon. Caring
for the cows would keep me gone for a couple of hours, at
least. Maybe by then, they'd be occupied with other chores and
leave me in peace.

I hoped. I knew better than to pray for it, but I hoped.

Star sensed something was amiss. She ignored her oats and
snuffled against my shoulder. I petted her soft nose, sad to think
that I would not be seeing much of her in the future.

"Yes, I love you, too," I muttered as I kissed her nose. "But
your owner is an ass."

I rarely swore. But that stab of rebellion warmed my belly,
even as Star rolled her eyes.

I led Star toward the western fields under an overcast sky.
Maybe now that Elijah was feeling well enough to be interfer-
ing in my business, he'd also be well enough to look after his
own chores. I would passive-aggressively fail to complete any
other chores on the Miller property today, but I would not ever
subject the animals to my ire. I would take care of them. But
Elijah's dirty clothes could rot. Or maybe Ruth could wash his
underwear and bring him lunch.

Tears welled up in my eyes. I wondered exactly what it was that I grieved for. I knew that I regretted losing the easy friendship Elijah and I once had, and of course our *Rumspringa*. But what about our life together after that? Would it have been like this — him changed to a pious flogger of anyone who breaks the rules? I began to suspect that there would be no infractions whatsoever permitted in our house.

And did I have any right to expect anything different? I knew what was expected of me. And I thought that those desires for the things of Outside would dim after *Rumspringa*. That I'd be ready to settle down, obey the rules, have children, and live under Elijah's direction. And the Lord's.

But those *were* my hopes for the future. Not now. Now I bristled against all these things. Even the Lord.

Star shied and pawed, so I grasped her harness and firmly led her into the field. The steers were clustered up against the fence, mooing in an agitated fashion. I could not see over their broad backs. I had to struggle to push the gate open against the wall of cow flesh.

"You must be hungry." I shoved them hard to move them out of the way, so that I could get the hay to their feeding area.

I noticed a swarm of flies buzzing through. I swatted at them. It was late in the season for flies, and perhaps that was what was irritating the cattle.

They didn't show much interest in the hay as it passed on the sledge. The whites of their eyes showed as I crowded through, and I had to mind my feet to avoid getting stepped on. Finally, I was able to grab the pitchfork in the back of the sledge to put out their breakfast.

But Star had stopped.

"Go on, girl."

She flicked her ears back at me but would not obey. From my vantage point behind her, I could see a shiver ripple through the skin of her back. Clutching the pitchfork, I came around to the front of her.

I stopped dead in my tracks and a fly landed on my cheek.

"Oh no," I cried.

Four dead cows lay in the field, three brown, one white. Flies matted them, creating the seething illusion of life. I approached slowly, my heart thudding behind my ribs so hard it hurt.

But these were not downers, sick cows who'd taken ill. The spine of the cow nearest me was bent at an awkward angle. Blood trickled from its nose and a gash in its throat into the mud, creating a lurid lipstick color. Two others had their heads torn clean off, the blind eyes covered in flies. The last one, the white one, showed the most blood on its pale hide. It had been torn open from stem to stern, its ribs splayed open in the shape of some terrible butterfly and its entrails soaking in the mud.

I covered my mouth with my hand to keep from retching.

I backed up slowly, my gaze fixed on that white cow.

The vampires were here.

"They're here!"

I reached the house, panting and terrified. My mother was washing laundry with Ginger in the backyard, with the spigot and steel basins and soap up to their elbows.

My mother grabbed me with soapy hands. "Who's here?"

But I was looking beyond her, at Ginger. She let her washboard slide back into the water. Her hands shook.

I forced myself to look at my mother. "The things. The things that destroyed Outside."

My mother knelt before me. "What's going on?"

I took a deep breath. "There are four cows in the west field. Dead. Ripped to pieces."

My mother's gaze dug deep into me as she smoothed a stray strand of hair from my bonnet. "*Liewe,* they could be wolves. Or coyotes." She was trying to be reassuring, but I could see the fear igniting in her gray eyes.

I shook my head. "No. Not like this. This is a . . . a savaging. No animal can break spines and ribs."

"They're here," Ginger whispered. "The vampires."

My mother's head snapped around to Ginger. "What are you talking about?" she demanded. Her grip tightened on my elbows, and I winced.

Ginger's breath was shallow over her words. "I got through to Dan on my cell phone. The contagion from Outside . . . it turns people mad. They are calling them vampires."

"I thought your cell phone was dead," a male voice said.

My gaze flashed beyond the clothesline. Elijah stood there, favoring his wounded ankle. He'd been listening to us behind the hanging sheets.

"What are you doing here?" I snapped.

"Katie. Mind your manners," my mother said.

I glared at Elijah. "I would have expected that you'd found something else to do other than hang around here. Isn't there anything going on at Ruth's house?"

"Katie."

Elijah looked hard at me, then at Ginger. "I thought your cell phone was dead," he said again.

Ginger lifted her chin. "I found a charger in the bottom of my car as I was cleaning it out."

"When were you going to say something about this?"

I hated his imperious air. I shrugged out of my mother's grip. "I don't think she owes you an explanation."

Elijah folded his arms across his chest. "She does when she's enjoying our hospitality."

"She's not enjoying *your* hospitality." I jammed my finger in his chest. "She's enjoying my family's."

"Katie." My mother's hand was on my shoulder, hauling me back.

"She's from Outside," he said, looking past me at Ginger. "Who's to say that she didn't bring something in?"

I reached back and slapped him.

It stunned him, and it stunned me. I'd never struck anyone in my life, and the roar of blood in my ears made me powerful. I could see the red mark spreading on his face where my hand made contact. My palm stung.

Elijah stared at me, incredulous.

"*Ja,* she's been Outside," I snarled at him. "So were you. And me. And your father."

My mother grabbed my wrist so hard I could feel the bones crackle. She began uttering an apology to Elijah.

"You had better get control of her," Elijah said, rubbing his cheek.

I laughed at him. "You certainly won't ever have control

of me. Go to that . . . *mouse* . . . who will allow you to tell her what to think. Now leave!"

Elijah lowered his hat over his eyes and moved away on his crutches. My mother led me up the back steps by my wrist into the kitchen. Her eyes were storm gray in anger.

"What is wrong with you?" she cried.

"What was *he* doing here?" I gestured through the open door with my chin.

"He came to check on you."

"He doesn't want me. He wants Ruth," I snapped. "He needs to leave me alone." I turned away.

My mother grabbed my chin, forced me to look at her. "He doesn't know what he wants. And neither do you."

"I—"

"Enough!" Her voice crackled like lightning.

I lapsed into silence.

I was dimly aware of a shadow in the doorway. Ginger.

My mother glared at her. "Come in. Sit down. Both of you."

Ginger obediently sat down at the table. My mother pushed me down in a chair.

Through gritted teeth, she said: "You two will stay here while I summon the Elders. They will sort out what to do with you."

"I'm sorry. I just . . . I didn't know how to say it." Ginger's voice was small.

"So you kept it from us?"

Ginger hung her head. "I wanted Dan to be wrong. I thought . . . I thought that he had lost it. Cracked under the pressure." She pressed the heels of her hands to her eyes.

My eyes widened. I had never seen an adult lie before, and I was fascinated to see how it was done.

Ginger went on: "I didn't want to believe it. I didn't want to believe that such a terrible thing could happen to my children." A sob escaped her lips. "My children."

Something in my mother's gaze softened. She put her hand on Ginger's shoulder. "I have been praying for your family. And I will continue to do so."

"Thank you. Thank you for everything you've done." Ginger put a shaking hand on my mother's. "I mean no disrespect."

My mother bent to kiss Ginger on the prayer bonnet she wore askew on her blond hair. "I know."

She went outside. Through the kitchen window, I saw her step up into Star's saddle. My mother and the horse headed north, to the next cluster of houses.

I stared at Ginger, incredulous. She took off her glasses and wiped them on her apron.

She looked at me through reddened eyes. "Now is the time that you and I have to get our stories straight. Or we'll both be dead."

"I think . . ." I blew out my breath. "I think we're dead already."

She leaned across the table and poked me in the sternum, blue eyes blazing. "Don't you dare say that. I wouldn't want any of my children to give up, and I won't let you do it, either."

I stared down at the table. There seemed precious little to live for.

"Hey." She pressed her hand to my face. "We are going to survive this. But you've got to fight for it."

Numbly, I nodded.

"Okay. We need to work out a timeline . . ."

And Ginger began to teach me how to lie.

———

The Elders and a handful of other men of the community descended upon our house. My father came with them. His face was tight and creased.

He grasped my hand. "Lead them to what you found."

I walked before the phalanx of men. I could feel their stares boring into my back. I forced my eyes forward, put one foot in front of the other, until we reached the field. I stopped at the edge of the fence, went no farther.

The men filed past me. The Elders surrounded the fallen cattle, whispering among themselves. After some time they finally nodded at one another, then streamed out.

The Bishop said to my father and the other laymen: "Burn them."

They walked back toward the house. The Hexenmeister remained behind, leaning on his cane.

My father asked: "What shall I do with the rest of the cows?"

Herr Stoltz frowned. "Put them in a barn. A barn with a Hex sign on the door."

"What did this?" my father asked.

The Hexenmeister gazed back at the dead cows with rheumy eyes. The other men were cautiously approaching the bodies with wood.

The old man looked back at me. "The Darkness. The Darkness took them."

"I don't understand." My father looked confused.

The Hexenmeister's face crumpled in heavy sadness. "You will."

He limped on after the others.

———

The Elders crowded into our kitchen, listening as Ginger recounted her story.

I noted that Ginger kept her story closely aligned with the truth. She clasped her hands in front of her on the table, telling them earnestly how it was God's providence that she had found the car charger buried in the junk under her seat. I corroborated her story, feeling guilty for throwing her to the wolves, but not wanting any of the attention to fall on me or my wanderings Outside.

"I don't know what to believe," she whispered. "Dan says that there are monsters out there. Vampires."

The Elders traded glances.

"And you said that he told you that people on holy ground are safe?" the Bishop asked her again.

"Yes," Ginger said. "As long as the evil doesn't find a way in."

I looked down at my shoes.

The Bishop nodded. He and the other Elders stepped outside to confer privately.

I stared through the kitchen window. I could see a smoke plume at the horizon where the cows were burning, like some offering to one of Alex's old gods.

Alex. My jaw tightened at the thought of him, and my palms began to sweat.

My father leaned against the table, rubbing his brow. My mother went to him, touched his sleeve. "Was it bad?" she asked.

He nodded. "Yes."

Her gaze rested on Ginger. "Do you believe her?" Her fingers tightened on his sleeve.

My father frowned. "I will believe what the Elders tell us to believe."

The Elders returned to the kitchen, their heavy footsteps creaking the floorboards. The Bishop stared long and hard at Ginger before he spoke: "There will be no more discussion of vampires. Or the Outside. Is this clear?"

"Yes, sir," she said.

"You will surrender your cell phone, and it will be destroyed."

Ginger gasped. She blurted: "But that's the last lifeline I have to my husband, my children . . ."

The Bishop was unmoved. "It is a link to Outside. If you want to stay, it must be destroyed. Otherwise"—the Bishop shrugged and looked out the window—"you are welcome to leave."

Ginger squeezed her eyes shut, and tears dripped down her pale face. They tapped on the tabletop for a long minute before she finally agreed: "Okay."

"Go get it."

Ginger pushed away from the table, went upstairs to collect

it. I could hear her footsteps on the wood above me, and my heart ached for her. This seemed such an unnecessary cruelty.

I opened my mouth, but my father shook his head. There was no undoing this.

Ginger slowly descended the stairs with her phone in her hands. She placed it before her on the table.

The Bishop nodded to one of the other Elders. He swept it to the floor and stomped on it. I could hear the crunch and shatter of plastic parts as the pieces skittered across the floor.

I put my arm around Ginger as she sobbed. The Bishop opened the back door to the throng of Plain men and women who had gathered in our backyard. They knew that something had happened, and I could hear the thickness of the rumors buzzing through them. I saw the Hexenmeister at the fringes, leaning on his cane. Elijah stared hard at the kitchen door, Ruth and Herr Miller flanking him. I looked away. The Elders would tell them all what was happening. I could feel the weight of guilt already being removed from me. One less secret to keep.

The Elders stepped down to the yard, the Bishop at the center.

"Brothers and sisters," the Bishop began. "Thank you for your concern. But there is no need to panic. God is with us. We have nothing to fear."

"But there is an Outsider among us," Elijah grumbled loudly. I shot him a murderous look. "An Outsider who speaks of vampires."

The crowd murmured.

The Bishop lifted his hands in a placating gesture. "We should offer our sympathies to the woman. The stress of the last week's events has caused her mind to become unhinged. She imagines fearsome things, things that are not real."

I gasped, stared at Ginger beside me at the table. Her face crumpled.

"She deserves our sympathy and our charity and our prayers that she should be restored to sound mind in accordance with God's will."

Another man shouted from the back. "What about the cattle?"

The Bishop shook his head. "Wolves. They have become bold. I entreat those of you with animals to keep them in the barns at night, to keep them safe."

My hands balled into fists. The Bishop was lying to them. I moved forward, but Ginger grabbed my wrist.

"Don't," she hissed. "Better that they think I'm crazy than both of us dead."

"But . . . we're all in danger!" I whispered back.

She grasped my hand and squeezed it. Hard. "No. Be quiet."

I bristled. All my life, people had been telling me to be quiet. To obey. And it had never gotten me anywhere.

I took a deep breath and stepped forward to face the crowd.

The Hexenmeister hobbled forward with his cane before I could speak. He faced the Elders. "The Darkness is coming."

The Bishop glared at him. "There is no Darkness, except for the poisonous thoughts of Outside."

The Hexenmeister pointed at the smoke plume in the distant field. "The Darkness is here. Someone has let it in."

"We are safe. God has chosen us . . ." the Bishop began.

The Hexenmeister had the temerity to interrupt him. "God has chosen those who will not listen to die."

He turned around and stumped away from the gathering. The crowd parted to let him, leaving the Bishop to fume impotently on our back step.

CHAPTER SIXTEEN

Nachtesse was brutally silent that night.

My mother and father did not speak, and Ginger sat at the table, staring at her chicken casserole. We were out of butter and ate our biscuits plain. Sarah, oblivious, filled the void with chatter until she realized that no one was responding. She settled down to push her casserole around with her fork, quiet like the rest of us.

After we ate, my father retired to his favorite chair by the fire to read the Bible to Sarah. Ginger slipped upstairs to go to bed. I wished that I could have done something to soothe her, but I could not have predicted today's events. I only know that I felt pity for her.

I helped my mother with the dishes, washing and rinsing while she dried. We worked mechanically until she spoke.

"I know it's difficult, *liewe*," she said.

I stared down at the dish that I scrubbed. I doubted that she understood any part of what I was going through.

She kept going. "I was jealous, once, of a girl your father used to know. She was a nurse."

I looked sidelong at her. Hard to imagine my father casting an eye at anyone other than my mother. "Oh?"

"Yes. Her name was Mindy. She was much more intelligent than I was. Better spoken." She rubbed at a spot I'd missed with a striped dishtowel. "She was prettier, too."

I crinkled my forehead. Mindy wasn't a traditional Amish biblical name. "How did he meet her?"

"On *Rumspringa*. We went to one of the nearby towns, a large group of boys and girls. He met her at the bowling alley. I think some of the other boys had a taste for English, and they egged him on."

I swallowed. "How did . . . how did you deal with that?"

She smiled into her reflection in a glass. "There is only one way to a man's heart. Through gentleness. Not by getting angry or jealous."

I frowned. "I don't understand." Maybe I didn't want to.

"Elijah still cares for you. Else, he wouldn't come around."

"I think he just wants to control me."

"He just wants to know that he has a place in your life, now that things have changed."

My fingers wrapped around the neck of a jar in the sink, hidden by the suds. "He has chosen to change things. I was happy with the way things were."

"You need to grow up. Things change. Once you accept that, you'll be happier."

I felt the jar collapse soundlessly in my hands, the glass bite into my palms. I lifted my hands from the water, speckling the suds pink.

"Oh no." My mother wrapped the dishtowel around my hands, pressing them together. The red soaked through the cloth, and she called for my father to get some bandages.

I passively watched my mother bind my hands, clucking under her breath. My father looked on anxiously, the worry mark between his brows deepening.

I looked from one to the other. I could not now imagine Elijah and I having what they did.

I began to cry. My mother held me, thinking it was from the pain of the cuts.

I let her, too exhausted to resist.

Night called me.

I lay in bed, listening to the soft settling noises of the house, to Ginger's snores, to the sound of the breath whistling through the gap in my little sister's front teeth. I could hear the crickets and the sound of the breeze through the trees.

Beyond that . . . I heard something more.

I wrapped the pillow around my head, muffling the night sounds so that I could hear my pulse thumping in my ears. But I still heard it, that strange sound in the darkness I'd never heard before. It was eerie. Seductive.

One of my classmates who'd gone on *Rumspringa* last year had brought back a shell. He'd gone as far as the ocean. He said that I could hear the sound of the ocean in the shell. Swallowing my jealousy, I pressed the shell to my ear, heard that soft roar. I closed my eyes, listening to that sound that was not unlike blowing across the lip of a bottle, that distant hiss of ocean captured in a pink whisper. I listened to the shell for an hour, imagining what that vastness must be like in person. I wondered what that broad blue horizon would smell like, how the sand would feel between my toes.

This was like that, that soft summoning. I could hear it in my bones, no matter how hard I tried to muffle it.

I rolled out of bed, padded across the floor. I shook Ginger's shoulder to wake her, to ask her if she heard it too. But she was deep in slumber and just mumbled and turned over.

I went to the window, slid it open. Cool dark air washed over me. The moon above had burned through the clouds, sketching out the landscape in black and white. I saw no sign of anyone in the yard below, only a rabbit hopping out of my sister's pumpkin patch.

I closed my eyes. I could still hear it, but louder. I shivered as it slid over my shoulders, tickled the hem of my nightdress. It sounded ethereal, soothing. My thoughts buzzed and felt fuzzy, much the way they did the time I got into hard cider at a party. The moon swam at the edge of my vision, and I clutched at the window sash.

Something was out there.

Something siren-soft, seductive. Beautiful.

For a moment, I wondered if it might be God.

As if in a trance, I put on my dress from yesterday and slipped down the stairs and out the kitchen door, not even bothering to put on my shoes.

The breeze played with the edges of my dress, teased a strand of hair free from my bonnet. I let the wind take it, pull it back, slide its hands through my skirts. I half closed my eyes, smelling honeysuckle and hearing the siren call of the night so loudly that it moved in my veins, the way the tides echoed in the back of that shell.

I stepped outside, closing the door behind me. The rabbit from the pumpkin patch peered up at me, chewing clover. Everything was serene, beautiful in the soft wash of moonlight. It was as if I were in a dream, moving in air that seemed thick and supportive of my limbs. My fingers splayed, feeling the movement of it, capturing a shred of that call I felt with every fiber of my being.

Dully fearless, I began to walk. I walked past the pumpkin patch, into the pitch-black beyond the house, where the field grass tickled the palms of my hands. The whole meadow was alive, seething with life. Deer grazed peacefully yards away from me, a doe and two fawns beginning to lose their spots. I stared at them dreamily, wondering if they'd seen the white horse.

The doe lifted her head, flicked her ears. Her head turned, her nostrils flared. She blinked, then bounded away with a flash of white tail. The fawns followed in their mother's wake.

The string of that call snapped, and the spell broke. It left me standing alone in the field, barefoot, shivering as a sudden awareness of danger slapped me in the face like a bucket of water.

I sucked in my breath, wheeled back to the distant light of the house.

Too late.

Something roiled in the grass. I could see it moving toward me, at terrible speed, zigzagging violently through the stalks. It kept low as it rushed toward me, but I spied a glimmer of red, like the eyes of the terrible creatures in the Laundromat, sliding through the shadows.

I ran.

It plowed into me, knocking me down from behind. My face pressed into the ground, and I tasted dirt. I felt something heavy on me, ripping at the skirt of my dress. Claws sank into my arm, and I shrieked.

The creature hissed like steam in a kettle, recoiled. It was then that I dimly realized that I was wearing yesterday's clothes. And the *Himmelsbrief* was still in my pocket.

I dug into my pocket with my free hand and grabbed the envelope in my fist. The creature released me, howling. The weight on my back vanished.

That was all I needed to run—run like the very dogs of hell were on my heels. I gave no thought to direction, just *away*. I plunged headlong into the field, my breath rattling in my mouth. The landscape bobbed around me, sharp grass slashing my bare arms, the wind whistling in my ears, tearing my bonnet off my head.

I saw the dim, shadowed hulk of the kennel ahead of me, the hex sign peeling away. I slammed up against the door, tried to work the latch, whimpering as my hands shook.

The door slid open suddenly, and I pitched forward into a pair of waiting arms.

I fought against them, kicking and snarling as they wrestled me back into the darkness. I was flung to the floor. The door reeled back, blotting out the night.

I scuttled blindly on the floor with straw in my fingers.

A light came on, the yellow beam of a flashlight. I blinked stupidly.

"Alex?"

The light showed his outline in the pitch-black. I saw that he was holding a shovel in his right hand like a weapon, the flashlight in his left. I could not see his face.

"Show me your teeth," I demanded.

The idea had crossed my mind, but I had shied away from it. I didn't want to consider that I may have been the one to bring this evil upon our community. That it was me who had let the Hexenmeister's Darkness in. Perhaps Alex was a vampire, and my stupid sympathy, my flouting of God's will, would kill us all.

The shadow remained still. Bile rose in the back of my mouth.

"Show me," I commanded, a note of hysteria creeping into my voice.

The flashlight turned back around to illuminate Alex's face, turned ghastly in bright planes and jagged shadow. I held my breath. His lips curled back around perfectly ordinary and smooth teeth.

I let out a sob.

The flashlight aimed back at my face. "Now you."

I pulled my lips back in a grotesque simulacrum of a smile. The light flashed on me, then receded.

I blinked in that red darkness. I heard footsteps, the clink of a chain. I gasped aloud as something wet and cold pressed against my neck. I reached up to discover it was a dog's nose.

"What are you doing here this late?" Alex kept the flashlight trained away from me, but I could still see his bare feet and chest. I glimpsed shapes of ink on his broad chest and his back.

I looked away, buried my fingers in Copper's ruff. "I don't know . . . I heard something. Where's Sunny? Is she all right?" Panic stung me.

"Eh. Sawing logs in the back paddock. Puppies are kicking her hard, and she's sleeping." I heard the note of worry in his voice. "What did you hear?"

"I can't describe it . . . It was like a whisper. Or music. It was beautiful." I pressed my hand to my forehead. I didn't understand why I did it. "I went outside. That was stupid. They're here."

I heard Alex suck in his breath. "They called you."

"They what?"

"There's folklore about vampires being able to hypnotize, to summon people they have a connection to."

I shivered, wrapped my hands around my arms. "I don't have a connection to them. But they came after me, anyway."

The flashlight washed over me again, and I protested the sudden light in my face. I felt my undone hair being thrust back from my neck, felt Alex's warm hands on my face, turning my head right and left.

"Did they bite you?"

"No . . . no."

He didn't believe me. He grabbed my arms, shoved my sleeves up to inspect my wrists. The light illuminated only a scratch on the inside of my right forearm, where the vampire had caught me.

"No one just escapes the vamps. Not at night," he said. "Not without holy ground."

His hand remained holding my wrist. I didn't protest.

"Holy ground doesn't matter anymore," I said. "They killed cows last night." I explained to him what I'd seen in the field that morning.

"I don't understand. If they've broken holy ground, entered this place . . . I don't understand how they had to lure you from the house to get to you. Why didn't they just kill you? Why didn't they follow you here?"

I was silent, feeling my pulse beat against his hand as he thought.

I cast my eyes down, reached into my torn skirt, and fished in my pocket for the *Himmelsbrief.* "I think it was this."

He took the envelope from me, and the warmth around my wrist was suddenly gone. He opened it, scanned it. "I can't read this. My German sucks."

I took it back from him. "It says: 'Keep thine own faith. Wear love around thee like a shield, and no harm shall come to thee, even when thou walk in the valley of darkness. God bless and protect thee, and keep the road before thee straight and open. In Jesus' name, Amen.'"

"A prayer?"

"More than that: a *Himmelsbrief,* constructed by our Hexenmeister." I struggled to put the concept into words. "It's a letter to heaven."

"I've heard of the Hexenmeister . . . kind of a throwback to the old days when kitchen witchery was practiced by Germans. It's not a typical Amish thing."

I protested. "He's not a kitchen witch. He's a man of God. And we have always had such men of God here."

"That's anthropologically bizarre, and I'd love to write a paper on that, but . . ." He shook his head. "More importantly, he writes spells that protected you from the vampires. What else does he do?"

I shrugged. "He makes all the hex signs on the barns." I looked up. "He painted the one here."

"He's a pretty powerful wizard, then."

I made a face that he couldn't see in the dark. The term "wizard" implied an old man with a pointy cap and a robe painted with stars. But . . . was that so far off from the bearded man who painted stars on the sides of buildings?

Alex sat, hunched over, his elbows resting on his knees and his hands steepled before him. "Even if the vamps are here, all might not be lost."

"It will take time for him to make a *Himmelsbrief* for each man, woman, and child," I began.

"Not just that. I'm thinking about their tactics. They didn't go into the house after you. Maybe they couldn't come in. Your houses, after all, are all churches."

"*Ja*. We each host church once or twice a year."

"Holy ground within holy ground. I'm betting that you'd have to invite them in, or they'd have to lure you outside in order to get to you." He looked up into the gloom of the barn. "And if your Hexenmeister is the genuine article, I'm betting that his hex signs keep evil away just as well as the *Himmelsbrief.*"

Hope flowered in the back of my throat. "We may survive this?"

"If you guys play it well, maybe. What happened with the cows? Do they understand what they're dealing with?"

My hands balled into fists. "*Ja.* And no. The Elders were told. But they chose to lie to the congregation. They told them that it was wolves. That the idea of vampires is simply a lie."

He shook his head. "If they're running propaganda, I think you guys are well and truly screwed."

"But what can I do?" I cried. "They would call me crazy."

"Even the Hexenmeister?"

I paused. Deep down, I knew that the Hexenmeister had a firmer grip on evil than the rest of us. "I'm not sure."

"Tell him. Tell him everything. He might believe you. Especially if those 'wolves' get more active."

"Well . . . I won't tell him *everything.*" I glanced at him.

He sighed. "I'm as good as dead. You do what you need to do to save your own skin."

"But . . ."

"Hey, I've had nothing but time to think about how this plays out. I can't stay here forever, like one of the dogs. You're gonna run out of food to smuggle to me. Or one of the others is gonna catch a glimpse of me stealing apples from the tree out back. That's if the vamps don't get me first." In the shadows, his mouth turned down. "I'm a goner."

"That's not true," I said, softly. "I will protect you."

Alex's gaze was resolute. "I don't mean to sound ungrateful, Bonnet. Really, I don't. But I know that I'm on borrowed time. Any additional sunrise I get is, in its own way, a blessing."

I lifted an eyebrow. "You're a strange one to talk about blessings."

He shrugged. "Hey, I've been hanging out in a barn for days with nothing to do. Osiris and I have made our peace."

My eyes flicked to the ink marks that covered his spine. "Are those more devotions to Osiris?" I asked timidly.

"Heh. I suppose." He turned the flashlight to his back. I saw a pillar that traveled the length of his spine, similar to the one I'd seen earlier on his arm.

"Another Djed pillar?" I scooted closer for a better look, and he handed the flashlight to me.

"Yeah. But I had to be drunk for three sittings in order to get that one finished."

It was intricate, much more so than the one on his arm. The architectural details of the pillar curved sensuously up over each vertebrae, flaring out to cradle the back of his neck. My fingertips hovered above the tattoo but didn't touch it. "That must have hurt."

"Actually, I don't remember the pain."

"You *must* have been drunk."

He turned in the light, showed me a mark on his chest, right above his heart. "This one hurt more. I was sober for that one."

"I was going to suggest that you spend a lot of the time drunk," I said dryly.

This looked like a stylized cross, burned black. I peered at it. "It's a brand," I said, in startlement. I'd seen enough of those on cattle. I reached out to touch it in spite of myself, feeling uneven skin.

"Yeah. It's what the hipsters called scarification. You basically let a couple of buddies hold you down while some tattoo-covered sadist who calls himself an artist drops a red-hot brand on you."

I glanced up at him. "Are you nuts?"

"Eh. Off and on."

I stared at the symbol. It seemed both familiar and foreign. "And what does this one mean?"

"It's an ankh. The Egyptian symbol of eternal life."

"Strange tattoo for a man who believes he's about to be dead." I pulled back my hand.

"Hey, you buy into the eternal life thing too. Just in heaven."

"Maybe. But we don't have to be branded to obtain it."

"I think I'd rather be branded than submit to some of the things that you have to." He said this without spite, just a soft statement of fact. "I'm not strong enough to do that."

I wrapped my arms around my knees. I had nothing to say to that. I didn't feel strong. I felt small and weak and not nearly worldly enough to face what was happening.

Alex reached out, pushed a tendril of loose hair behind my ear. His touch was light as a feather. Not the clumsy fingers that I was accustomed to with Elijah. I shivered.

"You're cold," he said automatically. He unfolded himself and stood. "I'll get you a blanket . . . see if I can haul one out from beneath the dog."

"Thank you," I said. "I should check on Sunny."

I followed him and the bobbing beam of the flashlight to the back paddock, Copper at my side. The flashlight's batteries were failing, and the glow was more of a dull ember, barely enough to see by.

Sunny was stretched out on one of her blankets and looked up when she saw me. I knelt beside her, stroking her belly. I could feel the puppies moving within her, restless. I kissed her behind the ear.

"She'll have her litter soon," I said. "Maybe in the next couple of days."

"Um. I don't know anything about puppies," Alex said. That was the first uncertain note I'd ever heard in his voice.

"I'll handle it. Don't worry about it."

"Good." He dropped a blanket over me that smelled like dog, tucked it up under my chin. There was a peculiar tenderness in that gesture.

He dug in his bundle of clothes for a shirt. I was a bit sorry to see him put it on. I was fascinated by the marks he'd put on his flesh . . . and more than a little fascinated by the flesh itself. Blushing, I turned away.

"Will they notice you're gone?" he asked.

"Probably not until morning," I said.

"At the risk of sounding incredibly forward, I think that you should stay here until the sun rises."

I opened my mouth to protest, but he leaned forward and put his finger to my lips. My lips buzzed, and I forgot what I was going to say.

"Look, I'm not really concerned about your standards of decency. I'm more concerned about your safety."

"I have the *Himmelsbrief*," I said in a small voice against his finger, but I didn't relish the idea of running the vampire gauntlet again.

"You mean you have it until the vamps glamour you into throwing it on the ground. Then you're a midnight snack. Here you're under the Hex sign." He withdrew his hand, settled up against a wall with his arms across his chest. "As sad as it makes me to say it, you're probably safer with me."

"I'm quite sure that you say that to anything in a skirt," I retorted primly.

"Historically, that's probably accurate," he admitted. "But I'm less of a monster than what's out there."

The flashlight winked out. I heard Alex scrape around in the straw to slap it twice, but it remained dark.

"Great," he muttered.

My eyes adjusted slowly. Streamers of moonlight filtered in through the chinks in the boards. It wasn't pitch-black, but I was accustomed to darkness. The Plain folk didn't sleep with night-lights.

Alex leaned back up against the far wall of the paddock. "You sleep. I'll keep watch."

I stood, crossed to the far side of the paddock, and sat down next to Alex. I opened the blanket like a wing. "I'll share if you promise not to bite."

He nodded, pulled the blanket around him. Gingerly, he put his arm around my shoulder. He smelled of straw and soap. I could hear his pulse thudding hypnotically in my ear.

And I slept the dreamless sleep of the dead.

CHAPTER SEVENTEEN

"Hey. Wake up."

"Huh." I was warm and didn't want to get out of bed just yet.

"Sun's rising."

I blinked. I wasn't in my bed. I was in the kennel, curled up next to Alex with my head on his chest. His arm was draped over me, his thumb resting lightly on my collarbone.

I was terrified. And I didn't want to move.

"C'mon, Katie. You've got to get back before they notice you're gone." Alex's voice was slurred in sleep. I thought for a moment that he had me confused with Cassia, but he'd called me Katie.

He kissed me on the top of my head.

That scared me. I slipped out from under his arm and the blanket and crawled over to where the dogs lay. Sunny's head felt warm, as it usually did. I ran my fingers over her sides. No sign of labor yet. But there would be soon. Maybe today, maybe tomorrow.

I turned back to Alex, who'd risen and was folding the blanket. "If she goes into labor before I get back . . ."

"Um, no . . . that's not gonna happen. I don't do labor." Sleepiness gave way to terror on his face. "You have to get back," he pleaded, cleared his throat. "For the dog."

I continued, firmly. "If she goes into labor before I get back, don't panic. This isn't her first time. Give her water. And watch her. The puppies will come on their own. Give her a couple of minutes to tear off the membranes for each pup. If she doesn't do it, you have to, or the pup will suffocate."

"Shit." Alex watched me with rounded eyes. He was awake now.

"Tie the umbilical cord off and cut it about an inch from the puppy's belly."

"Shit," he repeated. "With what?"

"There are scissors in the tackle box in the front of the barn. Expect about one pup an hour after she's gone into hard labor."

"Shit. How many will she have?"

I grinned. The look on his face was worth listening to his swearing. "Usually four." I stood and patted his sleeve. "You've faced the Undead. You can handle this."

He looked at me skeptically. "Um . . ."

"She does all the work. Just be there for her."

He pinched the bridge of his nose. "Okay."

"Don't panic," I repeated.

"Shit."

I walked to the front of the barn. Alex hauled open the door to the dawn.

The gray of night had given way to a red gash at the horizon. I glanced at him. "Is it safe now?"

He stood with his hands in his pockets, barefoot, shirt open, and hair mussed, blinking into the wan light. "Yeah. As soon as the sun comes up. As long as you stay out of shadows and shade."

I nodded, ran my fingers through my hair. I pinned it up in a loose roll with the hairpins I had remaining and straightened my apron over the tear in my dress. There was nothing to be done for the lost bonnet, but I hoped to be back before anyone noticed I was gone. I realized then that I looked very guilty. So did Alex. I blushed.

"Hey," he said.

I half turned toward him, eager to be on my way and escape this awkwardness.

He caught my hand. "Be careful, will you?"

His fingers meshed in mine. I nodded wordlessly and moved away, pulling against his grip.

But he didn't let go. He reeled me back in as if I were a fish. With a startled gasp, I stumbled and landed against his chest. A flicker of amusement glittered in his eyes.

He kissed me on my forehead, whispered against my skin. "Be careful, Bonnet."

He released me. I stumbled backwards, nodded again, and turned to walk the way back home with my heart thundering in my chest.

———

I let myself in the back door, wincing as the screen door banged against my calf. I heard footsteps above me, and I lurched to the cupboards to begin banging around with pots and pans.

My mother descended the stairs, tucking her hair into a

bun at the nape of her neck. She was always the earliest riser in our family. "Katie. You're up early."

I lit the kerosene stove burner with a match. I smiled at her and remembered what Ginger had said about the simplest lie being the best one. "Couldn't sleep. Would you like some eggs?"

"That would be lovely." My mother seemed relieved to see me in the kitchen and puttering about in an obedient fashion. I flopped a chunk of lard into the skillet and took some eggs out of the egg basket.

My mother plucked a piece of straw from my dress. I swallowed. My mouth was dry around the half-truth: "I saw Sunny this morning."

"How big is she?"

I wrapped my arms around an imaginary dog belly the size of a barrel. "Huge. Her temperature hasn't dropped yet. The puppies could come soon. Maybe tomorrow."

"Good." My mother slid into a chair at the table. "About yesterday . . ." she began.

I cracked four eggs, one by one, into the skillet of sizzling lard, waiting for her to continue.

She stared down at her hands, knotted together before her, as if in prayer, working the piece of straw between them. "I know that it's difficult to understand why the Elders do what they do. But it's for the best."

I turned over my shoulder, smiled reassuringly at her. "It's all right." As bad as things were, a tiny flicker of something had lit inside me. Hope. Despite the Elders.

I seasoned the eggs with salt and pepper, then scraped them out on two plates with a fork. They were tender and slightly runny, just the way my mother liked them. I took my plate and sat across from her. I was ravenous and rushed through my prayer to get to the eggs.

My mother set her fork down. "I just want you to accept that things are the way they are for a reason. We may not understand it. But we have to do as we're told."

I spoke around hot egg in my mouth, not meeting her eyes. *"Gelassenheit."*

"Yes. *Gelassenheit.*" She tapped the piece of straw on the table. "Sometimes I think that your father and I have been too lax with you."

I looked up in alarm.

She continued. "But then I remember the kinds of freedoms I had at your age. When I was on *Rumspringa,* I was riding a motorcycle."

My jaw dropped. "You . . . what?"

My parents had told me little of their time Outside, only allowing stories to come in bits and pieces as circumstances warranted.

Her eyes twinkled, and she nodded. "We are not nearly the sticks in the mud that you think. I know your heart, that you are a good girl. You are bright and a hard worker. I have faith that you will eventually come around to what's best. As we all do, sooner or later."

My stomach turned, and I pushed the half-eaten plate of eggs away. I forced myself to look my mother in the eye. She seemed in such a perfect state of denial of everything, clinging to her beliefs and the way things used to be. "Thank you, Mother. I will . . . strive to do better."

"That's my girl." She reached across the table to pat my cheek.

"May I go begin my chores?" I asked.

"Yes. And remember to bring more milk and eggs in today, *liewe.*"

"Yes, Mother."

"And one more thing."

I looked at her expectantly.

"Bring Elijah some supper today."

"Yes, Mother." I bit my tongue so hard it bled. More likely, I'd feed it to the dogs. Or the Outsider.

"You and I will talk later about getting baptized. Your father and I have decided that this is best for you." The set of her mouth showed that she would brook no argument.

I slid away from the table, scraped the remainder of my plate into the trash. I slipped down to the spring room to wash and retrieve a clean dress from the laundry before I left the house. I reminded myself to put the *Himmelsbrief* in the pocket of my clean dress. Apparently, the *Himmelsbrief* didn't seem to mind my wavering faith as much as my mother did.

The sun had climbed high enough on the horizon that I could see its full yellow body. I headed due north when I left the house. Not toward the chicken coop, the cows, or the Miller house. But to the Hexenmeister.

Herr Stoltz's house lay at the farthest northern edge of our settlement. His vegetable garden was overgrown and tangled with thistles, and the shade cast by the nearby forest over his small dwelling lent a palpable chill to the land. The whitewash on the house was speckled with mildew, and sprigs of pepper-mint grew wild around its foundations. The shade around it made me nervous, as I thought of things that could lurk there. I steeled myself, reasoning that the Hexenmeister's property would be better protected than ours.

As children, we avoided this place. The Hexenmeister was a bit frightening. He'd never done anything to harm anyone, but we feared the way he talked to himself and watched how the adults gave him a wide berth. But I needed him now.

I screwed up my courage and knocked at the door. It echoed back through the rooms of the house.

I waited and knocked again, more insistently.

Eventually, I heard shuffling and the thump of a cane against the floor. The door opened, and the Hexenmeister blinked dazedly at me. Well, not at me . . . He looked beyond me at the sky.

"Oh, it's sunrise already. Good thing."

I swallowed hard. "Herr Stoltz, may I speak with you?"

He stepped aside to let me in. I noted that the collar on his shirt was wrinkled and bore paint stains. He smelled like he needed a bath.

I had never been inside the Hexenmeister's house. When-ever it had been his turn to host church, he always did so from the yard. I could see why.

Every horizontal surface was cluttered with bits of wood, paper, paint, a T-square, rulers, and old brass compasses. I saw the petals of a hex sign beginning to unfold from a sketch on a perfectly sanded piece of wood, a jar full of blackberry ink. A fly buzzed past me, and I swatted at it. I didn't want to imagine the chaos in the kitchen.

The old man stumped to a worn rocking chair and sat down. "What can I do for you, Katie?"

"I wanted . . . to thank you for the *Himmelsbrief* . . ." I began. I perched uncomfortably on a stool at his feet.

His eyes narrowed. "Have you had to use it?"

I lowered my head. "Yes, Herr Stoltz. It saved my life."

"The Darkness has come." He leaned back in his chair, letting it creak against the scarred floor as he rocked. He looked up into space, at a cobweb in the corner.

"What do you know about the Darkness?" I asked timidly.

He rocked vigorously in his chair as he spoke. "The Darkness has always been a part of mankind. I have never seen it myself, mind you. Only heard stories about it from the Hexenmeister before me."

I laced my hands together in my lap. "What did he say?"

"Not all Plain folk came to America solely for reasons of political and religious persecution. Europe had become crowded. It was difficult to buy any land of one's own and not swear fealty to some minor land baron. Our little group of Plain folk could not have truly sacred land. Land that was immune to the Darkness."

"The Darkness . . . existed back then? In the eighteenth century?" My brow furrowed. I knew the stories of our ancestors being forced to worship in secret, at night, in secluded forests and caves. I now wondered if there was more reason than persecution for that.

"In those days, people were wiser to the true nature of evil. We were different than other Plain folk in that regard. We knew about the Darkness, and we fought it with the tools we had available to us: the hex signs, the *Himmelsbrief* . . . and in other ways. We would sever the heads of the dead, stuff their mouths with garlic, burn them with fire. It was ugly . . . but it worked."

I could not imagine desecrating a corpse like that. "And they were able to contain this contagion?"

"Then, yes. Remember that this was a long time ago. Fewer people. When we saw the glint of evil, we would destroy it before it grew too large to control. Now"—he waved a hand around the room—"we have forgotten. Become complacent. People saw no Darkness and no need to teach the means to stop it to recent generations. Now it festers."

"As it festers here," I whispered.

The Hexenmeister stared at me under bushy eyebrows. "You've seen them."

"*Ja*. I have seen them. They only come out at night, with their teeth and their claws." I rolled up my sleeve to show the Hexenmeister my scratch. "The Outsiders call these creatures vampires . . ."

Herr Stoltz frowned at the scratch, muttered: "Outsiders."

"You heard it. The Elders have decided that the Outsider woman is crazy," I said. I shied away from the topic of Alex.

The old man's eyes darkened. "They are fools. The Outsiders are no more or less pure than we are. We simply have . . . we have the knowledge to stop the Darkness."

I leaned forward on the stool. "*You* have the knowledge. You have the power to make *Himmelsbriefen*. And the hex signs." My hand swept around to indicate his workshop. "You can keep us safe."

The Hexenmeister snorted. "They would have to believe that I could help them, believe that the Darkness is here." He gestured to me with his chin. "That was why I gave you the *Himmelsbrief.* You would believe. You had seen it."

My mind froze in its tracks. "How did you know?"

A thin smile curled over his lips. "Few things escape the observation of a crazy old man with no supervision. I saw you leave the other day, saw you go over the gate with your bicycle."

I stared down at the floor. I'd been caught. I was finished.

"And I know that you are hiding the Outsider man."

I shut my eyes. Alex and I were both finished.

"I went back to the field after the Elders had left to look for the man myself." The Hexenmeister's chair creaked rhythmically against the floor. "I wanted to see what he was, to see if he had any Darkness in him. If he did, I brought my saw to take his head."

I shuddered.

"If not"—he shrugged—"I probably would have done the same as you did. But he was not there when I returned."

"How did . . . how did you know that it was my doing?"

"You left a canning jar beside the fence, half-full of water. Of all the people who saw that man, you were the only one who had any sympathy for him." He smiled. "I took your jar and roughed up the tracks in the grass you left with your sledge. I hoped that the Elders would think that he had recovered and walked away. Or that animals had taken him."

My throat tightened. "He's not a vampire. I have seen him in daylight."

Herr Stoltz chuckled. "I know, child. If he were, you would be dead." He leaned forward to cup my face in his hands. "You merely have a large heart. And a rebellious spirit." He tapped my nose with his index finger.

"Will you . . . will you tell the Elders?" I squeaked.

"No. There would be no good purpose achieved by that."

"Will you make a *Himmelsbrief* for everyone?" I asked.

"I will try." His mouth creased. "But they must believe in the Darkness first. They must believe that they are in danger, that evil has fallen upon us . . ."

A knock sounded at the front door, startling me. The Hexenmeister's runny eyes turned to the door. "Huh. I've had more visitors today than in the past year." He rose, stumped to the door.

One of the congregation members I dimly recognized was there. I'd seen him yesterday, with the gathering in my yard. He was the one who'd asked about the cattle, who had seemed most dubious of the Elders' explanation. He was out of breath, his beard shaking, hands braced on his knees.

"Herr Stoltz, come quick," he panted.

"What is the matter?"

"There's been murder . . . not just murder . . . a slaughter." He shook his head, as if to clear it, his eyes squeezed shut.

"Where?" The Hexenmeister reached for his hat.

"The Hersberger house."

———————

There had never been a murder in our community.

Never. Not in all the time that I had lived there. Not in all the time that my parents had lived here, or my grandparents. Not ever.

We were simply not capable of it.

I rode in the back of a buggy with the Hexenmeister and the man who'd raised the alarm in front, driving. He refused to speak of what he'd seen, despite our prodding. He just sat and sweated.

I saw Herr Stoltz slip a parchment envelope into his jacket pocket.

I asked him: "Is that—?"

He nodded and whispered, "This old man won't go anywhere unarmed these days."

I grasped his sleeve. I was glad that the Hexenmeister was protecting himself. He could be our only hope.

The buggy stopped in front of the Hersberger house and I climbed out with trepidation. There were already a half-dozen people whispering in the yard. The Elders had not yet arrived.

The crowd parted for the Hexenmeister. It seemed as if, in their fear, they recognized some of his ancient authority. He stumped up the porch, paused before the door. His hand pressed to his chest, he recited the Lord's Prayer.

I shied away, stepping down to stay with the rest of the Plain folk.

Herr Stoltz grasped my arm. "No, Katie. You come with me. I will need your help."

I nodded, my mouth dry.

He pushed open the door.

I smelled blood, immediately, and my stomach churned. Bile filled the back of my throat, and I vomited on the front step.

The Hexenmeister waited patiently for me, motioned for me to cross the threshold behind him.

"Gott in Himmel," he whispered.

Chapter Eighteen

I did not know that the human body could hold so much blood. I suppose that I must have had some concept of it. I helped on those weekends when pigs and cows were butchered in the spring and fall, watched as the blood drained from them into buckets. But that was outdoors, not in a confined space. And we only butchered one or two at a time.

Not a whole family.

Lurid red blood smeared the walls and the overturned table and chairs. A body lay just over the threshold. I knew it was female, judging by the nightdress and the long blond hair. The Hexenmeister prodded the corpse with his cane, turned it over.

It was Ruth. Her face was blank, rubbery, the eyes staring into nothingness. Her nightdress had been ripped open from neck to hem, and she was soaked in blood.

I jammed my fist in my mouth. Some small part of me, in the deepest, darkest part of my mind, had wanted her gone. Maybe even dead. But not like this.

"That one," the Hexenmeister said, "that one let the Darkness into the house."

I thought back to the seductive call I'd heard in the moon-light. I shivered.

Herr Stoltz stumped forward. The second body, the father, and the third, the oldest brother, were sprawled on the kitchen floor. Their heads were merely bloody pulp. A hunting rifle lay in the grip of the father. The Hexenmeister leaned on his cane. "I expect these two heard the commotion, came running . . ." His gaze slid upstairs, to the bedrooms.

My eyes widened. Ruth had a mother and four sisters.

The Hexenmeister sighed, trod heavily toward the steps. I followed him upstairs, clutching the oak railing. I could see on the wall that there were faint streaks of blood, as if someone had let their fingers trail along the wall. I shuddered, imagining the pale vampires slipping up the steps in the dark, knowing that their terrified victims were trapped on the second floor with nowhere to run. Cornered.

The Hexenmeister turned to the first bedroom. The door was ajar, and he pushed it open with his cane.

This was the parents' bedroom. Ruth's mother was impaled on the nearest bedpost of the four-poster bed. She seemed to be suspended in space, her back turned at an impossible angle and her chest torn out. I could see the white fingers of her ribs reaching toward the ceiling. Blood had poured down the bedpost, making a puddle on the floor. Where her arms were splayed out, I could see chew marks on her wrists.

I covered my mouth with my hand.

Herr Stoltz crossed the hall, to the girls' room. I crept behind in his shadow, terrified to look. But I knew that he would not shield me from the sight of violence. The door was open, and I glanced over his shoulder.

The ceiling was red. Red and dripping and turning brown.

I gasped and turned away, shaking.

The Hexenmeister heard that hitch in my voice. He turned to me, gripping my shoulder with the ironlike claw of his hand.

"Katie," he hissed. "You must be strong. There is hard work to do."

I blinked at him stupidly.

"Katie. We must stop the spread of the Darkness, keep this family from rising as Dark."

"How?"

"In my grandfather's days, they would have stuffed the mouths of the dead with garlic, cut off their heads, staked their hearts."

I recoiled in horror, but that brutality seemed tame in light of what I'd just seen.

The old man's gaze scraped the red ceiling in the room beyond. "But, in this case, fire might be best."

"Fire?" I echoed.

"Get some of the men hanging around outside. Tell them to bring me kerosene and matches." He peered into the red room, made a noise. "Lots of kerosene."

I was only too grateful to have the opportunity to flee. I rushed down the stairs to the front door, lurched into fresh air. I was surrounded by dark skirts and legs as I heaved what remained of my breakfast into the grass.

"Kerosene," I panted. "And matches. Herr Stoltz needs kerosene."

But no one moved away to gather them. The throng parted, murmuring, as the Elders flew through the yard. In spite of myself, I shrank back from them.

"There will be no kerosene," the Bishop said, loud enough for all to hear. "There will be no fire."

The Hexenmeister stood in the doorway. His milky eyes seethed. "The Darkness is here. It must not spread. We must burn the bodies."

The Elders climbed the porch, sidestepping my vomit.

"You spread the hysteria of the Outside world. You know better," the Bishop growled at him.

The Hexenmeister stepped back, waved his arm to usher him into the house. "Then come see for yourself." He looked out over the crowd. "All of you. Come see."

No one in the crowd moved. The Bishop's eyes narrowed, and he marched past the old man. The other Elders flocked after him. I saw one cross the threshold, then stop. He did not progress farther.

"They are here. Vampires," the Hexenmeister announced.

The throng chattered among themselves.

"But we are protected!" someone shouted.

The Hexenmeister shook his head. "Not any longer. We must protect ourselves."

The Bishop stalked out of the house. I noticed that he was pale, very pale. But he and the other Elders did a better job of controlling their breakfast than I did. One still remained on the threshold, frozen, with his back turned to the crowd. The Bishop pushed past him.

"This is a terrible loss," the Bishop shouted at the simmering crowd. "But it is a result of human evil. Human violence. Not vampires or some ephemeral Darkness . . ."

"You must burn them," the Hexenmeister insisted, jabbing a bony finger at him. "They are contaminated, and it will spread. You and your pious sensibilities are damning us to death."

"*No,*" the Bishop thundered. Spittle flecked his trembling lip. "They will be granted a decent burial, not burned like . . . like cattle. We are not animals. We have been chosen by God to survive. And we will not disintegrate into savages and fall into the fantasies of the Outside."

The Bishop glowered at the Hexenmeister. "There will be a funeral. Tomorrow, at noon."

He turned his glare on the crowd. "And *you* shall do as the Lord has instructed you to do for funerals. The men here shall wash and prepare the men, and the women shall attend to the women."

The throng visibly shrank back. Some of the Elders looked pale and doubtful, but they nodded in support.

"Remember *Gelassenheit.* Remember the will and the love of God. Be strong in your faith, even in the face of tragedy. Obey and be saved."

The Hexenmeister spat. "Faith is one thing. Survival is another."

The Bishop whirled on him. His voice was low, but I could hear it: "One more word from you, old man, and I will have you shunned, cast out into your own darkness."

The Hexenmeister watched with a level gaze as the Elders moved down the porch steps toward the gate. One Elder remained behind, still facing the interior of the house.

"I don't understand," I whispered. "Why can't they see—?"

The Hexenmeister interrupted me. "They *won't* see. They are a prideful lot, whether or not they choose to admit it. And the Bishop loves power. He'll love it to the very end."

Heads lowered, the men and women in the yard moved toward the house to accomplish the grim task of preparing the dead. The Hexenmeister gripped my wrist. "Find some garlic and stuff it into the mouths of the women, if you can."

"And then what?" I dreaded the answer.

"Then you and your young man meet me back here before sunset." The old man pursed his wrinkly mouth. "I'll bring the kerosene."

———

I scurried into the kitchen, unable to breathe. I opened up the window, let the breeze push the drapes aside. Behind me, above me, in the rest of the house, I could hear gasps and cries as those of us who had been assigned the unfortunate task of taking out the dead saw what had happened, what had become of our neighbors.

I rifled through the cupboards for garlic, at last locating three splintering bulbs in the bottom of a potato sack. I stuffed the bulbs into my apron pockets, confident that no one would smell the garlic on me above the hideous copper stench that clung to the walls.

I minced around the first floor, opening windows. I kept my back to the bodies. Many of the women and even some of the men fled the house in tears, unable to contemplate the job. Eventually, the Elder who had been frozen in the doorway was shoved to the side. He moved out onto the porch, where he began to pray.

I took a deep breath and walked toward Ruth, where she lay on the floor. I stared at her for a long time, overwhelmed by the task before me. I had been to funerals. I had helped prepare my grandmother for burial. I'd washed her with soap and water, lovingly dressed her and set her out on a table with my mother's help. But this . . . this was too much. I didn't know where to start.

"It's all right, dear."

A woman in her sixties stood beside me, Frau Gerlach, the midwife. I had always thought her to be somewhat uptight and disapproving. She always seemed to scowl. But I realized that she and I were the only women remaining in the house. I dimly remembered that her husband had been a butcher.

Frau Gerlach nodded to herself. "Let's take her to the spring room. You grab her head and shoulders; I'll get her feet."

I crouched down beside Ruth, gingerly slipping my hands under her arms. Frau Gerlach grabbed her bare feet.

"Lift."

As I heaved upward, an anguished howl emanated from the doorway. I looked up, half expecting to see that the lone remaining Elder had lost his mind.

But it was Elijah. He stared in horror at the body in our arms, then at my face. He limped into the house, elbowed Frau Gerlach aside. Someone must have driven him here, against all good judgment . . .

Frau Gerlach dropped Ruth's feet. Her legs thudded to the floor and the body pitched to the left. A piece of intestine hit the floor with a wet smack. I struggled to lay her body back down, while Elijah tried to take her from me.

"Elijah, no!" I shouted at him. "She's dead. Leave her alone!"

Elijah sobbed unintelligibly. I felt a short pang of sympathy for him.

Frau Gerlach shouted into the yard for some men who were able to stomach handling the living. Two men dragged Elijah from the house, kicking and yelling.

I sank to my knees with Ruth's heavy head in my lap.

Frau Gerlach bent down beside me. "We can make quick work of this. I promise."

I nodded numbly. We picked up Ruth's body again and descended down a short series of steps behind the kitchen to the spring room.

The Hersberger spring room was larger than ours and more modern, with running water. We awkwardly wrestled the limp corpse into a bathtub. Dim light filtered in from a basement window that Frau Gerlach tugged open. She reached for a lantern, lit it, and I was instantly grateful for the warm yellow light it cast. I didn't think that I could bear to be alone in the dark with Ruth's body.

"Now what?" I panted.

Frau Gerlach stared at the dead girl. She fingered the shower curtain. "Find scissors. And a set of clothes for her."

I scurried to the laundry area of the spring room, popped open the lid of the gas dryer. I prayed to find some of Ruth's clothes here. I did not want to go upstairs again.

I found one of her dresses, an apron, and a bonnet in a laundry basket. I located a pair of shoes that looked like they might fit her beside the door upstairs and snatched some scissors from the kitchen. I did not make eye contact with the two men who were staring at Ruth's brother and Herr Hersberger with their hands in their pockets. The Hexenmeister stood with them. His hand was behind his back, and I saw garlic in it.

I fled back downstairs to the spring room. Frau Gerlach took the scissors from me to cut the nightdress from Ruth's body. She clucked as she looked at the dripping mess in her abdomen. She handed me the scissors and gestured to the shower curtain with her chin.

"Cut that into two-foot-wide strips."

I ripped the shower curtain down, spread it out on the floor, and began to measure it out using my forearm. Frau Gerlach looked over my shoulder.

"Very good. I'm going upstairs for some twine. I'll be back."

Her footsteps receded, and I finished cutting the strips with my back to Ruth. I wasn't ready to face her. Not yet.

But I had to.

I turned around, crept to the bathtub.

Ruth lay like a gangly spider, sprawled on the porcelain. She was all legs and breasts, I noticed. Well, what wasn't torn open by the vampires. Frau Gerlach had turned her so that the remaining blood trickled from her belly down the drain. She had closed the girl's eyes. Her ruddy matted hair was stuck to one side of her head.

I touched her forehead. I was sorry that I'd hated her. Truly sorry.

I reached into my pocket, broke apart one of the garlic bulbs. I had only three, so I had to figure out a way to make this last. I plucked out three cloves, reached for her mouth.

Awkwardly, I stuffed my fingers into her mouth to pry apart her teeth. My stomach turned when I heard something pop. But I ignored my nausea and jammed the cloves under her swollen tongue. I thought I heard a small hiss of air escaping as I did so.

I shuddered, pulled my fingers back. I braced one hand on the top of her head, the other on her chin, and closed her jaws. I brushed away a small fragment of garlic at her lip, then let out a shaking breath. I wasn't sure exactly what this was supposed to accomplish, but I was more than willing to obey the Hexenmeister.

Frau Gerlach returned to the room with a spool of scratchy brown twine.

"At least those men are useful for something," she grumbled. "Ask them to do something that has nothing to do with blood, and they're all over it."

I cracked a smile.

She nodded at me. "Men are essentially useless for the difficult things in life. For births and deaths, one clearheaded woman is more useful than a half-dozen men."

She knelt beside the body. "Go get me one of those strips from the shower curtain you cut."

I brought one to her. I had no idea what she intended.

She blew a steel-gray piece of hair out of her eyes. "We're going to pretend that she's a package. We're going to wrap the curtain around her to hold the insides in and tie it with twine."

I swallowed. "What do you need me to do?"

"Get behind her at the back of the bathtub and prop her into a sitting position. I'll need you to hold her arms up while I wrap."

It was easier said than done. Ruth was simply dead weight, and it was difficult to keep her upright. Frau Gerlach quickly wrapped her with the shower curtain from her armpits to her thighs, trying to stuff bits of her intestines back into the cavity. She then followed her tracks with the twine, tying very tightly to make sure that nothing escaped, as if Ruth were a rump roast.

Then we washed her. Frau Gerlach was all business, scrubbing at the blood stains on Ruth's skin with a sponge and soap. She didn't fill the tub, not wanting to loosen the twine. I gingerly scrubbed at Ruth's hair with shampoo, rinsing red from it under the tap.

"Go ahead and scrub, girl. Ruth's in no condition to mind."

But, despite the garlic, I wondered if she really did.

We dragged Ruth out of the tub and awkwardly stuffed her into her dress. We were barely able to pin it shut over the bundle around her midsection, but we tried. Frau Gerlach tied Ruth's shoes on her feet, while I tucked her soggy hair into a bonnet. I tried to do a decent job, make it look good.

Not that it mattered. I knew that the Hexenmeister would see this house in flames before the night had fallen.

We laid Ruth on the floor of the spring room, then went upstairs to turn our attention to her mother. Frau Gerlach harrumphed at the men still standing around, staring at the two dead men.

We climbed the stairs to the parents' bedroom. Frau Gerlach put her hands on her hips, contemplating the woman impaled on the bedpost.

"Huh," she said. "I think it would have been easier if they let the Hexenmeister burn the house."

I swallowed.

"Katie, go tell one of those men to find me a hacksaw. There's no point in trying to save the furniture."

———

I remained at the Hersberger house until late in the afternoon, side by side with Frau Gerlach. I worked numbly, following her terse directions, dimly aware of the passage of time. Outdoors, a few men were making simple caskets out of sheets of pine. The Hexenmeister had disappeared, and I assumed that he had gone to make preparations for the evening. Everyone else avoided the house.

We had to take down the bedpost, and Frau Hersberger landed on the floor in an awkward pile. But we succeeded in getting her cleaned, wrapped up, dressed, and lined up next to Ruth on the spring room floor. I managed to slip some garlic in her mouth when Frau Gerlach's back was turned.

The four sisters were more problematic.

I followed Frau Gerlach into their bedroom with my eyes shut. I smelled blood, felt my shoes sticking to the floor. My breath was shallow, and I could feel my own living blood rushing in my ears.

I heard Frau Gerlach's footsteps in the sticky mess, tracking back and forth, and her breathing. I heard her open a window.

"Katie," she said, with unusual gentleness.

I forced myself to open my eyes.

The girls had been torn to pieces. Bits of flesh and bone were strewn from wall to wall. I saw a small arm reaching from under the bed and fixed my eyes on that. At first, I thought it was a doll's—but then it registered that it was the limb of a young girl.

I looked down. I was standing on a girl's finger. I backed up, balled my fists, and was preparing to flee. The room spun crazily around me: the reddened quilts, the smears on the walls, the human leg cast upon a half-full hope chest, a doll face-down in blood. I stared at it, unsure whether to retrieve it and clean it up or let it be.

"Katie," Frau Gerlach repeated. She shook me.

I forced myself to look at her. "How . . .?" I had no idea what the Elders expected us to do with this.

"Ask the men to bring us four boxes from the yard."

"But how . . ." I couldn't imagine trying to sort the limbs and cleaning.

"We will do the best we can," she said firmly. "God will understand. And if the Elders don't . . . Well, they're not here."

I nodded, then walked robotically away, down the stairs and into the sunshine of the yard to ask the men for the boxes.

My father was there. I blinked tears at him, relieved that he'd come. He put his arms around me, and I embraced him gratefully, willing myself not to cry, not yet. He smoothed my hair back from my face, offered me some water. I saw him staring at a red stain on my rolled-up sleeve, at the red on my apron. "I came as soon as I heard."

I nodded, taking a small sip of water before my stomach turned.

"She's a good girl." Frau Gerlach had come up behind me, put her hand on my shoulder. "She is a strong girl. The only strong one here. She is helping me attend the women. You should be proud of her."

My father looked at me with sad pride. "I know."

My lip quivered. "I have to help Frau Gerlach. There's . . . there's a lot to do."

He nodded. "I will tell your mother."

I kissed him on the cheek quickly and turned back to Frau Gerlach, who had chosen four small hollow boxes that stood beside the door. She left the lids on the grass.

We carried them to the girls' room, arranged them on the floor.

"There is not enough left to fill these boxes." Frau Gerlach sighed.

"How do we know . . ." I looked around the room. "How do we know what belongs to . . . whom?"

She shook her head. "God will take them however he finds them. And the congregation does not need to see them. We will just do our best."

We began with the larger pieces, putting them in the boxes according to size. I merely wanted to get through with the task. I slipped a clove of garlic into each box, though I only found two pieces of jaw and part of a scalp. I put the ruined doll into the box that had the smallest body parts in it.

We worked for an hour in silence, before Frau Gerlach stood and said, "*Ja,* that is enough."

She stared up at the late-afternoon light on the ceiling. "They will have to have the service outdoors. There will not be enough time to clean the house before then."

I was relieved. I could not imagine all the buckets that it would take to scrub this place clean.

"You have done well, Katie," Frau Gerlach said. "You would make a fine midwife someday, if you ever wished to learn."

I cast my eyes down, exhausted and shy and afraid and proud all at once. "All I have managed so far is to be a midwife to the puppies."

She reached out to pat my cheek with a bloody hand. "God smiles on those who quietly do his dirty work, my girl."

CHAPTER NINETEEN

The sun was slipping toward the horizon by the time I'd trudged back to the kennel. I hauled aside the heavy door. I was exhausted, but there was still work to do.

"It's Katie," I called softly.

Copper raced up to me, and I knelt down to rub his ears. He sniffed at me dubiously, flattened his ears.

"I'm sorry, boy." I surely reeked like a slaughterhouse, but there was nothing to be done for it. If I headed directly home, I knew that my mother would fling me into the bathtub, stuff me full of soup, and not allow me out for the rest of the day.

Alex ambled up to me, a sly smile on his face. He was eating an apple.

"Where did you get that?" I snapped.

He shrugged. "From the apple tree out back . . . They're a little wormy, but that's just extra protein. You shouldn't be outside, Bonnet. Sunset's coming." He fixed his gaze on my stained apron. "What happened?"

I blew out a deep breath. "A family was found dead this morning."

"Dead?"

"Killed by vampires." I shut my eyes. "It was awful."

He knelt beside me and put his arm around my shoulders. "I'm sorry."

I nodded, leaning into the warmth of his side. "I spoke with the Hexenmeister."

"Did he have any ideas?"

"He does. But the Elders don't believe him."

"Don't believe him? Or don't want to believe him?"

"Some of both. The Hexenmeister wanted to burn down the house with the bodies in it, but the Bishop wouldn't let him."

Alex looked at me. "This place will be overrun. Vamps pop up faster than Whac-a-Moles."

I didn't bother to ask him what a Whac-a-Mole was. I nodded. "I know. But the Hexenmeister wants to try to stop them. He's asked us to meet him at the Hersberger house before sunset."

"Wait . . . he wants 'us'?"

"I told him everything." I looked up at him. "He won't hurt you. He needs your help."

Alex lifted a brow. "Your wizard wants to play a little arson?"

"I assume so."

"I like burning things. I think." He screwed up his face. "Last thing I set fire to was a couch in college. This will be way cooler."

I elbowed him in the ribs. "There is nothing 'cool' about this."

"Just a little levity. Though . . . not every guy gets to go play firebug with a wizard and Bonnet the Vampire Slayer."

I was going to tell him that he had no idea what was in that house, but . . . maybe he did. Instead, I asked: "How's Sunny?"

"She's okay. I think. I keep staring at her and fidgeting. I think she's annoyed at that." His tone suddenly turned doubtful. I was reminded of what Frau Gerlach had said about men being useless in death and childbirth.

I lifted myself off the floor and trotted back to the paddock. Sunny was wrapped up in Alex's blanket. Her tail thumped when she saw me.

"Hi, girl. How's my mama-to-be?"

She licked my face. I unwrapped her from the blanket and ran my hands over her belly. The puppies felt calm. Her head was cool. I bent down to kiss her ear.

"Has she been drinking and eating?"

"She had dog food this morning. She hasn't had much of an appetite since then, though she's been drinking. She hasn't moved except to go outside to pee."

"I think she'll be ready to go in the next day, definitely." I arranged the blanket back over her body. "It's nice of you to share your blanket with her."

He sniffed his sleeve. "I think I smell like dog, though."

"Better than smelling like a butcher shop."

He leaned over and sniffed my neck. "I also detect garlic."

I grimaced at him. I wasn't much in the mood for play. Once Alex saw the Hersberger house, I was betting that he wouldn't be, either.

I was terrified to take Alex into our world.

I tugged his sleeves down over his wrist bones to hide his

tattoos, insisted that his suspenders were straight, and jammed Joseph's old hat over his eyes. I hoped that he would pass for Plain from a distance, hoped that no one would get too close. He let me fuss over him like a mother hen before reminding me: "Daylight's burning."

I led him out of the barn, my sweaty hand in his. The sun cast our shadows long over the striped fields. I hoped that anyone who spied us from afar would think that we were simply young lovers enjoying the molten evening and leave us be.

I hoped.

I took him the long way through the fields, away from the roads. "How far is it?" he asked.

"Just ahead." I pointed to a dot on the horizon. "That house."

We approached slowly, and the dot resolved to a white house surrounded by a white fence. The front door was shut. There were no buggies or horses tied up at the gate, but I was still uncertain that the house was empty. Pine boxes stood empty against the side of the house — the larger ones for Ruth, her brother, and their parents. The small ones were still inside.

"Stay here," I ordered, pointing to a tall hay bale.

Alex shook his head. "There are . . . bodies in there. There could be more than you're reckoning. I'm coming with you."

"I'll check and make sure that no one's there. I'll come out on the porch and wave for you to come in."

He looked at me dubiously.

"I have the *Himmelsbrief*." I patted my pocket. "You can hear me scream from this distance."

He acquiesced. "Five minutes."

Neither one of us had a watch, but it sounded good. I nodded sharply. "Five minutes."

I stepped out from behind the bale. Sweat broke out on the back of my neck. I was about to enter this house, full of dead, all alone.

Resolutely, I put one foot before the other, until I reached the gate. I unlatched it and let myself into the yard. The shadow of the house fell over me, the sun behind it. I was all too aware that the vampires only needed a shadow to survive, mentally calculating how many steps it was from the door to the patch of sun beyond the gate.

Something white moved in the corner of my eye, and a squeak escaped my lips. But it was only the white horse, standing at the edge of the fence.

I whistled to him. But he stood, rooted, on the other side of the yard. It was as if he sensed where the property line was. He could smell it. Smell the death here.

I walked up to the front step. The front door was closed but unlocked, and the windows were still open to give the house the opportunity to air out. The knob was slick on my hand as I shoved the door open.

"Hello?" I called. My voice was dry and cracked. I licked my lips. "Herr Stoltz? Frau Gerlach?"

Silence radiated through the building.

"Anyone there?"

No one answered me. And I was too afraid to continue farther alone.

I turned on my heel, walked down the step. I lifted my hand to wave to Alex but dropped it down to my side.

A plume of dust was lifting down the dirt road. I squinted, trying to distinguish who it was. A familiar figure held the reins, nodded to me as he pulled his horses up to the gate. The Hexenmeister.

I hurried to meet him.

The old man eased himself down from the step of his buggy. Herr Stoltz had a two-seated courting buggy, like Elijah. Only his was much, much older and showed bits of rust at the seams and along the inside tracks of the wheels. He tied his graying black mare to the fence post. The horse flicked her ears at the house, turned away.

"It's okay, girl," the Hexenmeister muttered at her. "We won't be long." He glanced at the opposite side of the yard, at the white horse frozen in place.

"I dinna recognize that horse."

My mouth flattened. "He's from Outside. I found him a few days ago . . . with a bloody saddle. And a foot still in the stirrup. I hoped that he would just go on . . ."

He whistled for the horse, muttered something in Hochdeutsch that the breeze ripped away before I could distinguish it. The horse picked its way carefully around the perimeter of the property and joined the black mare at the fence. Herr Stoltz shook some oats from his pocket, let the shy horse eat from his palm.

"*Ja,* there is evil in that house." He explained, "A white horse is a sign of God's purity. It will not willingly walk where the Darkness falls." He rubbed the horse's nose. "Where's your friend?"

I gestured with my chin. "There."

Alex emerged from behind the haystack, his hands loose at his side and his head lowered. I could not see his face beneath this hat. My heart quickened uncomfortably, and not just because I was exposing him to the possibility of discovery.

The Hexenmeister looked him up and down as he approached. "Good evening, young man."

The Outsider stuck his hand out. "I'm Alex. You must be the wizard."

The Hexenmeister took his hand, smiled. "*Ja.* I'm Stoltz. Thank you for . . . helping with this difficult work."

"No problem, sir."

I was startled at that bit of awkward politeness from Alex.

The Hexenmeister gestured to a brown paper bag on the seat of his buggy. "Please take that and come into the house. We must begin."

Alex grabbed the paper sack, and we followed the Hexenmeister into the house of the dead.

"Jesus Christ," Alex muttered.

The house had not been cleaned. Violence still stained the floors and walls. But the bodies were peaceful. On the kitchen table, Herr Hersberger lay, fully dressed, his hands folded over his chest. A hat covered the ruins of his face. His son lay on the floor beside him.

"Bring the bag here," the Hexenmeister ordered. Alex placed it on the kitchen table, and the Hexenmeister's withered hands dug into the sack. He laid out a crude wooden stake of green wood, a steel hammer, and a hacksaw.

I swallowed with an audible click.

The old man grasped the stake in one hand, the hammer in

the other. "It must go through the heart," he said quietly. "Like this."

He set the point of the stake on Herr Hersberger's chest. I flinched when he struck it with a hammer. No blood came from the wound as he hammered, with a soft sound like tenderizing a steak.

I swayed, and Alex put his arm around me.

I began reciting the Lord's Prayer in a small, quavering voice.

The stake hit the back of the table with a hard, solid sound, like a nail in a wood block.

I sucked in my breath. "Is it done?"

"No." The Hexenmeister set his tools down and rested for a few moments. "The head must be taken." His hands shook as he reached for the saw. He set the blade against Herr Hersberger's throat and drew it back like a violinist with a bow.

The first strokes were easy. The blade slipped through flesh until it hit bone. The Hexenmeister grunted as the blade skipped and embedded itself in the table, jammed. The hat fell off the remains of Herr Hersberger's head, releasing a handful of flies.

"Let me," Alex said, quietly. He took the saw from the old man, pushed Hersberger's neck to the edge of the table, and finished the job with two awkward strokes.

"Good," the old man said. "Now the son."

We repeated the process with the younger man. I held the stake for the Hexenmeister, and Alex took the head.

Herr Stoltz wiped sweat from his forehead, looked upstairs. "The little girls are still up there?"

"Ja." I cast my eyes downward. "What is left of them."

We clomped up the staircase to the bedroom. The girls' room was cheerfully drenched in sunlight, a breezed brushing through the ruffled curtains. The boxes had the lids pressed in place to keep the flies out, but they were not nailed shut yet. The Hexenmeister pushed the lids aside with his cane, inspected the contents.

"I put the garlic in the boxes," I said, helplessly, my fingers winding together at my waist. "I didn't know where to put it."

Alex sucked in his breath, glanced at my rust-colored apron. "This . . . this is what you've been doing all day?"

"*Ja,*" I said, numbly. "Picking up the pieces."

The Hexenmeister shook his head. "There is nothing more for us to do here." He patted my sleeve. "You have done well. Now, where is the mother and the other sister?"

"In the spring room," I said. "Frau Gerlach and I were able to . . . make them presentable."

The Hexenmeister frowned. "You should not have left them in the basement. It is too close to earth. Too dark."

My mouth went dry. I remembered the wraiths from the Laundromat, and my stomach twisted. "Frau Gerlach wanted to keep them where it was cool. Away from the flies."

"Come. We must work faster."

The Hexenmeister stumped from the room. Alex and I followed in his wake. We gathered in the kitchen, before the closed basement door. The old man opened it, and meager sunlight trickled down the steps.

"Katie," he said softly. "Bring a lantern."

I scurried to obey, turning up the wick of a kerosene lantern on the kitchen counter and lighting it with a long match.

I traded glances with Alex. The Hexenmeister puttered around the hall closet, then came back with Herr Hersberger's hunting rifle. He loaded it with bullets from his pocket.

"Guns don't work on vampires," Alex said automatically.

"No, they don't," the Hexenmeister agreed. "But they will slow them down."

"I'll go first," Alex said.

The Hexenmeister nodded slowly and handed him the rifle.

We descended.

The basement appeared as I had left it. A small square of sunlight came in from the window, between the bathtub and the washer and dryer. Ruth and her mother lay side by side, as if they slept. The sun shone down on them, casting artificial warmth on their chests.

Alex crept across the dirt floor, poked Frau Hersberger with the barrel of the gun. She did not move.

"*Ja*. We are in time." The Hexenmeister came to his knees beside Frau Hersberger. His arthritic hand shook on the stake. Alex took the stake from him and grabbed the hammer.

I took the bloody tools from Alex. "I can do it." I *should* do it; these were my people, not his. And I had seen to the other preparations for their deaths.

I set the point of the stake over Frau Hersberger's breast. "Here?"

"*Ja.*"

I lifted the hammer and swung. The first blow sickened me, and the stake went in at an angle.

"Keep going, Katie."

I straightened the stake and struck again. I felt a rib shatter and hit timidly.

"Harder."

I hit it harder.

"Again."

The stake sank deep into her chest.

"Again."

I struck again and the point hit the dirt floor.

"Good girl." The Hexenmeister clapped my shoulder to draw me back, and Alex set in with the saw.

I looked away. It seemed such a perversion, to care for the bodies with such reverence and now destroy them.

"Last one," the Hexenmeister said, as Alex pulled Frau Hersberger's body away to clear the path to Ruth.

I fished in the paper sack for a stake, my fingers tight around it. I pressed the stake over a pin in Ruth's dress, a pin I'd carefully set there. To be sure, I'd fantasized about slapping Ruth. Maybe even choking her. Or running over her with a buggy.

But this was different. This was real. Too real.

I swung with the hammer, missed. The hammer bounced off her sternum.

"Concentrate, Katie," the old man said behind me.

I pressed the hammer to the back of the stake, lifted it. I had to finish this job. I struck down hard. The stake tore her dress, split her skin, and drove the pin deep away from sight.

I struck again, without his urging.

Again.

Hate bubbled up in me, coursing through my arms. I hated Ruth. I knew that I should feel compassion for her, lying here on the floor, torn and dead and held together with twine and a shower curtain. And I was destroying her again. A tear rolled down my cheek. I grunted as I swung with all my might, feeling the anger course through me, as if she were the one to blame for the dissolution of my relationship with Elijah. Not God.

It was easier to blame her.

"Katie." Alex grabbed my arm on the upswing, and I struggled. Only then did I realize that I'd driven the stake deep into the dirt, embedding it beyond sight. I was simply pulping the flesh that I'd so carefully rinsed and tied together.

I landed on my backside, gasping, as he took the hammer from me. I drew my hands back to my chest, crept up close to Ruth on my knees.

I looked her full in her face. "Ruth, I'm sorry," I whispered.

"Ruth," Alex echoed. "*That* Ruth?"

My face flamed in shame. My rage at the dead girl was reprehensible. I was shocked that it had bubbled up now, at a time demanding compassion.

I closed my eyes. "*Ja.* That one." I wanted to feel the sun on my face now, to feel God's favor. But the sun and God's favor had moved away, leaving me cold.

I was slammed back to the floor by a hand on my shoulder. My eyes snapped open, and I scrabbled back on my hands and knees in startlement. Alex stood over me, the gun trained on Ruth.

I jammed my fist in my mouth, stifling a cry. The dead girl had turned her head toward me, her eyes burning red. She opened her mouth and hissed, reaching for me.

But she couldn't get to me with those pale fingers. She was

pinned to the dirt floor by the stake, squirming like a spider caught on a pin. Her fiery gaze boiled on me with hate. Maybe even more hate than I'd fixed on her.

"The saw!" Herr Stoltz cried.

I crawled along the floor, my hands closing around the saw handle. Alex stood on Ruth's nearest wrist, and the Hexenmeister fixed her head in place with his cane jammed in her frothing mouth. I smelled garlic.

I wedged myself between them, dodging her free arm. I set the saw blade against the tender white flesh of her throat. She kicked and howled as I drew the blade back, fighting and struggling until I hit the tough bones in the back of her neck.

I reached inside myself, for that last trickle of the cold well of hate, and ripped the saw through the bone.

The last bit of artificial life in her dimmed out as her head rolled free and came to a rest next to the dryer.

The three of us, tangled in silence, stared at the head.

Alex was first to speak. "There was talk of fire?"

"*Ja,*" the Hexenmeister said, struggling to stand. "There will be fire."

We scoured the house and the outbuildings for every drop of kerosene we could find: from the lamps, cans in the shed, even from the clothes iron. The Hexenmeister instructed us to cover Frau Hersberger and Ruth first, then the men in the living room. The last of it was cast about in the girls' room.

"The fire will rise," Herr Stoltz said. "And there's unlikely to be enough left for them to knit back together, anyway."

I stood at the top of the basement stairs and lit a match. I tossed it down like a falling star. At first, it seemed as if nothing happened. Then blue flames raced across the dirt floor to engulf the women.

I turned and ran through the kitchen. Alex lit a book of matches and threw them on the floor, beside the Hersberger boy. Flames swept up from his body to ignite his father on the kitchen table.

We raced from the house to meet the Hexenmeister in the yard.

"Come on," he said, gesturing for us to climb into the buggy. He was already perched on the seat and holding the reins. The white horse stayed at the side of the black one, and it seemed that there was no getting rid of him.

"There's not room," I protested. But Alex had already grabbed me by the waist and was shoving me up into the buggy.

"Scoot over, Bonnet," he said as he swung up. "We're gonna get friendly."

I wound up awkwardly sprawled on Alex's lap as the Hexenmeister drove the buggy away. I could see no sign of fire, except for a bit of smoke from the open living room window.

The sun was setting, blazing beautiful orange on the horizon as Herr Stoltz's black mare trotted down the road. The white horse fell into step beside her, as if he were part of a hitched team.

I turned around to watch until the house was out of sight.

The Hexenmeister took Alex back to the kennel and me to my house, leaving us with stern warnings to stay indoors. There were still more vampires out there. As the Hexenmeister said: "More work to do."

I let myself into my house while the sun was still at the horizon. As expected, my mother rushed to the door to meet me and hustle my blood-smeared appearance away from Sarah's eyes. She drew me a hot bath. I protested, not wanting to be in the dark by myself.

My mother stayed. As if I were a small child, she undressed me, then scrubbed my back with a washrag and fresh soap. She washed my hair, cared for me just as thoroughly as I'd cared for Ruth and her mother.

Guilt closed my throat, and I choked back a sob.

"It's all right, *liewe,*" my mother murmured. She gathered my head to her shoulder and let me cry, smoothing my wet hair. "You are such a good girl. I'm so proud of you."

When I looked at her, her eyes were brimming with such tears of pride that I hated myself.

After I dried off, my mother dressed me like a doll, in a nightgown and a pair of thick socks that she'd knitted for winter.

When we climbed the stairs, I saw that darkness had fallen. My father and Sarah sat by the fireplace reading the Bible. He smiled at me with that same heartbreaking expression of pride. Ginger sat beside them, looking at me with interminable sadness and fear. The afghan she was crocheting had grown longer, from her lap almost down to her ankles. She showed few other signs of life. Since her link to the Outside had been destroyed, she had seemed to collapse in on herself. I was afraid for her.

"I'll make you some soup," my mother said.

"Thank you," I said, around the guilty lump in my throat.

I crossed to the front window, turned the lock on the door. I saw a small dot of orange on the northern horizon.

I drew the curtains.

We were all learning to fear the darkness.

CHAPTER TWENTY

We gathered for the funeral the next day, circling around the ashes of the Hersberger house.

Unimpaired by rain or human intervention, the house had burned down to its foundations. The support beams, second floor, and roof had collapsed on the first floor, leaving a blackened mess. Smoke still issued from embers deep inside the structure.

Our funeral traditions had not changed in three hundred years. We did not bring flowers, drape caskets, or eulogize the dead. We did listen to a sermon and prayers, but there was no singing. And we did organize viewings at the home and bury the dead in our cemetery, all with feet facing east.

Those graves in the cemetery would remain open. The pallbearers were at a loss. The benches for church were brought to the Hersbergers' front yard and arranged as usual, but there were no bodies to weep over.

We looked to the Elders for what to do. They gathered in a tight knot next to the structure. I sat quietly with my mother and Sarah among the rest of the female side of the congregation, my head lowered. Ginger sat beside me, dressed in her

Plain clothes and looking defeated. She seemed locked in her own world, occasionally humming to herself.

Snatches of conversation swept past my ears:

"Is that the Outsider woman?"

"Do you think she's really crazy?"

". . . did you see the fire last night?"

". . . maybe someone was trying to cover their tracks . . ."

"Maybe it was the Hexenmeister. He is crazy."

"No, he's too frail to commit such an act on his own."

I glanced around and saw many of the men and women who were too fearful to enter the Hersberger house. Frau Gerlach nodded at me from a nearby bench, her posture prim and ramrod-straight. Her apron was pure white and her bonnet sharply starched. One would never know that she'd spent yesterday smeared in gore.

I didn't see the Hexenmeister, which worried me.

Elijah and his father sat near the front of the men's section. Elijah's shoulders were a broken line of grief. I shuddered, recalling the feeling of the hammer striking the stake into Ruth's chest.

I saw him rise, walk back toward us. I stared down at my hands, hoping that he didn't mean to speak to me. But his shadow stopped before me, and I was forced to look up.

"Thank you," he said. His face was open, vulnerable. "Thank you for what you did for Ruth and the girls."

I nodded, swallowing the lump in my throat. I could not meet his eyes.

"Can I . . ." he began. "Can I come by to see you sometime?"

I flicked a panicked glance up at him.

"Just . . . just to talk?"

My grip on my own fingers tightened. I nodded shortly, just to get him away from me.

He shuffled off. My mother reached over Sarah and put her hands on mine.

"See?" she whispered. *"Gelassenheit."*

Bile burned the back of my throat. I wanted to tell her that *Gelassenheit* had nothing to do with it.

The cluster of men in black at the front broke apart. The Bishop stood before us with his *Ausbund* in hand.

"God has taken the Hersberger family from us, brought them to his kingdom. We should be grateful to our Lord Jesus for bringing them home."

My hands tightened into fists. *Grateful?* I bit the inside of my cheek until I tasted blood.

". . . God has a plan for us, here on earth. It may seem inscrutable. Unknowable. But our faith in the Lord will bring us through this time of violence, to his kingdom and reunion with our loved ones in heaven. Only through faith, love, and obedience to his will shall we reach the kingdom."

I let his words wash over me. They were, I realized, meaningless to me. I watched him read aloud from the *Ausbund,* reciting hymns that we usually sung. My attention wandered to the smoke rising from the back of the house. It didn't smell like the slaughterhouse of yesterday. It simply smelled of burning wood. Pure. Cleansing.

Since there was no point in going to the cemetery, the funeral disbanded early. The congregation scattered like blown dandelion fluff. I still didn't see the Hexenmeister among them, not even when I climbed the high step on my family's buggy to survey the crowd.

His absence chewed on me as I worked my chores. I had little to do: laundry for myself and the Millers, picking pumpkins, searching for some wild sarsaparilla for tea and wild onions for stew. My mother had given me just enough to keep me occupied, to keep my thoughts from churning.

But they still churned, spiraling like blood down the dark drain of the Hersberger bathtub.

Self-loathing soaked through me. I hated what I had done yesterday. I hated how I had felt about it. I could feel myself falling into darkness, into a strange world that looked like my own on the surface but was full of bloody secrets underneath.

Only one of my secrets filled me with warmth: Alex. I was relieved to have someone beside me and the old Hexenmeister. Someone who was willing to do the Lord's dirty work with me. Someone who I could be honest with.

He was as far from Elijah as a man could get. But he was a good man. I knew it in my heart . . . my heart that skipped when he was beside me. I had not ever experienced that buzz of emotion with Elijah. I didn't know what to call it. But it — and he — fascinated me. And I was afraid that I was falling for him. Falling for a secret.

I ranged far from the house with my basket in search of the sweet root. I found that my feet took me north, and I followed them straight to the Hexenmeister's house.

But as his house came into view, I realized that Herr Stoltz was not alone.

One of the Elders stood on the front porch. And he was holding a gun.

My heart lurched into my chest. Had something happened to the old man? Had they hurt him?

Screwing up my courage, I crossed the road to the house. I held my basket primly before me, thankful to have it as a plausible excuse. "Is Herr Stoltz home? I have brought him some sarsaparilla and onions."

The Elder on the porch regarded me with skepticism. "*Ja.* He is home. But he is not taking visitors."

"Oh. I hope he is not ill?"

"No. He is not ill. But he is not allowed visitors."

I blinked. "He is not *allowed* visitors?" The old man had always done as he pleased. I glanced at the front window, through the glass, and my heart sank. I saw Herr Stoltz sitting at his desk. And the Bishop stood before him. The look on his face was such a wrath as I had never seen.

The Elder moved to block my view. "The Bishop says he is to stay here. He has violated the Ordnung. No one speaks to him."

My eyes slid to the rifle. I understood: Herr Stoltz was a prisoner in his own home. The Bishop has found out or suspected his hand in the fire that consumed the Hersberger house.

My eyes widened, and I blurted: "Is he under the *Bann?*"

"No. Not yet, anyway."

I lamely held the basket before me. "Could you please give these to him?"

"You can leave them here. I will give them to him if the Bishop says it's okay."

I nodded, handed him the basket, and walked briskly away from the house. I walked until I was out of sight of the guard.

And then I fled.

At first, I headed south, toward home. I wanted to tell my mother, have her comfort me. I wanted my father to listen, to feel his protective shadow over me.

But I was learning that some things were beyond them, their powers to understand or their strength. This was one of them.

I veered south and east, toward the kennel. There was one person who would listen to me.

I hauled open the barn door, flooding the straw floor with light.

Alex rushed to the sound of the door reeling back. His sleeves were rolled up to his elbows, and he was holding a bucket of water that splashed onto the knees of his britches. A worry mark deepened his brow.

"Jesus, Bonnet. Thank God you're here."

"What's wrong?" I dreaded his answer.

He gestured helplessly to the back. "The dog . . . she's in labor. I think. I don't know." He set down the bucket and rubbed the back of his neck with his hand. "You've got good timing."

"*Ja*," I said darkly. "I have excellent timing in all things."

He searched my face. "Look, don't worry about . . . about last night. Your wizard is working on it. The old man's got some vinegar in him. He'll have all of your folk outfitted with *Himmelsbriefs*—or is it *Himmelsbriefen?* Anyway, he'll have you guys set up before long. The vamps will move on, and maybe by then the military will have—"

"Herr Stoltz has been imprisoned."

He caught my elbow. "What do you mean, imprisoned? By the English?"

"No. By the Elders. There is a man with a gun, an Elder guarding his house. And the Bishop is there. I fear that they may put him under the *Bann*."

"The *Bann* . . . Excommunicate him?"

I nodded fiercely. *"Ja.* If he does not confess and repent.*"

"They'd be fools to do it!" he exclaimed. "The old wizard is their only hope."

"I know it, and you know it. But they will not allow him to flout the rules like that."

"But—"

"We will talk of this more. But show me Sunny," I insisted. I might have no control over what the Bishop did to Herr Stoltz, but I could at the very least make sure that Sunny was safe.

"She's here."

I followed him to the back paddock. The dog lay on her blanket, uncovered. Her sides twitched, and her front paws moved, as if she were dreaming. She rolled her brown eyes up at me.

"Shhh, girl. It's all right." I knelt beside her, stroked her sides.

"Gah," Alex said. "Is that what I think it is?"

I rinsed my hands in the bucket, then reached for the tiny gummy bundle that Sunny pushed out onto the straw. Sunny licked at it, worrying at the puppy while I pulled open the protective sack.

"Get me some scissors, would you? And some of the clean towels on the shelf beside the door."

"Got it." He sped away as fast as his feet could carry him.

I smiled to myself. The events of the last days may have left me shocked and stupefied. But this . . . this I could handle.

I rubbed the puppy gently in my lap with a corner of the blanket to stimulate its circulation. I lifted it to my ear, felt its heart beat and the flutter of its breathing. His tiny, delicate paws twitched, and I set him back beside Sunny's belly. She began to serenely lick the top of his head.

Alex returned with the towels and scissors. Copper peered around the corner, whining.

"It's okay, boys." I chuckled, setting the scissors to the umbilical cord. "I think that Frau Gerlach might be right about your gender."

"What?"

"Never mind."

There was something reassuring about the normal, orderly process of birth. I smiled and cooed at the puppies as they came, one after the other. Copper developed enough nerve to lay down in the stall, and Alex sidled in behind him. I handed him one of the puppies.

He held it in his hands — hands that I remembered decapitating people just yesterday. I could see the terror on his face that he might drop it. He cradled the puppy close to his chest. "So tiny. And his eyes aren't even open."

"Her eyes. That one's a her."

"Eh. How can you tell?" He picked up a puppy and squinted at its tail region.

"The usual way." I grinned as I rubbed the latest arrival down with a towel. There was little to see except to the trained eye.

"Bonnet, did anyone ever tell you that you're a smart-ass?"

"No," I said innocently. "Plain folk don't use that kind of language."

He snorted.

There were four puppies born over the afternoon. Four and the afterbirth, which Alex grimaced at. I took it away before Sunny had a chance to eat it. Though, in retrospect, it might have given me some small satisfaction to allow her to do it and disgust the Outsider.

I sat with my back to the paddock wall beside Alex, watching Sunny nose the puppies into position to nurse. Copper dozed in the straw, his tail slapping occasionally as he dreamed.

Alex casually draped his arm around me. And, for a moment, the world seemed right and good. The puppies were all healthy and perfect. Sunshine streamed in through the slats of the barn. I smelled sweet straw and snuggled up to Alex's chest.

As I felt the joy growing in me to see the puppies making their way safely into the world, I also felt a pang of sorrow.

Alex must have sensed me frowning against his chest. He tucked a piece of my hair behind my ear. My ear tingled at that light touch. "I've been thinking about what you said. About Stoltz. Your Elders. And your Bishop."

At this moment, in the dazzling sunshine, I was more afraid

of the men in black than the Hexenmeister's terrible Darkness. "You have a plan? A plan to free Herr Stoltz?"

"Not exactly. If they found Stoltz, they're going to be on a witch-hunt."

"We are a nonviolent people, but . . ." I sighed. "It seems that their word is law. Now more than ever . . . and for things beyond the Ordnung. Without discussion."

He kissed the top of my bonnet. "Then, I should go."

"Go where?" I blinked up at him. "No. The vampires will have you before the moon comes up."

"Yeah, well. Better me than you. And it's not like I'm going to last here for long, anyway."

"You are safe here, under the hex sign. And I will bring you food . . ."

"But what about winter? What about when it's hip-deep in snow and you guys have exhausted your food? You just can't."

"Don't," I said. My fingers were wound in his shirt buttons. "Don't leave."

His head dipped close to mine, and for a moment I thought he meant to kiss me. But then he drew away, slid his arm from behind my neck.

"Look. I don't want to make it any harder than it already is." His tone was flat, and he pulled his knees up to his chest, let his elbows rest on them and his hands dangle into space. "I'm a dead man, Bonnet. It's just a matter of timing now."

I reached for his hand. "Don't go."

He shook his head, stared up at the light in the barn. "Day's burnt. I'll be out of your hair tomorrow, bright and early. Get a head start, that way."

Tears prickled my eyes, but I nodded sharply. I let his hand go, rose to my feet.

"I will see you tomorrow morning, then," I said quietly, turning so that he couldn't see my face. "I'll bring you some provisions."

"Thanks." He looked up at me. "I mean it. You've done a great thing for me, Bonnet. Your God would be pleased."

I nodded. "And your god will be pleased to see you soon."

CHAPTER TWENTY-ONE

I had hoped . . .

Ja. I had hoped for many things. A normal life. A taste of freedom. Maybe some Coca-Cola and a movie once in a while.

But those things had dissipated, and I was left with smaller hopes. Like hoping that the stranger would stay. That, somehow, he *could*.

I had hoped.

After all, I had no one left. Not even to talk to about the Darkness falling over us.

I trudged back to my house, feeling the lowering sun on my back through the fabric of my dress. Maybe Alex was right. Maybe it didn't matter anymore. Maybe our fates were inevitable, and the rest was just timing.

I scrubbed my sleeve across my face.

A scrap of fate from my old life was waiting for me on the back step when I returned. Elijah. His crutches were nowhere in sight. Inwardly, I cringed when I saw him. I nodded curtly at him, sidestepped him to get to the door.

"Katie." He reached up and grabbed my hand.

I looked down at him frostily. "Good evening, Elijah."

"I wanted to talk to you."

"I have chores to do."

He shook his head. "They can wait."

He pulled on my arm, drew me down to the top step. I jerked my arm away and folded my hands in my lap. Maybe if I let him say his piece, he'd go away. I stared out at the field, back in the direction in which I'd come, toward sunshine.

"I'm sorry."

I flicked a glance at him, said nothing.

"I'm sorry. I'm sorry for pushing you. I . . . know that things have been hard. Hard on all of us."

I nodded, swallowed. "You did what you had to do. You miss your brothers." I felt their loss too, like a void in our familiar landscape.

"But I knew better than to push that on you. And I knew better than to take up with Ruth."

I didn't care to imagine what all "take up" encompassed. The shadow of a red-tailed hawk soared overhead. I envied him his freedom, his power as he hunted. He was beholden to nobody, to no one's rules. I wondered if he knew that the ravens had left.

"I was wrong."

"Ruth is gone," I said as I watched the hawk plunge into the field, his wings cupped to break his descent as he disappeared under the sea of blond grass.

"She's gone . . . but that's not why I'm here. I'm here for you."

I didn't say anything. I watched the grass rustle, thought I heard a squeak.

"I heard what you did yesterday for Ruth, for her family. You showed . . . such faith and courage. Such obedience to God. You did what no one else would do."

"Frau Gerlach was there."

"You know what I mean. You were . . . I am in awe of you."

"I did what needed to be done."

Elijah got in front of me, knelt down, obstructing my view of the field. He grabbed my hands in his clammy ones. "Katie, will you marry me?"

I stared at him, hard. My gaze felt like the hawk's, as if I saw beneath him. Saw the core of him. He wasn't a bad man. Just human.

I lifted my gaze to watch the hawk take off, soaring above the field with a mouse in his talons. My heart soared with him, singing and free.

"No," I said.

I disentangled my hands from his, turned around, and disappeared into the house.

———

My mother was making dinner. Sarah was helping, mashing potatoes with great concentration. My father sat at the head of the table. I noticed that there was an extra place set.

I walked past them, toward the stairs to my room.

"Katie," my father said, his voice stopping me on the second step. He was smiling, a smile that reached the wrinkles around the corners of his eyes.

"Yes, Father?"

"Do you have some news for me?"

I glanced out the back door. Elijah had asked for my father's blessing before he asked me to marry him. I balled my hand into a fist and hid it in my skirt.

"No," I said. "No, I don't."

I climbed the steps, hearing my mother whispering something below me. I walked into my room and shut the door behind me. My gaze fell immediately on the wooden *Rumspringa* money box Elijah had made for me. It sat on the floor. I knew it was empty. I kicked it under the bed.

Ginger sat up in bed, hands folded on her lap. She stared vacantly at the wall, her mouth turned down.

"Ginger?"

Her eyes slowly turned to mine. "Hello, Katie."

I came to sit beside her on the bed. I fingered the crochet work in her basket. "This is pretty."

"Thank you." Her hand stroked it softly, as if it were a kitten.

Her sadness was so real, so tangible. And more. I could see in her dead gaze that she'd given up.

I reached for her wrist, shook it. "Ginger."

She lowered her eyes. There was no spark of hope left in them. No tears, even. Just aloneness.

"The vampires are here, aren't they?" she whispered.

"Yes, Ginger. They're here. You know that they've been here. They took the cows."

She nodded to herself, stared at the quilt. "That's good. It'll be over soon."

I grasped her wrist harder. "You can't just lie down and give

288 — LAURA BICKLE

up," I insisted. She'd grown despondent since her cell phone had been destroyed. Without that link to the Outside world, she'd fallen into a deeper and deeper depression—one I could not shake her from.

She gave a small shrug. "There's nothing left for me. This isn't my world." She looked down at her dress. "This isn't who I am. I'm just"—she sighed—"waiting."

I put my arms around her, but she didn't cry. She just sat there, still as the bodies of the women I'd handled yesterday.

Waiting for the end of everything.

We may have been dead.

But I was determined to live.

I had gone to bed without *Nachtesse,* wrapping myself in a bundle of quilts. My mother attempted to speak to me about Elijah, about how he meant well. I just shook my head at her until she retreated back to the kitchen. Ginger sat in the falling darkness, staring at the wall, while I pretended to sleep.

I didn't move as Sarah climbed into bed beside me.

Through slit eyes, I watched the light below our bedroom door move, then become extinguished as my parents went to bed. I heard the murmur of their voices beyond, but I could not make out what they were saying. I think that they were arguing, but I was not sure. Eventually, their voices faded. I heard the creak of bedsprings as one of them turned around to present their back to the other.

I stared out the window, waiting for the moon to rise and paint silvery light inside the room.

I looked at Ginger. She had not moved, was still sitting up-right. I climbed out of bed, padded toward her.

"Ginger?" I whispered.

She didn't respond. I didn't know if she *could*. Tenderly, I pushed her back down on the bed, facing the ceiling. I pulled the quilt up around her neck. I could see the glassiness of her open eyes shining in the dimness, though her pupils didn't seem to follow me as I snatched my dress from the laundry. I reached inside the pocket to reassure myself that the *Himmels-brief* was still there, but I left my apron and bonnet behind.

I slipped down the stairs, through the dark kitchen. I grabbed my shoes, opened the back door . . .

And plunged into darkness.

The day had rendered this place gold, but the night was cool and silvery. I ran past the pumpkin patch, through the tall grass. Overhead, I could see the Milky Way, the trail of the dead, as I swam through the tall fields and heard crickets singing.

I scanned the silvery darkness for the vampires, but I was not afraid. Not like before. I had been terrified of the violence. But now I had already seen what there was to see. I knew that they could not harm me as they harmed the others. I had the Hexenmeister's power, however long it lasted.

Even so, I sensed that my time was measured. I wanted to wring every last experience out of it like juice from an orange, to feel, to touch, and to taste the juice as it ran down my chin. I did not want to lie down and wait for death like Ginger and the others, with their veil of ignorance drawn around them and surrendering their will to live to others.

I wanted my life to matter.

And I wanted to choose how it mattered.

I shoved the heavy kennel door open. Idly, I wondered if the vampires had discovered this place, if they had circled it in the dark. I knew that Alex was without light, without warmth, without any way to call for help. I wondered if that was part of the reason why he was leaving the settlement.

And I wondered if the other part was me.

"Bonnet? Is that you?"

I spied movement in the back. The moonlight illuminated him walking toward me, barefoot, shirtless, one trouser leg wadded up around his shin. His tattoos seemed to absorb the light, black and squirming against his pale flesh. Relief that he was still here flushed through my skin.

"*Ja,* it's me." I turned to haul the door shut, blotting out the light.

"What the hell are you doing, wandering around at night?" I could hear the spark of anger in his voice.

The door bounced a little against the frame, opening an inch and letting the moonlight stream in. I could hear his breath behind me, felt as it disturbed the loose hair on the back of my neck.

His hand rested on the door beside my head. His voice was softer: "Bonnet."

I turned to face him, bumping up against his chest.

"What are you doing here?"

I reached up with both my hands, lowered his stubbly face to my mouth, and kissed him. His lips were frozen, still, under mine. At first, I was afraid that he would reject me, tell me to go home — or worse, send me back to sleep with Sunny and Copper.

But then he sighed against my lips, kissed me back. He didn't kiss me like Elijah did, with that persistent fumbling I was accustomed to. Alex kissed me with his whole body, not just his mouth. His hands on the door, framing my face, inexorably pulled in and tangled in my hair. He leaned against me, the warmth of his lanky frame against mine, his tongue pressing past my lips.

My hands slipped down to his bare chest, timidly, to the ankh burned over his heart, circled behind him to finger the Djed column along his spine. I expected the skin there to feel different. Hotter. But it was as evenly warm as the rest of him.

His kiss slipped from my mouth, trailed along my jaw to my neck. One hand cradled my head while the other circled my waist, pushing my breasts against his chest.

"What did you come for?" he murmured.

"For you."

He reached up to brush a strand of hair from my eyes. "Are you sure that this is what you want?"

I nodded. I slipped my hands up over his bare shoulder blades.

"I've still gotta leave . . . I can't stay." He was being honest. I appreciated that. "I know."

"But—"

I laid my finger to his mouth. I knew that he wanted me,

too. I could hear it in the rough sound of his voice, feel it in the hard press of his body against my thigh.

"Just be gentle," I said. I was afraid. But this was what I wanted. Him.

He murmured against my finger. "I will."

Tenderly, he took my hand in his, turned it to kiss my palm.

I let him draw me down to the straw of the floor, down to darkness.

I did not believe much of anything that anyone else told me anymore.

But I believed him.

———————

I slept fitfully. I woke often, unaccustomed to having a man's arms around me. I stared into the darkness, listened to his breathing, plucked bits of straw out of my mouth.

I think it was because I wanted to savor each instant, knowing that it had to end. As the dark softened and the light grayed, I dozed. Once or twice, I sensed something was watching us, and I heard a scuff at the door. I froze.

Alex held me close. "If it's the vampires," he whispered, "don't move."

The footsteps seemed to go away, and I was able to relax against him, lulled into dreams by warmth. It was a beautiful spell. For a moment, I felt as if I were truly in control of my world, of my own destiny.

The spell broke after sunrise.

I woke to a rusty sound, the sound of the door being reeled back.

I jolted upright, clutching the blanket to my chest. I shaded my eyes from the bright sunlight with my hand. I could make out silhouettes at the door.

"There they are," said a voice, cold and bitter.

I blinked. It was Elijah. And the Elders.

I felt Alex behind me rising to fight, as I scrambled for my dress.

"Don't move," the Bishop said, aiming a rifle at Alex.

I closed my eyes.

My little dream was over.

Chapter Twenty-Two

The Elders let us dress, then marched us back through the fields to my house. I glared murderously at Elijah's back the whole way. How dare he . . . how dare he destroy the last little bit of a dream I had for myself?

I knew then that I hated him.

Hated him more than Ruth. More than the vampires, even.

I would never forgive him. Though "never" was shaping up to be a very short time for me.

My father marched down the steps, shock on his face. My mother was fast behind him, wiping her hands on a dishrag. It was clear to me that they were just as surprised as Alex and I.

"What's happened?" my father demanded.

Elijah was the first to answer. "I came by to see if Katie was home. She wasn't. You said that she was likely looking after the new puppies, so I thought to go look for her there."

"*Ja,* I remember. You woke us up." My father's tone was harsh. I couldn't tell if it was for me or directed at Elijah.

I traded glances with Alex. The "vampires" we'd heard at dawn . . . it must have been Elijah. Spying.

"I thought she was up to no good. I peered in between the

slats of the wall . . . saw *her*"—he cast a contemptuous glare at me, then pointed to Alex—"lying with *him*."

My father's angry gaze landed on me. I lifted my chin in defiance.

"Is this true?"

I stubbornly refused to answer. But my father took in my disheveled appearance, my unbound hair, and drew his own conclusions.

He turned back to Elijah. "Why did you not come to me? I am her father. This is none of the concern of the Elders."

The Bishop raised his voice. "It is our concern when she lies with an Outsider." He grabbed Alex's wrist, yanked up his sleeve to show his tattoo. "The Outsider we ordered to be left beyond the field."

I opened my mouth to issue a scathing protest, but Alex interrupted me.

"It's true. She came to me to bring me water in the field that day. And I forced her to take me to shelter."

I shook my head. "No."

"I told her that I'd kill her family if she didn't obey. That I'd kill all of you if she didn't bring me food. I even threatened to kill the pregnant dog with her puppies." His jaw jutted out, and his voice was harsh. "She's a good little obedient girl, that one. Does what she's told."

"That's not true." Tears sprang to my eyes. I knew what he was trying to do.

He stepped forward, raising his voice. "Shut up, you dumb bitch. And, yeah, I raped her. I forced her when she came to check on the dogs this morning."

My mother choked back a sob and pressed the dishtowel to her face.

"She fought hard, but . . . how could any of you resist a piece of ass like that?" He gestured contemptuously at me, then Elijah. "How about you?"

Elijah slugged him. Alex didn't fight back, didn't fall, just turned his cheek and stared at him.

The Bishop stared at me. "Is this true?"

I shook. I knew that Alex was trying to save me, that he was as good as dead. But he was trying to buy me a little time. Tears blurred my vision, and my mother came to me and wrapped her arms around me.

"How could you ask such a thing?" she snarled at the Bishop.

"It's not true," I said. I lifted my chin. "He's lying. I took him in willingly. He was injured, and none of you would help."

Alex sneered at me. "See? I've got her wrapped around my little finger."

My father shoved him in the chest. *"Enough."*

I swallowed hard. I had never seen him get violent with anyone before.

"I went to him willingly," I cried. "I went to him willingly then, as I did last night."

My mother sobbed behind her fingers. "Katie, please . . ."

Alex closed his eyes.

Rage stained my hot cheeks. "And I went to him the night before when he helped the Hexenmeister and I keep the contagion from spreading, when we kept the Hersbergers from becoming monsters . . . from becoming vampires. What the Englishwoman said is right. There are vampires among us."

I stabbed my finger at the Elders, aware that my voice was shrill and hysterical. "I have seen them. And the Hexenmeister, with his *Himmelsbriefen,* is the only one who can save us. But you have silenced him, so he cannot help us."

My voice echoed in my ears, full of tears and rage. It felt useless, against the black wall of the Elders. But at least I had spoken the truth.

The Bishop looked from Alex to me, nodded to the Elder holding the rifle. "Take them both Outside."

"No." My father stood between him and me. This was the first note of defiance I'd ever seen in him. "My daughter is a victim."

"Your daughter has let an Outsider inside. He is likely the one to blame for all the other—"

"No!" I shouted. *"He didn't do it. It was the vampires. Ask the Hexenmeister."*

My mother flinched. The Bishop cast a murderous gaze on me. "She goes with him. She is now under the *Bann.*"

"She may be too trusting," my father said. "She's been abused, and we will take care of her."

"She is still under the *Bann.*"

"You cannot do that," my father protested. "You can throw the Outsider beyond the gate. He is not one of us. But you cannot place an unbaptized person under the *Bann.*"

The Bishop's pale eyes narrowed.

"You cannot," my father said, his voice shaking in anger.

I saw in that moment how truly strong he was. "It's against the Ordnung. She has not formally accepted the church. If you place her under the *Bann,* you must place every child in this settlement with a pair of blue jeans in his closet or a radio in her dresser under the *Bann.* The Ordnung cannot be suspended in times of crisis. The Ordnung is law, and we will continue to follow it."

A heavy silence hung over the yard. I'd never seen anyone challenge the Elders, argue with them on a point of law. My father was correct. He'd called the Bishop out on his selective interpretation of the Ordnung.

But what remained to be seen was whether or not the Bishop would acquiesce. Whether he would try to save face or fight.

After a long moment, the Bishop grudgingly nodded in my direction. "Get her under control. We will decide about her later."

Another Elder entered the yard leading the white horse on a bridle.

My heart sank to see the horse captured. They must have found him at Herr Stoltz's house with the black mare. And they must have known that he did not belong to any of us. Or else Herr Stoltz had been forced to tell them.

The Bishop nodded at the horse. "Tie the Englisher to the horse. Turn them loose beyond the gate."

"No!" I shouted, remembering the single bloody boot I'd found in the horse's saddle. "That's certain death. The vampires will devour him. You're a murderer, just the same as if you shot him the day you found him!"

My mother clapped her hand over my mouth. Elijah grabbed my wrists, and they began to pull me back into my house.

I kicked and fought against them, biting my mother on the hand. I saw the Elders turn and march Alex away before the door slammed and cut me off from the world.

My mother dragged me down to the spring room. She cried when she saw the blood on the inside of my thigh, scrubbed me so hard that I ached. I would not look at her. No matter how hard she tried to wash the sin away, I was a defiled woman. Her hopes for me, the future that she wanted so desperately for her child, was ruined.

She watched me dress. As she did so, I heard another crying jag begin. I stole that moment to steal the *Himmelsbrief* away from my dirty dress and hide it in the pocket of my clean apron. I waited expectantly for her to wash her face, blow her nose, and send me upstairs to my room. When I got up there, Ginger was still sitting upright in her nightgown, staring at the wall. I noticed that the beds had been stripped and Sarah's things had been taken from the room. Only a Bible and a copy of the *Ausbund* lay on my naked bed.

As soon as the door shut behind me, I heard a key turn in the lock.

I snarled in frustration and collapsed on the bed.

I felt Ginger's vacant gaze upon me. "Sounds like you pissed them off."

"*Ja.* I really pissed them off."

She slowly reached beside her for her basket of yarn and

offered me a ball. "Would you like to start a project of your own?"

I started to bite off a snide remark, but then I looked at the thick yarn she was winding around her fingers. My eyes flicked to the window.

Ginger lifted an eyebrow.

I flattened my mouth and reached for the yarn.

———

I was a fast hooker.

Well, at least, that was what my mother said about my crochet skills.

I worked on the yarn all day, using up all the balls of wool in Ginger's basket and unraveling part of her afghan. The yarn was stretchy, and I tried to make stitches that were tight and inflexible. Looking out the window, I gauged the distance between the lintel and the ground to be about twenty-four feet.

When I heard footsteps on the stairs, I jammed my project under the bed and grabbed my *Ausbund*. I succeeded in getting it open on my lap when my mother came in with lunch for us.

She looked at me, teared up, and left the dishes on the bed. When the door was shut and locked, I heard her crying.

I gave my food to Ginger and continued crocheting. I tightened my stitches angrily while the tears fell. I was angry for having endangered Alex with my selfishness. I was angry at Elijah for being rigid and possessive. I was angry at the Elders for their abuses of power. I was angry that the Hexenmeister was imprisoned, that our last hope for survival was under lock and key.

But, most of all, I was angry that they had killed Alex. The image of the blood-smeared white horse was burned into my memory. I knew that after the sun set, it would be his blood pouring from his shoe in the stirrup onto the ground. Tears splashed onto my work, but I didn't stop. I continued even though my fingers ached and the needle was blistering hot in my hand.

I had enough of this world. I knew what lay Outside, but I would not stay here.

I was fast, but the sun was faster. As I worked, it moved across the sky, moving toward the horizon. Part of me hoped that I could complete my work before the moon rose, that I could find Alex and save him. But I was forced to put my half-finished escape plan away when the sun disappeared and the stars came out. There simply was not enough light left to work by.

I lay on my bed, listening to the clank of pots and pans downstairs and the crickets outside. Despair fell on me, and tears ran from the corners of my eyes into my ears. I rubbed at them. I knew that the vampires were coming out now, probably treating Alex's remains like those of the dead cattle.

We were all soon to be dead cattle.

A knock sounded at the door. I lifted my head to see who it was, lowered it again.

Elijah. Elijah the rat. He came in bearing the golden light of a lantern and a tray of food. My mother came after him to take Ginger downstairs, leaving me alone with the last person on earth I wanted to talk to.

I stared up at the ceiling. The shadows on it moved as he set the lantern down on the nightstand. The bed squeaked as he sat down beside me. I edged away from him; I wanted no part of my leg touching his.

"Katie . . ." he began.

I said nothing. I laced my fingers behind my head tightly. Or else I was going to strangle him.

"Katie, this is for your own good."

I turned my bright, angry gaze upon him. "And who are you to judge that?" I propped myself up on one arm, jammed my finger into his chest. "Who are you to judge me?"

"What you did is——"

"You are not God. The Elders are not God. The Bishop is not God. You may want to play as if you are him, in your own screwed-up shrinking little world, but you have no jurisdiction over me."

His eyes were wide, shocked. "I just came to tell you that . . . I forgive you."

I put my face close to his, snarled: "*I don't care.* I don't care what you think of me, what you approve of, what you forgive. You are not my God."

"But we're to be together," he said plaintively.

"No," I said. "Not you. Not ever. Not even after the vampires chew us up and spit us out, and we're all dead, rotting meat waiting in line for the kingdom of heaven or the road to hell. Not ever."

His gaze darkened. It wasn't the blasphemy that angered him. It was the rejection.

He struck me. He hit me hard across the face, sending me

tumbling to the floor. I lifted my head and growled at him, "Get out!"

He stood over me, his hand clenching my dress collar. His breath was hot on my face. "How could you give yourself to that Outsider? That stranger?"

I lifted my chin. "Because he didn't try to control me."

"I'll show you control." He grabbed my wrist and the hem of my dress, then sat on me.

I opened my mouth to scream, but he jammed his hand over my mouth.

"You never screamed in his arms," he snarled.

Something struck my window. It sounded small, insignificant. Like a pebble hitting glass. It barely registered to me, but Elijah froze.

"Oh no," he cried out.

I reached up, dug my thumb into his eye.

He howled and fell back against the bed. I kicked him off of me, backed away.

"You get the hell away from me," I said. "You monster."

He pressed his hand over his wounded eye, but the other eye rolled fearfully to the window. "I'm not a monster. Not like them."

I glanced at the window, down into the yard.

And then I understood. I understood everything with perfect clarity.

I understood why the Darkness had fallen over us. Why my parents had not come running when they heard the scuffle on the second floor. I even understood why Ruth had died.

Two vampires stood in the backyard, staring up at my window. They were pale and gaunt, like spiders, the shadow cast by the moon driven before them.

"Elijah," one of them said. "Come to us."

"Elijah," the other said. "Don't you miss us?"

They were dressed as Plain folk, but their white shirts were stained with blood from neck to waist. I knew them. Seth and Joseph.

"You left us a note that said you missed us."

I turned to Elijah, who sat stupidly on the floor, crying and holding his eye. "You knew they were here."

"Ja," he sobbed. "I saw them at dusk, five nights ago. I took my father's wagon to go and get some fresh air . . . I was tired of being cooped up in the house. And I saw them, standing just beyond the gate, on the road. They called to me. Like now."

I sucked in my breath. *"You let them in."*

I heard a scraping outside the house. I stifled a scream as I whirled and saw Joseph peering through the window, stroking the screen. I reached up and slammed the window glass so hard it cracked a pane. Joseph laughed, and I heard him drop to the ground as lightly as a cat from a fence.

I whirled back to Elijah. "How could you let them in?"

He lowered his head. "I was so happy to see them . . . you can't imagine. But they blew past me like leaves."

"Why didn't they kill you?" I demanded.

"I don't know," he said. "I think they remember me."

"No. They have no sentimentality." I kicked him in the ribs. "Why didn't they kill you?"

"I don't know," he whimpered.

I grabbed his jacket, dug through his pockets. My fingers closed around a piece of paper. When I pulled it out, it was parchment. I shook it in front of his nose like a dog who'd had an accident. "Where did you get this?"

"Herr Stoltz made it for me."

I opened it up, expecting a *Himmelsbrief.* But it was an elaborately painted document, showing stylized doves and hearts and tulips. In the Hexenmeister's hand, the words *Grow old with me* were printed in Hochdeutsch. A list of ministers' signatures endorsed Elijah's character. Both our names were printed on it, with space for us to sign.

It was a *Zeugnis,* a marriage contract. I let it flutter to the floor. Some of the Hexenmeister's magic must have worked into it, enough to keep Elijah safe.

I looked down into the yard, and my breath clotted in my throat.

Seth, the youngest, was kneeling down with his arms open. The door creaked open, and a small figure ran across the yard into his embrace.

"No!" I shrieked.

Seth stood up, cradling Sarah. He grinned over his shoulder at me, displaying long teeth and inhuman eyes.

"Come down here, pretty one," Joseph said. "Come here and we'll let the little girl go."

I glared down at Elijah. He rocked back and forth, his hand pressed to his eye. "How dare you bring this to our doorstep!" I cried.

He didn't answer me. I grabbed the lantern and stepped on the *Zeugnis* as I left the room.

I descended the stairs. My parents were seated at the table with Ginger, their heads bowed in prayer. I touched my father's shoulder, but he didn't respond. I shook him hard, but he didn't move. Neither did my mother. Ginger stared at her plate with the same catatonic, glassy-eyed stare that I'd grown accustomed to. The vampires had put them under their spell, the same spell that had drawn me out of the house two nights ago. The same spell that had drawn Ruth and Sarah to the door.

My hands balled into fists. I would not allow them to hurt my family.

I clutched the lantern close to my chest, so close that I could feel the heat through my dress. I shoved open the screen door and into the darkness.

Joseph smiled when he saw me, lips peeled back from his teeth. "I was always a bit jealous of Elijah."

"You had Ruth," I said, my voice quavering.

He gave a small, boneless shrug. "Ruth was not very interested in me. Not until the end."

I shuddered, remembering the corpse at the threshold of the Hersberger house. It had not occurred to me that he had slaked appetites other than for blood with her mutilated body.

"Unfortunately, it seems as if Ruth will no longer be the recipient of my ministrations."

"Ruth's dead," I said.

His eyes narrowed. "Did you have anything to do with that?"

"No." I glanced at Seth, who held Sarah, squirming in his grip. "Let her go. Let my family go. You can have me."

Joseph laughed. "You overestimate your value. I pressed my ear to your kitchen window. I heard your mother whispering about you being a defiled woman. So Elijah finally got some?"

"Let her go," I said. "I'll do anything you want. Willingly."

Joseph flicked a glance at Seth. "For a moment."

Seth placed Sarah on her feet. As if sleepwalking, she stumbled back toward the house. I saw her through the safety of the threshold before I turned my attention back to the vampires.

Joseph crooked his finger. "Now. You promised."

I took a step toward him. Then another.

Then I flung the lantern at his face. He shrieked, clawing at the burning kerosene.

Seth was fast. He grabbed me by the waist, then howled. I struggled to reach into my pocket, hauled out the *Himmelsbrief,* and waved it in the air like a flag. It seemed to burn him to hold me, and his grip faltered.

"Get off of her."

I was thrown to the ground by a force that knocked the wind out of me—and Seth off of me. I rolled, gasping for breath, to see a Plain man brandishing a shovel. It made a ringing sound as it collided with the vampire's head.

My heart soared as I saw the stain of a familiar tattoo on the man's arm.

The *Himmelsbrief* had fluttered to the ground a yard away. Instinctively, I reached for it.

But something clutched my ankle. Something that burned.

I shrieked. Joseph, engulfed in flames, had latched on to me. The fire lit the edge of my skirt. I kicked and fought against him, desperately reaching for the *Himmelsbrief.*

And Joseph abruptly let go. I rolled away, slapping out the fire on my skirt and stuffing the *Himmelsbrief* in the top of my dress.

"Ginger!"

She stood over the flaming man, beating him with a fireplace poker. In the glare of the fire, I could see hate and fury boiling in her eyes, the first emotion I'd seen in days.

"No . . . more . . . killing . . ." she panted.

Joseph snarled and hissed at her, snatched the poker away as if she were a child.

"Bonnet! Here!"

I turned. Alex threw me a garden hoe. I turned the metal end away from me and charged Joseph.

The shaft of the hoe pierced his chest, slammed him to the pumpkin patch. I put my full weight against it, driving it into the soft, tilled soil. He flailed liked Ruth had, squirming and spitting. Fire splashed onto the pumpkins, and I smelled roasted pumpkin seeds and meat.

I held on until he stopped flailing, until his burning chest cavity was pressed into the earth.

I released the hoe, turned back to the house.

Alex stood over Seth. The shovel was embedded in the vampire's neck. Black, viscous fluid leaked onto the earth. But his eyes were closed.

I ran to Alex, threw my arms around him. I wound my fingers in his open shirt. It smelled like blood. "You're alive."

"Yeah. Well . . . not for lack of trying by your Elder guys."
He kissed the top of my head. "They roughed me up, tied me
to the horse. Spooked him with gunshots to send him running
west. Horse ran for what seemed like forever."

I fingered scratches on his face. "Like the cow in your
myth?"

"Like Io."

"And the vampires didn't find you." I hugged him happily.

"Well . . . not exactly. They did."

I drew back, stared at him. I began to run my fingers over
his neck and wrists.

"Horse ran out of steam, eventually. I was busy trying to
cut the rope on a stop sign beside the road when the vampires
turned up. And it should have been easy for them, since I was
still trussed up like a pig." He looked down at his arms. "I think
it's the tattoos."

"It is," the Hexenmeister confirmed. I turned to see the old
man limping across the yard toward us. "I cannot read them,
but they are just as powerful as the *Himmelsbrief.*"

I ran my fingers over the black ink. "They're holy to you."

Alex flexed his fingers. "They are now."

"How did you escape?" I asked Herr Stoltz.

The Hexenmeister's eyes twinkled. "My guard likes to
sleep. He does not pay much attention to the back windows.
Though my old joints do." He rubbed his knee.

"What will happen when they find out you're gone?"

The old man smiled. "There is little they can do to me.
They will need me. They know it, even though they refuse to
admit it. I shall confess, ask forgiveness. I will allow them to

swear me to silence, immerse myself in making ink and paint."
He made a dismissive gesture.

"More *Himmelsbriefen*. More hex signs."

"*Ja*. I will do what I can do." He glanced at the bodies
of the vampires before stumping away, muttering to himself.
"But for now, we need more kerosene. And some kindling . . .
maybe salt . . ."

"I'll get the kerosene and the salt." Ginger ran into the
house.

Alex took my hands. His hands were warm and solid. I
rested my head against his, a prayer of thanksgiving on my lips.

———————

Dawn seared the horizon pink and red, burning away the violet of night.

I stood at the gate in a clean dress, with a heavy pack on my
shoulder, watching the sun rise.

"What happens now?" I asked.

I would be lying to say I wasn't afraid. I glanced back, seeing the line of Elders in the distance, like crows on a telephone
wire. The Hexenmeister was with them, but he was silent. I
knew that he would do his best to protect our community. I
think that my parents believed what had happened last night,
after Elijah had told them. But the Elders couldn't allow that
belief to spread. It made me angry, leaving everything I loved
behind. But, on some level, I also craved it. I turned my face to
the sun.

I was sad that my family would not come with me. Some
sliver of me hoped that they would not send me out into the

world alone, knowing that I spoke the truth. But I knew that they had Sarah to care for. And that this was the safest place for them.

Baptized or not, I was an adult woman now. Time to make my own choices. I chose not to repent and ask for mercy. I chose to go beyond the gate.

Alex shrugged, adjusting his pack. His sleeves were rolled up over his elbows and shirt unbuttoned to show his tattoos, and his hat was pulled down low to shade his eyes. His black jacket with the zippers was tucked under one arm. He led the white horse on a bridle behind us.

"What happens now?" I asked again.

"I dunno, Bonnet. But we'll figure it out."

"Wait! Wait for me!"

I turned. A round figure in Amish dress ran toward us, kicking up dust and clutching a pink purse. Ginger. She broke past the startled line of Elders as if she were playing an adult version of red rover, launched herself over the fence with a degree of agility that shocked me. She skidded to a stop in the dust before us, the sun reflecting off her eyeglasses.

"Um. You guys want some company?"

"*Ja.*" I grinned and nodded. I unlatched the gate and we stepped through into the unknown together.

LAURA BICKLE's professional background is in criminal justice and library science. When she's not patrolling the stacks at the public library, she can be found dreaming up stories about the monsters under the stairs. She has written several contemporary fantasy novels for adults, and *The Hallowed Ones* is her first young adult novel. Laura lives in Ohio with her husband and five mostly reformed feral cats. For more about Laura, please visit her website at **www.laurabickle.com**.